"Have you fallen so low that you now conduct your flirtations in backrooms? Or perhaps," he said goadingly, "it has gone beyond *mere* flirtation?"

Samantha flamed immediately. "We were *not* flirting. The earl has been most civil to me. *That* I assure you is more than I can say about you whose manners always give offense! And you've no right to chide me on this matter, I don't even know why I bother to stay in this room with you!" She moved at once to pass him, but he caught her wrist and pulled her close.

"Let me go!" She cried out.

"Not yet," he muttered grimly and lowered mouth on hers.

For one maddening moment Samantha surrendered to the passion that had been building within her, then she struggled free. The amusement in his dark eyes incensed her. Without hesitation she brought one hand up swiftly and slapped him as hard as she could across his cheek.

SAMANTHA

CLARICE PETERS

for Adrian

A Fawcett Crest Book
Published by Ballantine Books

FAWCETT CREST • NEW YORK

Library of Congress Catalog Card Number: 82-90907

ISBN 0-449-20217-8

Manufactured in the United States of America

First Ballantine Books Edition: May 1983

~ ONE ~

The three ladies seated on a sadly worn satinwood sofa in a sorely depleted Yorkshire parlor could have been excused for staring so rudely at the sole male occupant in the room with them, since they were unaccustomed to entertaining London visitors, particularly those of the masculine sex.

Mr. Augustus Phelps was neither a Corinthian nor a Tulip, who might have been expected to hold the riveting attention of three pairs of eyes, two blue and the third green. He was instead a balding man of fifty plus years who had served as solicitor to their aunt Lady Kendall in London. Indeed, he had just imparted news of such import to his listeners that even Pamela Langford, the pretty brunette alleged to be the best mannered of the trio, as befitted the eldest, could do little but gape at Mr. Phelps.

Miss Miranda Curtis, the youngest of the three and as blond as her eldest sister was dark, was herself well past the gaping stage and had turned to embrace their other sister, Samantha, in what amounted to a hug of felicitations.

Miss Samantha Curtis, sandy-haired, green-eyed, and blessed with the same upturned nose as her sisters and a chin that hinted of a temperamental nature, patted Miranda distractedly with one hand and then struggled to free herself from this affectionate display, simultaneously requesting that Mr. Phelps be so obliging as to repeat his last statement to them once more.

"I said that you have inherited your Aunt Kendall's fortune, Miss Curtis," he repeated, thinking that for someone rumored to be on the shelf at twenty-three, Miss Curtis was looking quite animated this afternoon despite the dreadful dowdiness of her walking dress, a garment that, like so much in the Curtis household, had seen much happier days.

The new heiress by this time had managed to free herself from her sister's rush of questions and congratulations. Her green eyes kindling with excitement, she turned to the solicitor.

"Are you certain of all this, Mr. Phelps?" she asked. "I don't mean to suggest that you are tottyheaded, but Aunt Kendall never paid any of us the least attention, not even after Papa's death—which I cannot hold against her, for they always quarreled so during his lifetime. Papa," she acknowledged ruefully, "could get on his high ropes. But to have chosen me! I am certain I saw her only a few times in my life."

"That may be as it may be, Miss Curtis," the solicitor murmured, wise in the ways of the Quality he served. "Despite your aunt and your father never seeing eye to eye, she did keep herself informed as to your welfare."

"Indeed," Samantha breathed.

Pamela coughed delicately. "Is there any possibility that the will might be in error, Mr. Phelps?" she asked.

The solicitor's shock was etched clearly on his bony face. "None at all, Mrs. Langford," he said energetically. "I drew up the document myself. You must not think this merely a freakish whim of an elderly dowager," he went on, visibly unbending under their rapt gaze. "Your aunt felt that she had done more than was usually required for her other relations through the years. They, I might add, were so accustomed to applying to her for assistance that she often complained that she was nought but a moneylender to them. She wished to leave her fortune to a relation who had need of it but who hadn't hung on her sleeve."

"Well, we certainly have need," Samantha said, waving a hand toward the walls and floor, which had long ago been stripped of anything remotely of value. "But I am still curious as to how it all came about."

Mr. Phelps settled himself against the Windsor chair

with an audible creaking of his joints. "Lady Kendall knew that the three of you had been in difficult straits for years, ever since your father's death in fact, and she stood ready to help you if you had applied to her—which you never did. And that did pique her interest. After satisfying herself that you were all honorable young ladies, she put your names into a hat, an Oldenburg hat, it was," he confided, "and drew one out."

"And it was mine?" Samantha asked.

He nodded.

"Heavens! It is too absurd! And exactly the type of thing our aunt would do, if all the stories Mama used to tell me about her were true!" Her face sobered suddenly. "I am sorry she is dead, however, for she sounds so wonderfully eccentric that I would have enjoyed knowing her, however much she and Papa may have quarreled."

"Yes," Mr. Phelps agreed. In deference to his late and much valued client, he paused a moment, then whisked them all briskly back to the present by stating that Lady Kendall's largesse came to ten thousand pounds.

Samantha stared at him. "Ten *thousand* pounds?"

The solicitor basked in her obvious delight. "And," he added, "should you desire any advice about the management of your fortune, Miss Curtis, I shall be more than pleased to assist you."

"That is good of you," Samantha said sincerely. "And I do hope you shall stay on as my solicitor, for I am certain you are the very one to advise me. But I must confess that I have some plans of my own on how to use the money Aunt Kendall has so obligingly left to me."

Mr. Phelps paled noticeably.

"Plans? My dear Miss Curtis, what can you mean?" he asked nervously. "I had presumed that for the time being you would exercise prudence and caution and leave the money where it has been, in the Funds." His brow knitted suddenly. "You can't wish to dabble in the Exchange, can you? Risky business, that," he said, remembering that her father, the late Mr. Reginald Curtis, had been reputedly a notorious gamester, known to risk huge sums on the Exchange. It was in large part his deplorable luck there as well as at White's that had reduced his three daughters to the station they now commanded in life.

"Oh I don't mean to *dabble* in anything," Samantha assured him, her green eyes dancing with pure mischief. "I mean to spend it."

"Spend it!" Mr. Phelps babbled. "Spend the *money*, do you mean, Miss Curtis? My word, what a curious idea. You must be funning!"

"Oh, no, I am quite in earnest," Samantha said, noticing that both Pamela and Miranda were staring at her with the same thunder-struck expression as Mr. Phelps. "I have had this plan for years," she told them all, "and now, thanks to Aunt Kendall, I have the money to put it into action. And it's not really spending, Mr. Phelps. I'd call it an investment. One that I'm certain even our mother, who frowned on all forms of gaming, would approve of."

This cryptic statement did little to assuage Mr. Phelps's fears. "What do you plan to do with the money?" he asked, mopping his face with a handkerchief.

"I plan to take us to London!" Samantha annnounced.

"To London!" Pamela exclaimed.

"Oh, Samantha, do you mean it?" Miranda asked as they pounced on Samantha together.

"Certainly I mean it. Have you all turned to doubting Thomases?"

"No!" Pamela protested. "But London!" Her voice dropped to a hush. "It shall cost you dearly."

"Yes, but we have the money now, thanks to Aunt Kendall! And do just think, Pammy. London. None of us has ever done the Season there, and now we shall. You shall come with us," she beseeched her sister, two years married. "I shall speak to Donald myself and make him see that you and he deserve a holiday. All of us shall have a grand time!"

Pamela, only too aware that her husband was putty in the hands of any Curtis female, replied that she was certain he would make no serious objection to the London expedition. She thus left the way clear for Mr. Phelps to supply the bulk of the objections himself.

Samantha, a usually obliging young lady, listened to him

paint the excesses of town life in quite vivid colors. Had he only stopped to think, he might have realized that this made her and her sisters more determined than ever to see London in this spring of 1817.

"But the sheer expense of a Season, Miss Curtis," he said, taking another tack. He was seated now with a plate of biscuits and a cup of tea balanced on his knees. "You have no idea of the cost of gowns, day dresses, pelisses, not to mention hats, gloves, boots, sandals, reticules, and other necessaries!"

"Mama was wont to say it would cost an arm and a leg," Samantha agreed, handing a cup of tea to Pamela. "But surely with ten thousand pounds at our disposal we shall be able to afford some dressmaker's fee."

At this blithe statement the biscuit Mr. Phelps had been nibbling on lodged itself in the middle of his throat, and he turned a desperate purple. He was rescued at last by Miranda Curtis's vigorous pounding on his back.

"You can't mean to spend *all* the money," he gasped when he finally could speak.

"Mr. Phelps is quite right, Samantha," Pamela said quietly. "Aunt Jane left the money to you, and you must not squander it. A Season in London would be the very thing for you and Miranda, since you are both unwed, but I'd liefer stay at home."

"You shall do no such thing," Samantha retorted, in no way persuaded by her sister's air of martyrdom. "Aunt Kendall did leave the money to me, but what of it? From what Mr. Phelps told us, it could just as easily have been your name or Miranda's plucked from the hat. We shall all three of us enjoy it together. Now no more protests, I have made up my mind: we are going to London."

"But where will you stay?" Mr. Phelps asked. "The town is quite filled these days. And you shall be arriving in the middle of Season."

"We shall find quarters somewhere," Samantha said, undismayed. "I shall put up in a hotel, if I must, but I assure you, Mr. Phelps, we are going to London!"

The note of finality in her voice, strongly resembling that of Mr. Phelps's late client, Lady Kendall, caused his instant capitulation, and after presenting her with a large roll of bills to pay their way to London and extracting a promise for her to call on him immediately when she did arrive, he departed, to endure all the discomforts of his return journey by mail coach.

As Mr. Phelps began his trip back to London, Samantha turned his objections over one by one in her mind. Despite what anyone else might think, she considered herself at twenty-three to be no green girl and her plan no mere fairy tale. Since that awful day a year and a half ago when her mother had succumbed to a fever, Samantha had taken charge of the family, a circumstance that had greatly relieved Pamela, who was two years her senior but disliked making any decisions, particularly those which might prove to be unpleasant. In the intervening months there had been a great many unpleasant decisions for Samantha to face, including the selling of most of their possessions in order to keep the family together.

It was, however, Miranda and not their past struggles that occupied Samantha as she strolled about in the Shakespeare garden her mother had planted years ago. At eighteen Miranda displayed the unmistakable bloom of beauty, with a complexion akin to a peach, blond curls that never failed to win praise, and a figure that even an ill-furbished wardrobe could not fully disguise. And till now it had all been going to waste in the backwaters of York.

"But with Aunt Kendall's windfall," Samantha told herself, "I have the means to right that wrong."

They would of course need a place to stay in London, she acknowledged farther down the garden path. It was all very well to declare her willingness to put up in a hotel if necessary, but such lodgings were bound to be uncomfortable. And she could not hope to launch Miranda into the *ton* from a hotel!

The problem continued to absorb her for the rest of the afternoon and well into the dinner hour, which she and Miranda habitually shared with Pamela and Donald Langford, Pammy's cheerful, red-haired husband who claimed the impecunious status of being a younger son of an impoverished country squire.

Between the mutton and the roast chicken, the answer flew into Samantha's mind.

"Cousin Wilhelm!" she exclaimed, laying down her fork.

Pamela, who with some difficulty had been attempting to follow the story of her husband's latest stormy attempt to breed a champion racer from the deplorably short-boned creatures on their meager estate, turned toward her sister with eyebrows raised in surprise.

"Pray, what has Cousin Wilhelm to do with Donald's horses, Samantha?" she asked, quite astonished.

Samantha chuckled. "Not a thing that I know of." She pushed away her plate, too excited to consume another morsel. "Do listen, all of you! I have been thinking of where we shall reside while in London, and I have found the answer: Cousin Wilhelm!"

"Do you think Wilhelm shall agree to that?" Pamela asked, looking doubtful.

"I don't see why he should not," Samantha replied. "We are his cousins, after all. Third cousins, to be sure, but cousins nevertheless. And he really doesn't *know* us, so there can be nothing for him to dislike about us. Really, when one considers that he lives all by himself in that great gloomy house on Cavendish Square, I am bound to believe we shall be doing him a great favor, for it is certain to get lonely for him there."

Pamela, while willing to grant the remote possibility that Mr. Wilhelm Curtis might be at times troubled by loneliness in his large house, was by no means persuaded that their plan to reside with him would win any favor from their would-be host.

"I don't see why not," Samantha said blithely. "There must be some rooms he is not using, for he is still a bachelor. And it stands to reason that he can't occupy them all himself at the same time. We shall contrive to be as quiet as churchmice and he shan't even know we are about!"

At this improbability Miranda hooted out loud, and Donald, being of a sporting disposition, was obliged to point out that it would be coming a bit too brown all around.

"Well, perhaps not churchmice," Samantha conceded, "but we shan't put him to the blush—at least we shan't once we have some new dresses commissioned. And Pammy, I do wish you would try and remember the name of that London *modiste* who used to dress Mama ages ago when we once visited London."

Assisted by a fierce wrinkling of her brow and not by the copious hints from Miranda, who, as both sisters took pains to remind her, had been a mere babe in arms at the time and hence could have no memory of London *modistes* to begin with, Pamela came up ultimately with the name of Madame Fanchon.

"That's it," Samantha said, nodding. Her eyes brightened. "That's where we shall go the day after we arrive in London. We shall have the very latest in everything," she promised her sisters, "walking dresses, ball gowns, hats, pelisses, everything the well-dressed lady of the *ton* must have!"

The images her words conjured up were so pleasing that none of the Curtis ladies had the slightest compunction about wearing their dowdy rigs to the city, since they knew that they would be shortly donning the very best that fashion had to offer.

After Pamela and Donald left for their small estate, situated a few miles away, Samantha and Miranda sat down with the latest issue of *La Belle Assemblée* between them, for if they were to meet a London *modiste* they must know what to ask for.

Miranda became absorbed in the magazine, turning the pages with an eager hand and prattling on about hems, necklines, muslins, and silks. Samantha scarcely heard her. Fashions and silks for the Season were all well and good, but she yearned for much more for her sister. In fact, the one wish of her heart was to contract a brilliant match for Miranda while they were in London, a match that would keep her from ever worrying about Miranda's future again. And with Aunt Kendall's legacy and Miranda's own undeniable beauty, that might not be as impossible as it used to seem.

Leaving her sister to peruse the magazine further, Samantha seated herself at a small escritoire in the corner of the room and immediately put pen to ink.

"Dear Cousin Wilhelm," she wrote, "No doubt this shall come as a surprise to you, but I have a favor to ask ...."

Two weeks later an antiquated travel chaise meandered down the Great North Road bound for London. Having heard not a word from Wilhelm in the intervening days to discourage their removal to London, the Curtis contingent had departed from York the previous day, enduring all the discomforts of a bone-shattering ride made even more unpleasant when a bout of carriage sickness afflicted Pamela.

By the time they departed the spartan quarters of the posting house where they had been obliged to pass one night, the excitement of going to London had subsided into the tedium always associated with travel. The dust, the rattle of the carriage wheels, and the cramped chaise—last used to conduct Mr. Reginald Curtis from London to York a full decade ago—all combined to set Samantha's temples throbbing.

It was approaching nine o'clock when they finally reached London, and Samantha, longing for nothing more than her supper and a warm bed, let out a thankful sigh as they neared Cavendish Square. This emotion took a turn for the worse as the vehicle halted and she peered through the window at her cousin's establishment. From top to bottom the building blazed with lights. Judging by the numbers of people clustered about and their voices hailing one another joyfully, she saw at once that a ball was in progress.

"Good heavens," she murmured, "Cousin Wilhelm would have to be entertaining tonight of all nights!"

Miranda, peeking over her shoulder, stole her first envious look at the elegantly gowned London ladies.

"Oh, Samantha! What shall we do?" Pamela asked, her face white with fright.

"We shall go in, of course," Samantha said encouragingly. "It is unfortunate that a gala is going on, but we have come a good distance from York, and we can't wait out here in the chill all night."

Donald Langford was a good-natured sort of man who rarely objected to any of his sister-in-law's schemes, but he roused himself now to lodge a mild protest.

"Samantha, have you seen the people out there? Tulips and Corinthians would be as nothing to them, I vow!"

Samantha, having been blessed all her life with two sound eyes, assured her brother-in-law that she had already taken in the exquisitely garbed ladies with jewels shining in their hair and the gentlemen in their swallow-tailed coats and striped silk stockings.

"But there is nothing to be disturbed about," she reassured him. "Now do come along. We must let Cousin Wilhelm know we have arrived!"

The others were by no means sure they must do anything of the sort. But, swallowing their doubts, they followed their leader out of the chaise and onto the street that seemed the sole domain of those forementioned ladies and gentlemen, who were not above lifting their quizzing glasses at the peculiar spectacle the Curtises made.

Samantha, knowing quite well that her travel dress was dusty as well as out of mode, put up her chin and attempted to sail pass the waiting crowd into Wilhelm's residence. Pretending not to notice the sea of scandalized faces and the tittering voices whispering of provincials, she led the way to the front door of her cousin's establishment, only to find her entrance blocked at the last moment by a very superior butler.

～ TWO ～

"Good evening, Miss," The butler said, looking as impassive as any Medusa.

"Good evening," Samantha countered, with the smile that her mother had often vowed could charm snakes. Its effect this evening on butlers, however, was sadly wanting. The manservant continued to stare woodenly back at her.

"I should like to see Mr. Curtis," Samantha said briskly. "I am his cousin, Miss Samantha Curtis, from York. He is expecting us."

For a fleeting moment a skeptical look crossed the butler's face. "I'm afraid, Miss, that Mr. Curtis has given me no such information concerning relations from Yorkshire. Perhaps if you returned tomorrow."

"But we can't!" Samantha said, exasperated by this unwillingness to understand a perfectly simple chain of events. "We were supposed to stay here with him, I tell you. It is all arranged. I wrote to him myself a fortnight ago. He must be expecting us by now surely."

"I'm afraid, Miss, that you are in error," the butler said, not unsympathetically. "I am fully cognizant of all Mr. Curtis's household matters, and he has made no such arrangements concerning relations from Yorkshire or anywhere else. So if you would please . . ." His eyes moved discreetly back toward the chaise.

This gesture was not lost on Samantha, nor on any of the others, who had already taken a step back to do the butler's bidding. But Samantha had not traveled two days in a cramped and antiquated chaise only to be put off now on the very doorstep of her own cousin's establishment.

"I am not budging one inch until I speak to Wilhelm,"

she said now, much to the astonishment of not only the butler and her sisters but also several of Wilhelm's guests, who would never have dreamed that anyone in such a dowdy rig would presume to speak with such an air of self-importance.

"We have traveled a goodly distance in order to see Wilhelm," she explained now to the butler. "And I must say, it is the shabbiest trick to be fobbed off now. If he didn't wish us here, he had only to write and tell me so. While I regret that a ball is in progress, I can scarcely be blamed for that, can I? So, if you would please oblige us by fetching him, we can settle the matter quickly between ourselves."

Accustomed as he was to the voice of authority, the butler recognized it now in Samantha's voice and acquiesced in ushering her and her companions across the threshold. As Miranda stepped in after Samantha and Pamela, she gave a small involuntary cry and gazed up raptly at the shimmering chandeliers, the great hall awash with flowers, and the music that floated down from a ballroom located up the flight of stairs. Here and there footmen scurried from one task to another.

Well aware that she could not have chosen a more inauspicious moment at which to arrive, Samantha did her best to appear unmoved by the amused looks emanating from Wilhelm's guests. One guest in particular, a tall, statuesque blond garbed in white satin, was not satisfied with merely looking but took it upon herself to cross the black and white lozenges, a frown on her pretty face.

"Trouble, Horace?" she inquired coldly of the butler.

Listening to Horace explain just who they were, Samantha discovered that the questioner was a Miss Horick, who served as hostess to the ball now underway. Was Wilhelm due to forsake the ranks of the bachelors? she wondered to herself.

"I do beg your pardon if we have intruded on you and your guests," Samantha said as Horace halted and moved off, leaving them alone with Miss Horick. "But we are Wilhelm's cousins from York and should like to speak to him for just a moment."

Miss Horick's gray eyes swept majestically from the top of Samantha's head to her shoes, which were deplorably dusty. Looking satisfied with herself, the Beauty shifted her gaze back to Samantha's face.

"Wilhelm's cousins, did you say?" She asked at last and with no sign of pleasure. "I would not have thought it. You don't have the look of him."

"No," Samantha agreed, rather flustered by this impertinent remark. "We are third cousins, after all. And we are said to resemble my mother."

Since Miss Horick was unacquainted with the late Mrs. Curtis, it was not to be expected that she would find this comment very edifying.

"If you are Wilhelm's cousins," she said in a tone that cast no little doubt on that fact, "you have come at quite the wrong time. Horace has erred to even allow you in. What could he be thinking of. I shall speak to him myself on that later. As for now, if you would kindly remove yourselves." She nodded imperiously toward the door and, taking it for granted that they would meekly take themselves off, trod back to her group of friends clustered near the stairs.

"Oh, Samantha," Pamela whispered and tugged at her sleeve. "Do let's go. Everyone is staring at us; it's so disagreeable. And it's quite obvious that Cousin Wilhelm doesn't want us here. Donald knows of a hotel where we can put up for the night. Let's go now."

"We shall do no such thing," Samantha replied so grimly that her sister felt genuine alarm. "We have come all this way to see Wilhelm, and we shall not be deprived of that pleasure!"

Conscious of the eyes that followed her movements, Samantha put up her chin again and advanced until she was shoulder to shoulder with the elegant Miss Horick, who was suddenly made aware of this fact by the discreet cough of one of her companions, a robust matron in a red turban.

The Beauty turned an exasperated face toward Samantha.

"I do apologize, Miss Horick," Samantha said swiftly, coloring despite herself under the shrewd appraisal of the robust matron. "But I do have a need to speak to my cousin. It's not an unreasonable request, I should hope, since, as far as I understand, this is still his residence. So I do hope you shan't think me too disobliging if I ignore your civil request to leave. If Wilhelm doesn't want me here, he can tell me so himself."

Two spots of color appeared on Miss Horick's cheeks.

"Now, see here—"

"Are you Wilhelm's wife?" Samantha asked.

"Certainly not!" Miss Horick replied, appearing affronted by the question.

"His betrothed?"

"Well, no," she was bound to admit.

"So actually," Samantha concluded, "you have no real standing in this establishment other than that which you assume for yourself. And now I should like to see Wilhelm, if you please, for I have come a great distance and am fagged to death. If you would tell the butler—Horace, I believe you said his name was?"

Miss Horick had not reached her twenty-first year by being addressed in such a high-handed fashion by any mere country miss; the fury that had been building rose in her throat. The lady in the red turban was beset with another emotion, however. She gurgled with laughter, looking highly diverted by the scene she was witnessing.

"If I were you, Frieda," she said, wiping her eyes, "I'd do exactly as this one asks you to."

Whoever the lady was, it was clear to Samantha by the way Miss Horick swallowed her anger that her consequence must be enormous. But she had no further opportunity to discern her identity, for Horace had reappeared. She hastened to follow him into a small drawing room to await her cousin.

It had been more than a decade since Samantha had last laid eyes on Wilhelm. The image her memory conjured up as she sat waiting nervously for him with the others was that of a callow youth running to puppy fat and struggling with a cravat several sizes too large, which he had insisted on twisting about a scrawny neck.

She had hoped for some change for the better in him during the years that had passed, but she was wholly unprepared for the vision of sartorial elegance that descended upon them now. The figure frowning in the doorway appeared to excellent advantage in a swallow-tailed coat, white waistcoat, and frilled shirt, the garments emphasizing very broad shoulders, a narrow waist, and an excellent leg. Reddish brown hair sat on the crown of a well-formed head, accentuated by two lazy brown eyes.

"Are you Miss Samantha Curtis?" he inquired, his eyes focusing on the nearest female, who happened to be Pamela.

This unexpected question threw Pamela into a quake, and she shot a quick supplicating look at Samantha.

"I am Samantha, Cousin Wilhelm," Samantha answered from the Egyptian couch where she was sitting. "I daresay it is no surprise that you are unable to recognize me, for it has been fully ten years since you saw any of us. In truth, I must own that I would scarcely have recognized you myself." She saw with some surprise that he was advancing unhesitantly to sit next to her on the couch. "And I am pleased to see you, since that Miss Horick all but accused us of being imposters. And I really could not comprehend what would be the point of anyone pretending to be *us*."

"None whatsoever, as far as I can see," he replied, the brown eyes appearing at closer range to be more animated than she had supposed.

"I am sorry for disturbing your ball."

"Don't fall into a pelter over it," Wilhelm replied calmly. "It was a tedious affair until your arrival." He paused a moment as he polished his quizzing glass. "But you shall I hope forgive me for inquiring how it comes that you are here in London instead of—where the devil is it you hail from—York?"

"Yes, cousin," Samantha nodded, pleased at him for even remembering. "But surely you know the reason. I explained it all most thoroughly to you in the letter."

"What letter was this?" Wilhelm, having finished with his quizzing glass, opened his snuffbox and extended it to Donald, who was so much surprised by the civility that he took an eager pinch. Perhaps too eager, for a sneezing fit overcame him.

"Try a little of this," Wilhelm commanded, holding out a glass of sherry.

"You did get my letter, didn't you?" Samantha asked, the only one in the room ignoring the problems of her sorely afflicted brother-in-law. "You must have! I sent it to you at least a fortnight ago."

A shake of Wilhelm's craggy head confirmed her worst fears.

"Good heavens," she said, looking mortified. "Then your butler wasn't funning. You *weren't* expecting us at all. And here I thought that nothing but a hum. We have arrived on your doorstep like gypsies. No wonder you are staring at us as though we had the plague."

"Am I really?" Wilhelm asked, helping himself to a pinch of snuff. "If so, I apologize heartily, for nothing is more uncivil than staring. I hope that you are jesting about that business of plague, for if word of *that* ever got out, ball or no ball, this establishment would empty like a shot and that would send Frieda into the boughs."

"Frieda?" Samantha asked, a question in her eyes.

"Miss Horick," he explained dutifully.

Samantha, although still curious about the relationship between the Beauty and her cousin, managed to keep a firm rein on her emotion. "Of course I was just jesting about the plague," she said now, "for I daresay no one could find four healthier specimens. Although Pammy did suffer from carriage sickness, and I myself fell prey to a migraine. But these two conditions hardly constitute a plague, cousin."

Wilhelm's brown eyes glinted appreciatively. "Quite true," he acknowledged as he sat back with one arm flung carelessly across the back of the couch. "How would it be if you started from the beginning and told me exactly how you come to be here."

"It all had to do with Mr. Phelps," Samantha began, then paused as Wilhelm directed a mild look of inquiry at the now fully recovered Donald Langford. "That's not Mr. Phelps, cousin," Samantha said, unable to repress a laugh.

"That's Donald. Donald Langford. Pamela's husband. You do remember Pamela and Miranda, do you not?" She asked, indicating her sisters on the chairs opposite them. "Mr. Phelps was Aunt Kendall's solicitor—perhaps you may have met him?"

"Unfortunately not. But now that you put me in mind of it, I seem to recall a solicitor by that name in the City. Does your presence here have something to do with him?"

"It has everything to do with him!" Samantha hesitated, wondering how best to break the news of her inheritance. She decided to take her fences in a rush. "I daresay this may come as a blow to you, cousin, but Aunt Kendall left her estate and fortune to me. That's why Mr. Phelps came to York.'"

A lanky forefinger ran up and down Wilhelm's chin. "A bit of a surprise that, I should imagine?"

"Of course it was! I only saw her once or twice, and I do hope you are not going to cry craven because you cherished hopes for her fortune, for that would be uncomfortable for us all. You see, we have come to London to enjoy the Season. Mama was wont to talk about it so much when she was alive."

"That seems a plan of considerable merit," Wilhelm agreed, "yet I still fail to see my role in your venture."

A mild blush suffused Samantha's cheeks. "Well, naturally we would need a place to stay while in London."

"Naturally," he said drily.

"And," she went on, acutely conscious of those brown eyes lingering on her face, "you own this huge house on Cavendish Square, and I *did* write to ask your permission, and if there had been any reason for you not to wish us here it would have been the civil thing to write back promptly and tell us so."

Wilhelm looked amused by the force of her accusation. "Quite true. *If* I had received your letter, which I did not. And as for your staying with me, it's not a simple matter of what I wish—"

"Do you mean to say you occupy all the rooms?" Samantha asked skeptically.

He had the grace to look momentarily abashed. "Well, hardly that. To occupy all the rooms would necessitate a full dozen or more of me."

"Exactly what I thought!" Samantha agreed. "You needn't worry that we shall get in your way. You shall go your way and we shall go ours. And we shan't put you to the blush. I know you must be wondering how we could even bear to arrive in public looking like this, and yet it didn't make a jot of sense to me to commission new dresses in York when we would be coming to London where all the prime *modistes* have their shops. Tomorrow I mean to set off to Madame Fanchon's. She is still on Bruton Street, I think?"

"As far as I know, yes," Wilhelm replied, a thoughtful expression on his face. He glanced across at her. "Just how long a visit are you contemplating?"

Samantha shrugged. "I have no notion," she confessed freely. "I presumed that we would stay as long as the Season lasted. After that we shall return to York. You mustn't think that I intend to hang on your sleeve."

Wilhelm smiled. "That is a relief. From what little Frieda told me, I was beginning to think—"

"That we were mushrooms, I suppose?" Samantha's lip curled involuntarily at the mention of Miss Horick's name. "You needn't scruple to deny it. I can well imagine just what she said about us. Really, Wilhelm, how could you give her the right to ride roughshod over your poor butler!"

"I don't give her the right," Wilhelm said testily. "She takes it upon herself. Frieda is quite accustomed to giving orders and having them followed. You must not let your chance meeting with her tonight dissuade you from becoming friends."

"I suppose not," Samantha said, thinking to herself that all the same she would sooner make friends with an asp than with Miss Horick. "I still fail to see why you allow her to assume command of your affairs, cousin. Unless—" She looked up with real consternation. "You are not planning to *marry* her, are you?"

Wilhelm laughed. "That thought had occurred to me some weeks ago, and in fact it has occurred to Miss Horick as well. We have what you might call an understanding between us."

Samantha, who was beginning to like her cousin Wilhelm very much, much more than she had anticipated back in York, was genuinely dismayed.

"An understanding!" she exclaimed. "You mean marriage, of course. But Wilhelm, you must not!"

"Samantha!" Pamela burst out, unable to resist the interruption as she attempted to silence her sister.

"I think Cousin Wilhelm has the perfect right to marry whomever he wishes, even someone like odious Miss Horick," Miranda offered up her opinion.

Wilhelm's shoulders shook. "It appears that we have heard from everyone in this room concerning my marriage except you, Mr. Langford."

Looking nervous, Donald replied that he had no opinion to offer.

"Very wise," Wilhelm murmured.

"Perhaps I ought to apologize for speaking so frankly," Samantha said.

"By no means! Your candor is refreshing."

"All the same, I can't have you thinking us ragmannered, and I do assure you, I do not talk this way to everyone I encounter. But there can be nothing amiss in frankness among family. And we are related."

"Only third cousins," he pointed out, "and hardly members of a close-knit family."

"Yes," Samantha admitted, remembering several stormy quarrels her father had initiated within his family. "But blood is thicker than water."

Wilhelm plucked a speck of dust from his coat. "I have always wondered about that myself. But before we continue any further, you must tell me all that has happened since we last saw each other. Ten years, did you say it had been? I'd have put the time at rather longer."

With this for an opening, Samantha filled in the details of their lives in Yorkshire, aided in part by Pamela and Miranda, who had abandoned their bashfulness. Indeed, the gentleman listening proved to be a perfect audience, murmuring appropriate sympathies at the untimely demise of their father and then their mother, and turning quickly to congratulate Donald on the marriage he had contracted with Pamela two years ago.

Wilhelm, to his credit, even found occasion to be interested in Donald's tales of woe regarding Langford, his small estate, and, after asking several pointed questions concerning the cattle Donald was attempting to raise, offered his advice on the advantages of the Arabian strain.

"You can see the truth of that for yourself at Tattersall's. We'll go there sometime."

"I should like that very much," Donald answered, conscious of the favor Wilhelm had bestowed on him. "Most civil of you."

Wilhelm brushed aside his thanks and then inquired of Samantha if Mr. Phelps knew of their arrival.

"No," she answered. "I plan to see him tomorrow as soon as we are settled. I mean to put my financial matters in his hands, so you needn't worry that you'll be responsible for my bills!"

"Good. For I have more bills than I care to contemplate myself at the moment."

"I suppose a goodly number of them related to Miss Horick?" Samantha asked.

"Some are from Miss Horick," Wilhelm said with a smile. "But perfectly understandable, don't you think, that someone like me would wish to bestow gifts on my nearest and dearest?"

"Oh, quite understandable," Samantha agreed. "And I do hope you see how shortly you might be up the River Tick by such a creature." She noticed Pamela's appalled look. "Don't blush so, Pammy. It's not as though Wilhelm were a stranger. He is family. And as such I do think I have the obligation to point out, for no one apparently has, that while Miss Horick is undeniably beautiful and elegant, she seems destined to be the sort of female who shall drive a man to an early grave or, barring that, a debtor's prison!"

Wilhelm accepted this rude scoring of his betrothed-to-be with amazing grace.

"You might be right on the first of your charges," he said to Samantha, "but I daresay being driven to an early grave by a beautiful woman is more advantageous than to fall on a battlefield or languish from consumption or the other modes of death that currently afflict us. And as for driving me to debtor's prison, that is highly unlikely, since Miss Horick is an heiress."

"An *heiress!*" Samantha's eyebrows shot up. "Well, that does explain it. I daresay nothing could be more provident for you, Wilhelm."

"Oh, I'm not after her fortune," he said quickly. "After all, I have one of my own."

This comment came as a profound shock to Samantha, for Wilhelm's branch of the family tree was alleged to be almost as far into Dun Territory as her own. But perhaps, she mused, in the past years he had had a run of luck with the dice that had righted his previous misfortunes.

"I shall have to explain, I see," Wilhelm began, but broke off as Horace entered the room. "Yes, what is it, Horace?" he asked.

"It's Miss Horick, my lord," the butler said apologetically. "She has requested Your Lordship's presence in the supper room."

"Good God, it can't be time for supper already! Tell her I shall be there directly."

"Your *Lordship*?" Samantha exclaimed after the butler had left. She gazed at the gentleman, whose eyes were displaying a most sardonic gleam, and felt her heart sink.

"You're *not* Wilhelm!" She accused.

"No," he agreed. "I certainly am not!"

~ *THREE* ~

"Who are you?" Samantha demanded, rising wrathfully from the sofa she had been sharing unwittingly with a perfect stranger. "And what have you done with my cousin?"

The gentleman they had presumed to be Wilhelm remained seated where he was, the benign expression on his face having given way to one of amusement that he made no attempt to hide.

"My name is Sheffield," he explained. "My friends call me Warren. And as for Wilhelm, I haven't done a thing with him, and certainly nothing criminal, as you seem to suspect, Miss Curtis. As far as I know, Wilhelm's exactly where he planned to be, in the middle of some wretched Derbyshire stream that is teeming with trout. He always goes there this time of year to try his luck."

"Unconscionable!"

Although Sheffield did not share Mr. Curtis's enthusiasm in the sport, he was taken aback by the vehemence in her tone.

"Unconscionable, you call it, Miss Curtis? I suppose some might consider fishing in that light. I myself have never seen the lure of angling, but I should warn you, quite a few favor the sport hereabouts."

"I am not talking about Wilhelm's fishing!" Samantha said, her cheeks flushing with anger. "I am speaking of your behavior, sir. I find it unconscionable and your manners execrable. The idea of your pretending to be Wilhelm."

"What an extraordinary accusation," Sheffield said. "And quite a false one."

Samantha crossed her arms on her chest. "Do you deny claiming to be my cousin?"

"Of course I deny it," came the prompt rejoinder. "And while my memory is alleged to be shockingly bad, I do think yours must be even worse, Miss Curtis, if you do not remember how you took it upon yourself to believe I was your cousin the minute I entered this room, whereupon you launched into a full litany, unassisted, of the affairs that had brought you to London. Perhaps a more courageous man whould have attempted to point out your error, but I'd sooner stop a deluge than you!"

"I see what it is," Samantha said, far from mollified by any of his remarks. "*She* put you up to it, didn't she."

"Don't be a ninnyhammer! *She* put me up to nothing of the sort! *She*, in fact, was in a high dudgeon because of the way a mere country miss—her words not mine—" he added hastily as Samantha's chin rose, "treated her in front of several august ladies of the *ton*, and she ordered me forthwith to deliver one of my odious setdowns to you. Not that I could have done any such thing if you really were Wilhelm's cousins."

"Which we are," Samantha said arcticly.

"Yes, I know. I had occasion to learn that, among a good many other things about you and your charming family, in this last hour."

"Of course you did," Samantha said. "By worming your way into our affections—"

Sheffield's brows shot up. "Come now, Miss Curtis. Worming?"

"—inducing us to feel comfortable in your presence, and encouraging us to divulge the most intimate things to you!"

"It is surely not that bad!" Sheffield protested. "And nothing so intimate was divulged to me. No family skeletons, more's the pity. And before you launch into a fresh recital of my misdeeds, let me state that you did not need any encouragement to confide your opinions of me or anyone else."

"Yes, but I thought you family!"

Having said this, Samantha fell silent and dropped into a chair opposite Sheffield. This allowed Miranda the opportunity to ask if Sheffield were really a lord.

"Yes," he replied, laughing a little.

"How famous! What sort of lord? An earl, perhaps? A marquis?"

Sheffield smiled at her emotion. "Nothing so uncommon, I do assure you, Miss Miranda. Merely a viscount."

Faced with such singular modesty, Miranda clapped her hands and turned to her sisters. "Did you hear that, Samantha? I vow, I have never even met a viscount before."

"Don't be a peagoose," Samantha implored. "You haven't even met a baronet much less an earl or marquis before today. I wonder, viscount or not, Lord Sheffield, if Wilhelm knows you are using this residence."

This question, which as good as implied that Sheffield was accustomed to entering any establishment that caught his fancy and making himself at home, brought the viscount up short. And he strove instantly to correct such an addled notion.

"Certainly Wilhelm knows I am here," he answered crossly. "Bad *ton* just to arrive at a fellow's house and use it! I am here, Miss Curtis, at the express invitation of your cousin."

Her green eyes locked momentarily with his brown ones. "How peculiar, then, that Wilhelm chose to go off on his fishing expedition if he *had* invited you to stay with him."

"Wilhelm invited me to stay when he discovered my residence in Berkeley Square was in need of repair. A leaky roof, or so my housekeeper informs me. Since Wilhelm was not using this establishment, he offered it to me."

"And you in turn have lent it to Miss Horick in order to throw her ball?"

The viscount suffered a distinct shock. Whatever he had expected when Frieda had commanded him to set a provincial straight, it was not to be called to task for abusing Wilhelm's hospitality. The incident, however, was not without novelty, and it appealed, as most things did sooner or later, to his sense of the ridiculous.

"I did not think Wilhelm would mind greatly," he said now apologetically. "And Frieda had been yearning to give a ball. I've paid for everything myself, and I assure you we haven't broken the china or stolen the silverware, if that is what troubles you. You may even ask Horace about it."

This suggestion met with strong objection from Pamela, who earnestly protested that they trusted him. "Don't we, Samantha?"

Samantha, who was scrutinizing the viscount with no great confidence visible on her face, replied drily that, under the circumstances, they had no other choice.

"It does warm my heart to see your confidence in me, Miss Curtis," Sheffield drawled so languidly that she forgot all about being angry with him and laughed.

She had, he noticed, a most charming laugh.

"When do you think we might see Wilhelm?" she asked.

"I haven't the slighest clue," he confessed. "Another week at the least, I should think. When he is fishing he loses all track of time. Something to do with being hip deep in water, I should imagine. Although I for one fail to understand the fascination fish can exert on a grown man."

Before anyone could scruple to point out the joys peculiar to anglers, the door to the room opened and in stomped Miss Horick looking blond, beautiful, and piqued.

"Warren, haven't you finished yet with these people?"

Sheffield dealt a quelling look at his soon-to-be-betrothed. "These are Wilhelm's cousins, Frieda," he explained in a civil but forceful tone. "He had invited them to stay with him while they were visiting London."

Samantha's back had stiffened at the Beauty's entrance. She was not at all surprised to see now that Miss Horick boasted a theatrical nature.

"Invited them to stay?" the Beauty asked, clutching one hand to a heaving bosom. "My dear Warren, that is outrageous. You are already staying here, and you must tell them so at once." As though, Samanatha thought, no one in the room other than Sheffield possessed any ears.

Miss Horick, having claimed the floor, continued to rail. "Really, Warren. This is too naughty of you. You have been in here for the greater part of an hour. Supper is waiting, and several of our guests have begun to wonder where you could be. Not that it isn't civil of you to be polite to people, whatever their station in life."

"Since I am Wilhelm's guest myself, Frieda, I can do no less than see to the comfort of his cousins," Sheffield answered urbanely. "But you needn't concern yourself about this matter. Go into the supper room. You are quite right. Our guests shall be hungry. Perhaps a little nourishment shall make you feel better."

"Go in to the supper room?" Miss Horick asked, looking as though Sheffield had just ordered her forthwith to a nunnery. "Do you mean without you?"

"I shall be in directly," he promised.

With a last fulminating look directed at Samantha, Miss Horick turned and flounced out of the room, banging the door hard on her heels.

Wincing slightly at this overt display of temper, Sheffield gazed at the others. "Now where were we?"

"Wilhelm's whereabouts," Donald supplied helpfully.

"Yes. I was saying I didn't know just where he was or how long he would be gone from London. It appears that he left before your letter reached here, Miss Curtis, otherwise he would have informed me to expect you." He paused, noticing for the first time the signs of fatigue on the four faces in front of him. "Good heavens. Here you are so tired. And you must be hungry as well. Let's have a bite of supper. We'll thrash it all out while we eat."

Although the merest mention of food caused Samantha's mouth to water, she had no wish to subject herself or her sisters to the odious remarks sure to come from Miss Horick again.

"You do eat, don't you?" Sheffield asked, puzzling over her silence.

"Of course we eat," Samantha answered with some exasperation. "And we are hungry, or at least I am. But as you can plainly see, we are not fit to be ushered into any supper room."

"You have been traveling," Sheffield said imperturbably. "No doubt all of our guests have at times undertaken a similar task. No one will care a rush about how you look."

"I care, my lord!" Samantha shot back. "And I have borne with quite enough snubs for one evening. You are kind to invite us to sup with you, but I think a tray in our rooms shall suffice."

Sheffield cocked his head at her. "Your rooms, Miss Curtis?"

"Yes, of course. We were relying on Cousin Wilhelm's hospitality while in London."

"Unfortunately," Sheffield pointed out as he helped himself to another pinch of snuff, "Wilhelm does not know a thing about you. As far as he is concerned, you are still in York. And he gave *me* command of his establishment."

"But you said yourself you are not using all the rooms!"

The Sevres snuffbox closed with an audible bang. "My dear Miss Curtis, if you are remotely considering the possibility of staying the night here under the same roof with me, I beg you to give that over. I am a bachelor."

"But not a rake, I should hope?" Samantha demanded.

Not unexpectedly, the viscount was stunned by this question and did not attempt to answer it straight away. *"Not a rake, I should hope?"* By Jove, just what sort of female was he dealing with.

"Have you qualms that Miss Horick shall not like such an arrangement?" Samantha inquired. "I daresay you may be right. I think you had better go to a hotel."

Sheffield stared at her as though at a ghost. "You want me to go to a hotel?" He asked, so faintly that Pamela, who had just heard her own sister inform a peer of the realm to take up residence for the night in public lodgings, hid her face in her husband's coat.

"Why yes, my lord," Samantha said blithely. "It is not that uncommon, even among those of your rank. And it would be easier for you to find a room than for us. Four is so awkward a number. Or else," she said as a flash of inspiration struck, "you could put up the night with a friend. I daresay you must have a large number of friends who would be only too happy to put you up. You might ask Miss Horick, if you are hard pressed for assistance."

"I might if I were a more courageous fellow," Sheffield said with a broad grin. "And I'd give a monkey to see her face if I ever put such a thing to her. But I shan't, for that would undoubtedly make her fly into a pet, which is always so tiresome." He rose to his feet. "I shall apply to John Steed. I saw him here earlier, and he owes me a favor. I suppose I could always sleep in his library or something of the sort. I should thank you, Miss Curtis. Frieda's party would have been devilishly boring if not for you. And as a reward, you shall have your rooms, and a supper tray as well. I shall just pop out now and inform Horace."

Before Samantha or anyone else had a chance to thank him he was out the door, leaving Pamela free to chide Samantha on her audacity in suggesting that the viscount put up in a friend's bookroom.

"I suggested nothing of the sort," Samantha said, too

pleased at being allowed to stay to take her sister's criticism to heart. "I suggested a hotel, which is a perfectly respectable place to stay the night. 'Twas he who conceived the notion of a bookroom. Perhaps he has slept in bookrooms before."

"Samantha!" Pamela said, shocked.

"I am only funning, Pammy!" Samantha laughed. "Surely you didn't wish to wander about looking for lodgings at this hour?"

"Well, no," Pamela admitted. "But you have been much too free with your tongue tonight, my dear."

Before Samanatha had the chance to refute this Horace returned, requesting them to follow him. Together they mounted the marble stairs and headed toward the east wing of the house, their journey marred only by a slight altercation they were obliged to witness near the supper room. It was, Samantha noted in passing, a rather emotional exchange between an agitated Frieda Horick and a cool, elegant Viscount Sheffield.

⟞ *FOUR* ⟝

Samantha's resolution to think no more of Sheffield or Miss Horick was not so easily kept. Marie, one of Wilhelm's maids who had undertaken the task of dressing Samantha, informed her that Sheffield and Miss Horick had been seen at Rundell and Bridges not a week ago, admiring a matching set of ruby necklace and bracelet. Rubies, Marie confided, were Miss Horick's favorite jewels, a fact she had straight from her cousin, who had once worked for the Beauty but who was now employed elsewhere, the Beauty's whims being notoriously fickle.

"Rubies have always struck me as unlucky," Samantha

murmured as Marie toyed with her hair. "But there is no denying that they are very pretty."

"Yes, Miss," Marie agreed as she frowned over a curl that would not obey her brush. "Still, it wouldn't surprise me if His Lordship does buy the rubies for her, unlucky or not. He dotes on her so. Do you know, his mama used to despair that he never marry, or if he did he would marry an American, and you know how they are."

Samantha had never met an American and felt ill qualified to pass judgment on them now. To her relief, for she felt that she would disgrace herself if she heard another syllable about Miss Horick, Marie deemed her hair fit to be seen, and she passed out of the room and into the hallway.

Maids and footmen were occupied in cleaning up after the ball, overseen by Horace, who greeted Samantha at the bottom of the stairs with the news that neither of her sisters had as yet arisen. He led her into a breakfast room, and a plate of buttered eggs and ham were whisked before her.

"Horace," she asked, after her first bite, "are you acquainted with a Mr. Augustus Phelps?"

"Is that Mr. Phelps the solicitor, Miss?" the butler asked discreetly.

"Yes. I have some matters to discuss with him, and since I am a virtual stranger to London, I shall rely on you to provide direction to his office. If you would."

"No direction will be necessary, Miss Curtis," Horace answered with a smile. "Kenrick will drive you. Lord Sheffield had informed me earlier that you were certain to have errands to run. Kenrick can find Mr. Phelps's office for you, and later, if you wish, he can stop at Madame Fanchon's. Lord Sheffield anticipated that you might wish to call there later this morning."

"Did he indeed," Samantha said, a little annoyed that Sheffied had anticipated her every move. However, she smothered her annoyance, finished her breakfast, and then willingly placed herself in the hands of Kenrick, a Scot whose garrulousness belied the taciturn nature of his forebearers. It was Kenrick who pointed out the sights they encountered on the way to the City, including Guildhall,

Whitehall's Banqueting House, Carlton House, and Westminster itself.

Samantha had not set foot in London since she was a child, and she craned her neck back and forth as she rode in Wilhelm's barouche. The carriage crossed the Strand and pulled to a stop in front of Mr. Phelps's office, located conveniently in the hub of the city not far from Mr. Wren's great cathedral.

Mr. Phelps himself appeared to more advantage amidst his legal clutter of books, papers, and briefs than he had in Samantha's parlor in York. He greeted her quite cordially and inquired meticulously after her sisters, then launched himself into a full explanation of Lady Kendall's tangled fiscal affairs.

"The bulk, as I explained back in York, is the ten thousand pounds," he said, squinting at her slightly over his pince nez. "There is unfortunately no land."

The lack of land did not dismay Samantha. "The ten thousand pounds is windfall enough for me," she told her solicitor.

He beamed back at her. "Of course it is. Oh, there is just one point I feel duty bound to pass on to you. Your inheritance has caused talk among some of Lady Kendall's relations."

"Indeed?"

"Yes," he tittered. "Some of it not very nice."

"I am not surprised," she revealed with a faint smile. "As a matter of fact, I don't count anything they might say as anything but *on dits*. They washed their hands of Papa long ago, you know. And I feel sure they have no real liking for us. But I shan't allow anyone to spoil my visit here."

"No, indeed." Mr. Phelps agreed. "You are bent on doing the Season, are you not?" He wagged a finger playfully at her. "You see, I have remembered what you told me back in York. And I have taken the liberty of establishing your credit with all of the prime shopkeepers. Quite the usual sort of thing, I do assure you."

"Mr. Phelps! You are a Trojan! What should I do without you?"

The solicitor blushed at her praise. "Nonsense. Just glad to be of service. Now, where are you staying?"

"At Cavendish Square. My cousin Wilhelm's residence."

Mr. Phelps looked puzzled. "I had heard he was out of town."

"Yes, following the fish, or so they tell me. He had loaned his establishment to the Viscount Sheffield, and it was he who actually consented to let us stay the night there."

Mr. Phelps's eyes bulged from their sockets, an event magnified by his spectacles. "You stayed the night under the same roof as the Viscount Sheffield?" he inquired.

Samantha choked on a laugh. "No, Mr. Phelps. The viscount removed himself to a hotel, at our suggestion."

The solicitor appeared fascinated and astonished by the news.

"Actually," Samantha continued, "now that I think of it, he didn't stay at a hotel but in a friend's bookroom. Mr. Steed was the friend's name."

Mr. Phelps patted his lips with a folded handkerchief. "Miss Curtis, have you any idea? No, I daresay you cannot, being a stranger to these parts. But do you know just who the Viscount Sheffield is?"

"Not really," Samantha confessed. "Although judging from your reaction, he must be someone of enormous consequence. However, Pammy did tell me that all peers are vastly important, so I really am not the one to judge. I do know that Sheffield is planning to marry that odiously starched up Miss Horick."

Mr. Phelps leaned back in his chair, ignoring this blunt reference to one of the *ton*'s leading ladies.

"Viscount Sheffield," he said with a low voice, "is one of the twenty richest men in the kingdom. He has estates in Kent as well as in Warwickshire, and his yearly income has been put in the neighborhood of forty thousand pounds."

"Which is four times my entire fortune," Samantha said with aplomb. "Now I see why he turned up his nose in that fashion last night when I merely hinted that he might be marrying Miss Horick for her fortune. That was when I was still laboring under the delusion that he was my cousin."

Mr. Phelps's confusion multiplied. "You thought Viscount Sheffield was your cousin?"

She laughed. "I know it sounds odd. Of course I knew I was not related to him, I just mistook him for Wilhelm. But his identity came to rights by the end of the evening. But do go on with what you were saying about him."

"I was saying that he is one of the richest men in the kingdom," Mr. Phelps answered. "And one of society's best traveled. He has been to Spain, the Americas, and Africa, all within the past four years."

"All within the past four years?" Samantha said, rather struck by this facet in Sheffield's character. "How intriguing! I must remember to ask him about that when next we meet, although I daresay I shan't know when that shall be for certain." She paused and then inquired offhandedly if Miss Horick's fortune was the equal of the viscount's.

Mr. Phelps permitted himself a ghost of a smile. "Hardly any lady's fortune would be the equal of Lord Sheffield's, Miss Curtis! But in spite of that, Miss Horick shall not want. Her father left her a substantial fortune, which she invested very wisely in the Funds—as you should," he could not help advising.

Samantha smiled. "But how is it that two such fortunes, Miss Horick's and the viscount's, contrived to meet?"

"Nothing could be simpler! It is true that Lord Sheffield is very much the world traveler, but after his last trip abroad, he settled in London. In fact, he had not been in town more than a week when he clapped eyes on Miss Horick, who is after all an acclaimed Beauty as well as an heiress. And such attractions—"

". . . are fatal to any bachelor," Samantha concluded. "Yes, any gentleman would fall under such a spell, even Sheffield—who seems to be rather poor husband material to begin with, if he is so addicted to travel. I do hope, however, that he is not the last well-pursed gentleman to be married off."

Mr. Phelps laced his fingers on his bony chest and threw her a curious look. "I should say he is not. Forgive the question, Miss Curtis, but perhaps you are contemplating matrimony in your future?"

Laughing, she shook her head. "At twenty-three I am acknowledged to be on the shelf, Mr. Phelps, and I find it a rather comfortable position to be in. I was thinking of my sister Miranda at the moment. You have seen yourself how beautiful she is. I have come to London expressly to see if I could arrange a suitable match."

A look of comprehension crossed the solicitor's face. "Miss Miranda is very beautiful," he agreed. "A suitable match, you said. Would you like me to keep my ears and eyes open?"

"If you would," Samantha said gratefully. "I daresay you know more about the eligible gentlemen in London at this point than I. Not that Miranda would ever consent to anything so coldblooded, and I for one do not mean to foist a match on her that she does not desire. But with a little assistance, I think I can arrange for her to meet a suitable gentleman, and with luck, she may find herself in love with him!"

After a half hour, during which she won Mr. Phelps's approbation by consenting to lay aside half her inheritance in the Funds, Samantha quitted his office in the City and journeyed back across the Strand to Madame Fanchon, who remembered vividly the Beauty that had been the late Mrs. Reginald Curtis.

Although Fanchon did not say anything untoward about the outmoded walking dress Samantha appeared in, her keen eyes did not miss a thing. After her customer had made her first tentative selections from the silks and satins in the shop, the *modiste* promised that her girls would work night and day in order that Mademoiselle Curtis not feel it necessary to hide her face when in public view. Feeling properly chastened, Samantha made an appointment for her two sisters on the following day and then rode off with Kenrick in the barouche.

As the carriage wheels rolled over the cobblestoned streets once again, she persuaded the groom to point out some of the more interesting sights that London boasted.

Although the Scot balked at the impropriety of her rather civil request to see the Manchester Square residence of the Regent's Lady Hertford, he did consent to point out New Bond Street, where he warned that no self-respecting lady would dare walk unaccompanied after the noon hour, as well as the bay window of White's, where the dandy set were known to congregate for the express pleasure of hurling insults at all the passersby.

"If you heed my warning, Miss, you'll have nought to do with them," Kenrick said, by now on excellent terms with his passenger.

"Is Viscount Sheffield part of that set, Kenrick?" she asked idly as he turned the carriage around a corner.

The groom snorted. "No, he ain't. And what's more, he wouldn't have a thing to do with such a passel of man-milliners! Now mind, I'm not saying that they are all that way, but a goodly number are. And the viscount has too much sense in his cockloft to involve himself in such a set."

Samantha smiled and inquired absentmindedly just what set Sheffield did belong to.

"To his own," Kenrick answered with some satisfaction. "Sets his own mode, does His Lordship."

The evident pride in his voice piqued Samantha's curiosity.

"You seem well acquainted with His Lordship, Kenrick."

The groom emitted a deep chuckle. "I ought to be, Miss. Been with him nigh on fifteen years. 'Twas I who taught him how to handle a whip—not that he had that much to learn, for if ever I saw one who took to the reins straight off, 'twas he."

Samantha wound the strings of her reticule tight about a finger. "Fifteen years?" she said, confused. "But I thought . . . Surely you are *Wilhelm's* groom, are you not, Kenrick?"

The Scot, who had been about to launch into one of his favorite stories concerning the viscount and himself, turned around in the seat. "Whatever gave you that idea, Miss? Not that I'm saying your cousin is a downy one, for he ain't. Everything up to snuff about him. But he can't lay a hand on an out-and-outer like the viscount, if you excuse my saying so."

"You work for Sheffield!" Samantha exclaimed, her confusion giving way to chagrin. She had been chatting so comfortably with the groom thinking him one of Wilhelm's servants, and all the while he was Sheffield's man—no doubt left behind with the express purpose of spying on her!

"Why didn't you tell me, Kenrick?" she demanded quietly.

"Didn't seem to be any reason to," the groom replied, darting a quick look over a hunched shoulder. "But truly, Miss, it's nothing to get on your high ropes about."

"When we arrive at Cavendish Square," Samantha ordered, "you shall leave and return to Lord Sheffield. I would be obliged if you told him that I requested him to do me no further favors. I am quite capable of taking care of myself. Why he would leave you behind quite escapes me."

"Now, now, Miss," Kenrick said, growing quite alarmed himself by the vehemence in her voice and relieved that they were fast approaching Cavendish Square. "It's nothing to be in the hips about, I do assure you. His Lordship was only trying to be helpful, seeing that you were new to the town and might fall into the briars." He brought the horses to a halt in front of Wilhelm's residence. "And if you do wish to speak to him you're in luck, for that's his phaeton on the flagway."

Samantha, who would not have recognized Sheffield's phaeton if it sat up and spoke to her, suffered herself to be handed down from the barouche, then brushed past the waiting Horace at the door, desiring to know the viscount's whereabouts.

"In the blue drawing room, Miss," Horace said placidly.

Since Samantha was not as yet thoroughly familiar with her cousin's residence, a few maddening minutes passed before she located the room. To add to her ill temper, when she finally reached it she discovered present not only the viscount but also her sisters and Donald as well, all seated enjoying a comfortable cose under the disapproving eye of a Curtis ancestor glowering from a canvas on the wall.

"Samantha, there you are," Pamela cried out in welcome. "Do come in. We are just trying this tea from the Berry Brothers. Horace says it is Wilhelm's favorite."

Samantha advanced into the room wearing a scowl that matched that of her forebearer over the mantle. Ignoring Pamela's invitation, she glared at Sheffield, wondering how he dared look so much at home.

"What are you doing here?" she demanded.

"Samantha!" Pamela hissed in acute mortification.

Sheffield, however, had risen at her approach and was undismayed by her unconventional greeting. He chose to take her question quite literally.

"I am having tea," he said, pointing to the cups on the table in front of them. "Perhaps you would care to join us, Miss Curtis?"

"Not until you explain yourself, my lord."

The viscount's expression turned quizzical. "Do you know, Miss Curtis," he said affably, "in the past twelve hours that I have known you, I detect an evident flair for the dramatic in you. I wonder if it would be demanding too much if you merely sat down and told us why you have suddenly flown into the boughs."

"I am not in the boughs," Samantha retorted, remaining on her feet. "You have been interfering in my affairs!"

"Don't be a skittle-brain! Not in my nature to poke my nose into things that don't concern me. Much too fatiguing, for one thing."

"I suppose you deny leaving Kenrick here to report back to you on what we do? He's *your* groom, not Wilhelm's!"

"Certainly he's my groom! And a deuced fine one at that. But he's hardly a spy, if that is what you are accusing him of. And peculiarly enough, that does appear to be your charge. I daresay you have become fascinated by the cloak-and-dagger tales in the papers of late, reminiscences of Bonapartist doings. You must contrive to remember that the war is at an end, Miss Curtis. It happened the year before last. Napoleon is vanquished. It happened at Waterloo. Chap named Wellington had something to do with it."

"I know that!" Samantha said between gritted teeth.

"Well, I couldn't be certain, what with all your talk of spies," he pointed out. "And Kenrick is not a Bonapartist. Now that I think of it, the man can't even speak a syllable of French."

"I know that!" Samantha said exasperatedly. "At least," she amended, "I know he is not a Bonapartist agent—not that I was ever aware of his problem with the French language, which I daresay is no great disgrace for half the English do not speak French."

"And the other half speak it abominably," he agreed. "But tell me then, why does my leaving Kenrick and my barouche with you make you so Friday-faced?"

"Good God. Don't tell me the barouche is yours too," Samantha ejaculated and dropped into the nearest chair. This relieved Sheffield of the necessity to stand, and within seconds he was once again seated in the Windsor chair sipping his tea.

"Look here, has Kenrick done anything to offend you?" he asked after a moment. "Deuced out of character, I'd call it. Known him all my life, but still—"

Samantha put a quick end to this speculation. "Oh, no! Heavens! On the contrary, he's been most helpful, pointing out all the sights of interest along the way to the City. But still," her voice hardened, "I should have been told he worked for you."

"Did you ask him?" Sheffield inquired.

Samantha admitted that she had not.

"Then it's entirely your own fault for not knowing," Sheffield said. "It appears to me, Miss Curtis, that all your mistaken impressions, including several of last evening, stem from your inability to ask a simple question at the proper time. If you had merely asked me if I were Wilhelm last evening, I would have said no, thus saving us both considerable vexation. And had you merely asked Kenrick if he were Wilhelm's groom, he would have assured you that he was not."

Samantha found herself in the odd position of being

bested. "There is no winning this battle with you, is there?" she asked.

He grinned. "None at all. Now do take that tea before it goes cold, and listen to me. I knew you were planning to see your solicitor and probably Fanchon today, and since you don't have a town carriage, I left one at your disposal. Did you dislike it, or Kenrick?"

"Of course not," Samantha said putting her tea cup down. "It's just that I don't wish to be beholden to you or any other gentleman."

"A perfectly understandable reaction in a female of your tender years," the viscount said. "It shall perhaps relieve you of your anxiety if I said that although Miss Horick and I have not made an announcement in the papers we do have an understanding. So your fears about me and any favor I may wish to extract from you are groundless."

"Don't talk flummery," Samantha said crossly. "I am not in the least afraid of you or what you might do, although perhaps I should be. I have been informed by Mr. Phelps that your consequence is enormous. However,"—a mischievous grin crossed her face—"I judge it much too late for us to stand on ceremony, don't you?"

"Decidedly yes, you minx," Sheffield answered. "And now do let us put an end to this tedious discussion. What will you have me do with the barouche and Kenrick? Do they stay or go?"

Samantha's hesitation did not last more than a moment. To have the carriage and the groom at her disposal would ease things during her stay in London.

"Since you have placed them at my disposal, my lord," she said demurely, "we would be ill-bred to refuse, so I do thank you."

"You're welcome," he said with an ironic gleam in his eyes.

"But," she continued, "henceforth you shall oblige us by staying completely out of my affairs?"

"Completely?"

"Completely."

"As you wish," he said with a smile.

With that problem successfully negotiated, Samantha relaxed long enough to take a sip of the fragrant tea and inquire what Sheffield was doing at Cavendish Square at such an hour.

"I thought people like you rarely woke before noon."

Her words nearly overset him again, but he managed to control a quivering lip.

"As a rule you are correct, Miss Curtis, but an early rising was dictated this morning."

"The viscount took Donald to Tattersall's," Pamela explained to Samantha. "They've only just returned."

"And quite a time we've had of it," Donald offered, his ruddy face flushing with pleasure. "Can't believe the quality of horseflesh there. No short-boned creatures for certain, and I can't thank you enough, my lord."

Miranda, who had even less interest in horses than either Samantha or Pamela, knew from long experience that, if encouraged, horse-mad Donald would be pelting Sheffield with questions and comments about his cattle. She tugged at Samantha's sleeve, demanding to know if she really had seen Fanchon.

"Yes," Samantha said with an emphatic nod. "And I have made appointments for you and Pammy to see her tomorrow."

The conversation thereupon in the blue salon turned, much to Mr. Langford's disappointment, from horses to fashion. Sheffield displayed such a marked knowledge of the details of the female toilette that Samantha was obliged to believe that he was quite accustomed to the commissioning of dresses, gowns, and heaven knew what else for Miss Horick—or perhaps one of his *chère amies* who had preceded her.

That thought, combined with his own undisputed elegance, made her feel more countrified than ever in her outmoded walking dress.

All the talk about clothing had reminded Sheffield of his own, which had been left abovestairs, and he went out into the hall to dispatch a footman to bring his things down. Recalled by this to certain deprivations he may have suffered the night before, Pamela inquired about his night spent with Mr. Steed.

"It went tolerably well, Mrs. Langford," Sheffield an-swered. "As it always does when John is in his cups. You will be relieved, Miss Curtis, to know that I wasn't obliged to put up in his bookroom after all. I had a chamber next to his, and one night there was more than enough. Upon awakening I posted off to Berkeley Square, to find my own residence had been repaired. I shall remain there for the duration of Season."

"Best thing for you, I should think," Donald agreed, and then took advantage of this opening to solicit Sheffield's opinion on his possibly buying some Arabian stock with which to refurbish his cattle in Yorkshire. As the two men debated the merits of such a plan, which Samantha for one fully realized would cost Donald dearly if he ever put it into action, they heard Horace's shocked exclamation from the hall: "Mr. Curtis!"

Hardly had these words left the butler's lips than Wilhelm himself strode into the blue drawing room, a rotund figure with a walruslike mustache and an expression of complete bewilderment on his face. His eyes darted from face to face until it fell on the only one in the room he recognized.

"Sheffield? What the devil are you up to, man?"

"Nothing whatever, my good Wilhelm," Sheffield replied at his most languid. "But do give me leave to introduce you to some of your own family. Mr. and Mrs. Langford, the Misses Curtis, Samantha and Miranda. They are cousins and guests, Wilhelm."

Wilhelm had been acknowledging the introductions with a curt nod but now drew himself up at the word "guests" and shook a pudgy finger at the viscount.

"See here, Sheffield. I'm in no mood for your pranks. Damn fishing stream. Bah! That blasted Farrington bought up the whole stream, aye, and the land, strictly to satisfy his own taste for angling. I'm fagged to death and need a bath, so let's have no more nonsense about guests."

"It's not nonsense," Samantha asserted, having decided from this wretched beginning that she might as well take the bull and her cousin by the horns. "I am your cousin, Samantha Curtis, from York, and I daresay none of this would be happening if you had received my letter, which you didn't on account of that fishing expedition, and I am sorry to hear that it all came to nought and someone bought up the stream, for that does strike me as unfair."

"Hmmph." Wilhelm snorted and glared at her fiercely. "Cousin did you call yourself? And what's this about York?"

"Yes, cousin," Samantha said patiently and furnished him with a quick explanation of who they were and what had brought them to London.

"Lucky you," Wilhelm said when she had finished speaking. "I could do with ten thousand quid myself. Not that I begrudge it to you, because your father did leave you all without a feather to fly with. But what in blazes does any of it have to do with me?"

"Well, we had to stay somewhere," Samantha said, feeling as though she had made this explanation at least a half dozen times since she had set foot in London. "You are a bachelor, after all. And your establishment is going to waste."

"It is not going to waste," Wilhelm contradicted, his mustache bristling indignantly at the very suggestion. "But I am a bachelor, right you are, and you can't stay with me! Cousin or not, bound to be talk. Not good for your reputation."

"Why?" Samantha demanded. "Are you a rake?"

The audacity of this question stopped Mr. Curtis cold in his tracks.

"Rake?" He thundered. The viscount followed the exchange with some interest, wondering if Miss Curtis were determined to ask this question of all the gentlemen she encountered in London. If she did, there would be diversion aplenty for the rest of the Season.

"No," Wilhelm said now, having recovered his powers of speech, "I am not a rake."

"No," Samantha agreed. "You are not even said to like females, are you? And as for reputation, cousin, that needn't concern you, for I am on the shelf. However, Miranda isn't, so I daresay we must observe the rules on her account."

"Of course," Wilhelm agreed and shifted a malevolent eye toward the viscount. "Did you stay the night here with them?"

"Don't be a dolt," Sheffield answered. "And pray don't glower at me as though you were on the verge of challenging me to a duel for besmirching your family honor. I removed myself to spend the night at Steed's, who, I might remind you, snores like a donkey. I've only just returned here to fetch the rest of my things. I'm obliged to you for your hospitality, Wilhelm, but it appears the work on my establishment has been completed. You, however, needn't scruple to stay here with your cousins, since blood is thicker than water."

"Bound to be talk," Wilhelm said, shaking his head. "A fellow my age and these young females and no older ones about. You know what the quizzes shall make of it. I might even be forced to *marry* one of them," he said, looking suitably shaken at the very prospect.

Samantha had heard enough nonsense for one day. "Don't be absurd, cousin," she said sharply. "None of us has the slightest intention to marry you. So you may rest easy on that score."

"You'll still have to leave," Wilhelm growled.

"Come now, Wilhelm," Sheffield said, interposing his lanky frame between the two cousins. "You can't mean to throw your cousins out, I should hope! How would that look in the *ton*. Definitely shall be talk, then."

"I suppose so," Wilhelm acknowledged, "but Warren—"

"I have it!" Sheffield snapped his fingers. "The very solution, even if I do say so myself. You'll come with me."

Wilhelm recoiled. "With you where?"

"To Berkeley Square. I'm on my way home, and I daresay nothing could be easier than to bring you with me to stay while your cousins use this establishment."

"But, Warren! I need a bath!" Wilhelm protested.

"Oh, we have soap and water at Berkeley Square," Sheffield said with a reproachful look. "And you needn't bother to thank me. After all, you can't throw your cousins out without causing talk, and you can't stay here, so you say, without causing talk, and they can't stay with me without causing talk. So the only sensible solution is for you to stay with me!"

"Perhaps so. But Warren," Wilhelm said as he found his friend's hand under his elbow, "this is my establishment!"

"Of course it is," Sheffield soothed. "But temporarily, I fear, it belongs to Miss Curtis and her sisters."

And without giving Wilhelm a chance to bleat out any further protests, he bustled his friend out the door and toward the phaeton, bound for Berkeley Square.

~ FIVE ~

For the Curtises the days flew by in a riot of excitement over hats, gloves, dresses, and calls to the silk warehouses and linen drapers. On their first visit to Bruton Street, Madame Fanchon proved to be as impressed as anyone could have wished over the sublime figure and countenance of the youngest member of the Curtis family and soon predicted that Mademoiselle Miranda would be the rage of the Season just as her *pauvre maman* once had been.

"If properly gowned, of course," she said with a sidelong glance at Samantha.

"Of course," Samantha answered as Miranda moved off, her attention drawn by some shimmery satin on a table. "It is my wish, Madame," Samantha confided to the *modiste*, "for you to supply Miranda with everything she shall need for the Season."

These words acted as a powerful restorative on Fanchon, who had thus far into the Season failed to discern the Beauty who would do justice to her genius. She briskly clapped her hands, summoned her girls from the back rooms, and began to measure and cut, promising that within the next week the morning dresses and ball gowns would be readied for *la famille* Curtis.

Fanchon was as good as her word. When the promised dresses at last arrived, she sat back gleefully waiting for the *ton* to descend upon Cavendish Square and hail Miranda as the brightest star on the horizon.

The members of the *haut ton*, however, being unacquainted with Samantha's plans, were engaged in various pursuits of their own, including the attending of routs, balls, breakfasts, and *soirées*, the accounts of which Samantha read daily in the *Morning Post* with mounting vexation.

"It is the outside of enough," she stormed one morning to Pamela as she crushed a newspaper in her fist and flung it into the fire. "The Season is upon us, but we have no part in it. It is enough to drive me to distraction."

"I know how disappointed you must be," Pamela said. "And indeed, I too own to feeling a bit cast down on account of Miranda. But perhaps someone shall turn up shortly."

"No one shall turn up," Samantha said gloomily, giving vent to her anger by striding up and down the length of the room, "except perhaps Wilhelm. And you know very well that he only comes here to pinch and scold and demand that we vacate this establishment at once."

Eventually her frustration led her to Mr. Phelps. No sooner had her solicitor greeted her and Pamela one morning than she quickly laid in front of him the whole sorry story of her failure to launch her sister.

"And there is no use to show me any list of gentlemen who might be looking for a wife," she said bitterly, "for no list shall be of any help unless Miranda were able to meet them. And I don't know how she shall do that!"

A bit surprised by his visitor's vehemence, Mr. Phelps still forebore to extend to her the list of eligibles he had so carefully drawn up.

"The Season is by no means at an end yet, Miss Curtis," he said reassuringly.

This attempt at optimism did not sway Samantha. "It might as well be the end of Season for all I have been able to accomplish. Mr. Phelps, just how does any Beauty attract the attention of the *ton*?"

Mr. Phelps appeared momentarily shocked that any female, even one from the country, would be unacquainted with such an elementary fact of life. "Why, at Almacks, of course, Miss Curtis. You must go to Almacks with your sister. Anyone desirous of marrying well must! I daresay the Assembly Rooms boast all the eligible males, as well as every new Beauty."

Samantha mulled over this news for a moment. "I had heard Mama mention Almacks now and then, of course, but I never knew it was so vastly important. Where is it, pray? And how does one get there?"

"Almacks is on King Street," Mr. Phelps informed her. "But there can be no question of just going there, Miss Curtis." He tittered nervously. "No one can just enter the Assembly Rooms without first procuring vouchers, which must of course come from the Patronesses."

Once again Samantha was obliged to admit her ignorance by inquiring just who the Patronesses might be.

Mr. Phelps clucked his tongue. "I see you have no idea of what is ahead of you," he intoned, and settling himself more comfortably in his chair and ignoring the clerk who had tottered in with a load of papers, he passed the next half hour telling Samantha and Pamela about the Patronesses who ruled over the august assembly at Almacks and whose number included the Countess Lieven, Mrs. Drummond Burrel, the Princess Ectzerdhady, Lady Sefton, and Lady Jersey. Before any female were even allowed into the hallowed halls of Almacks she must be approved of by the Patronesses, whose whims were notorious.

Here Mr. Phelps diverged momentarily on a tangent of his own to relate several horror tales concerning certain females ill advised enough to anger the Patronesses and whose subsequent attempts to secure a voucher were doomed to failure.

"Good heavens," Samantha exclaimed as he came at last to the end of this torturous recital. "I had no idea it would be so difficult. Cannot a match be contrived without Almacks?"

"I supose so," the solicitor said, looking doubtful. "But that would be leaving something to chance, which most marriage-minded mamas do not wish to do." He wiped his spectacles with a handkerchief. "You see, at Almacks they are assured that their daughters shall be seen and appreciated by the most eligible gentlemen of the *ton*. The *crème de la crème*, as the Countess Lieven likes to call it."

"Then that is where Miranda must go," Samantha said decisively. "But have you any notion how I could meet these Patronesses? I don't know one of them, but perhaps you might."

At this naive utterance Mr. Phelps turned nearly as white as his shirt and emitted several garbled protests.

"Miss Curtis," he said finally, "my circle of acquaintances, while large, does not boast any of the Patronesses."

"That is a pity," Samantha said sadly.

"The best advice I would have to offer would be to find someone who does know one of the Patronesses. Perhaps not Mrs. Burrell, for she is the highest stickler of the lot, nor the Countess Lieven, being Russian and so prone to whims. Lady Jersey and Lady Sefton are the better-natured of the group."

Samantha scowled. "But I know no one of any use, Mr. Phelps. Aside from you and Wilhelm. And I assure you that my cousin is not about to introduce us anywhere, since he is still livid at us for usurping his house on Cavendish Square. And that was not so much our doing but Sheffield's, who did so only to amuse himself!"

"Sh-Sheffield!" Mr. Phelps stuttered a little in his haste to speak. "I beg pardon, Miss Curtis, but there is the answer to your prayers. Since you are acquainted with Viscount Sheffield, there shall be no difficulty in getting to know the Patronesses. He is at first oars with Lady Jersey."

This announcement came as no great surprise to Samantha. Sheffield did have the look of an out-and-outer who was probably given entree to Almacks and anywhere else he wished to go. But she was by no means certain that she wished to apply to him for help, particularly when she remembered the way she had all but demanded at their last encounter that he keep his nose out of her private affairs.

It was approaching eleven-thirty when Samantha and Pamela returned to the barouche. After settling herself comfortably against the squabs, Samantha ordered Kenrick to take them to his employer's residence.

"To the viscount's, do you mean, Miss?" Kenrick asked, looking startled—but not as startled as Pamela.

Samantha nodded to the groom.

"Samantha!" her sister hissed as the carriage rolled along. "What can you be thinking of! You know very well that Lord Sheffield is not expecting us. And I hope you are not brazen enough to call on a gentleman—and a bachelor!"

"I am not calling on Sheffield," Samantha interrupted as she clapped one hand to the hat that was in danger of flying off in the wind. "I am calling on Cousin Wilhelm, which I have every right to do, being his relation. It is the sheerest coincidence that Wilhelm is staying now with Sheffield!"

Pamela, however, saw through this ruse at once. "Donald told us both last night that Wilhelm would be spending the morning at Tattersall's!" she exclaimed. "Really, Samantha, you are all about in your head! Have you no thought of your reputation?"

"Don't be a goose, Pammy," Samantha said, rather exasperated by such talk. "You speak as though Viscount Sheffield were a rake. He is no such thing. And as for my precious reputation, you know very well I am on the shelf." She grinned and leaned over to pat her sister on the hand. "If you can't bring yourself to step into the devil's lair, I shall go in and speak to Sheffield alone. You may wait in the barouche."

In the face of this threat, which Samantha was more than capable of fulfilling, Pamela quickly capitulated. "How can you even jest about such a thing," she scolded. "As though I would allow you to do anything so foolish. Since you are determined to see the viscount, I shall have to accompany you."

"Thank you, Pammy," Samantha said with a smile.

Her sister was not so easily placated. "But why do you wish to see him?"

"To get the vouchers for Almacks!" she exclaimed. "Don't you wish Miranda to be a spelndid success? Mr. Phelps explained it all most thoroughly to us. We need Sheffield to sponsor Miranda and introduce us to Lady Jersey."

"Oh, Samantha," Pamela murmured helplessly, "there must be someone else we can apply to for help. You were barely civil to the viscount when last you saw him," she reminded her, "and he cannot have forgotten that so soon. I was thinking only last night about Lady Alice North, Mama's great chum. Do you remember? She might help us."

Samantha, while willing to acknowledge this remote possibility, replied pessimistically that they had not seen or heard of Lady Alice in years and that she might be deceased for all they knew. "Whereas I do know the viscount is hale and hearty! Or at least he was five days ago! And with a little persuasion, he might lend us his assistance!"

Despite the confidence with which Samantha tossed off this blithe assurance, even she was obliged to own to some qualms when the carriage pulled up at the elegant town mansion that was the residence of the viscount. Its corniched doorway and Roman entrance hall all but announced the fact that a Nonpareil dwelled within. Nor did Samantha's nervousness abate when they were ushered into the ivory saloon by a butler every bit as superior as Horace.

"I shall inform His Lordship of your presence, Miss," he intoned before withdrawing.

"Oh, Samantha! Do let's go," Pamela pleaded, what little courage she had possessed earlier having taken flight immediately.

"Good heavens, Pammy, we can't leave," Samantha answered, gazing with curiosity at one of Mr. Constable's finer landscapes above the mantel and several rather exotic looking artifacts, including a bronze vase that was no doubt a remnant of His Lordship's travels. "Don't be a 'fraidy cat, Pammy," she said, seeing her sister's worried face. "He shan't eat us."

Of this, however, Samantha herself was uncertain when

the viscount finally loomed in the doorway looking complete and to the shade, his lanky frame couched in a coat of Bath blue superfine augmented by a cream-colored waistcoat, matching pantaloons, and gleaming black Hessians. No eye could miss the snowy white cravat done in the Mathematical style by the expert hand of a master.

"It is you!" he said, dropping his quizzing glass and advancing toward Samantha. "I thought Charles was roasting me about two young female visitors. What the devil brings you here?"

Samantha had no way of knowing that Sheffield had been roused from his dressing room, an occasion which always put him out of temper, and she thought it just like him to ask such a rude question straight off when the civil thing would have been to greet them kindly.

"We have come to see you, my lord," she responded now.

"So I observe," he said, highly entertained by the tone of voice that definitely indicated something was afoot. Intrigued in spite of himself, he sat down on a gilded Hepplewhite chair, informing her that she had his complete attention.

"It occurred to me," Samantha began slowly, "that I may have spoken too harshly to you on the last occasion we met. Now that I have had time to reflect on the matter, it was more than civil of you to loan us Kenrick and the barouche."

"If it were an apology you wished to offer, Miss Curtis, you could have penned a full dozen to me in the time it took Kenrick to drive here," Sheffield observed.

"Perhaps so, but Mama told us that an apology should be made in person," Samantha said with aplomb.

Sheffield laughed. "And did your mama also tell you not to try and hoodwink people? If she neglected this facet in your education, I should take that charge on myself and warn you not to try and gammon me. Apology! I have never heard such fiddle in my life. Females blessed with half your spirit, Miss Curtis, do not come meekly hat in hand unless they desire something. Even though I now observe that your hat is on your head, and,"—he resorted again to his quizzing glass—"it is quite a handsome rig, all in all."

"I did not come here to win your approval of my wardrobe," Samantha said frostily, although secretly pleased that she had won the approbation of one of the *ton's* leading men of mode.

"The color green would suit you to excellent advantage," Sheffield said now as he abandoned his glass, "and do avoid yellow, for it shall make you look hideously sallow. And now, my good Miss Curtis, the truth, if you please?"

"Oh, very well. I want you to sponsor my sister in the *ton.*"

Sheffield had been toying idly with his riband but now stiffened with incredulity. "You want me to do *what*?" he demanded. "No, never mind, don't repeat such a request. How came you by such a harebrained notion?"

"It's not harebrained," Samantha retorted.

"No? Pray forgive me, perhaps you are just foxed."

"I am no such thing!" Samantha glared at him. "And I have never heard anything so uncivil. I'm not asking for myself, for I daresay you may not feel kindly disposed toward me, but for Miranda. She fully deserves to attract the notice of the *ton.*"

"Miss Curtis—"

"Why, even Madame Fanchon, who met her only this week, says she has rarely seen such perfection in both form and face, and Fanchon has been dressing all the ladies of the *ton* for decades."

"I am well aware of Fanchon's expertise—"

"Miranda would be the rage of the Season."

Sheffield stopped and looked at her more closely. "With perhaps a brilliant match to follow?"

Samantha blushed slightly at this rather bald and all too accurate evaluation of her motives. "Yes," she said defiantly. "That is my wish. But if she is ever to meet the right sort of gentleman, she will need entree into Almacks."

Sheffield's interest in Miranda's fate was beginning to wane. "These confidences are perhaps interesting to you," he said now, "but I confess to finding myself at a loss."

"The vouchers for Almacks are granted only by the

Patronesses," Samantha said, goaded beyond endurance by this striking example of male stupidity. "And you are at first oars with Lady Jersey, or so I have heard. So I thought if you were obliging enough to sponsor a small party for Miranda, which I would pay for myself, we could meet Lady Jersey. Once she has seen Miranda, I am sure she would grant her the vouchers."

A malevolent smile flashed across Sheffield's face. "Lady Jersey," he said with great relish, "has already seen your lovely sister."

Samantha looked bewildered. "When was this?" she demanded.

"She was among the guests who witnessed your arrival at Cavendish Square," Sheffield said, not unkindly.

"Good God!" Samantha said. However, her spirits rallied almost at once from this mortal blow. "Then you must see that it is even more important that Lady Jersey meet Miranda under more auspicious surroundings."

Sheffield groaned. "My dear child, you have windmills in your head. Have you even stopped to think what the *ton* shall say, let alone Lady Jersey, whose tongue does seem to run on wheels at my giving a party, even a modest one, for your sister—especially after your arrival the other night? I am a bachelor," he reminded her, "and not a relation to either you or the lovely Miranda."

A stricken look appeared in Samantha's eyes. "Good gracious, do you mean there will be talk?"

"A good deal of talk," Sheffield said diplomatically. "If you do wish your sister to be the success you envison, you shan't have her making her comeout under the wing of a bachelor without the slightest family tie to her."

He saw that she was for once looking cast down by his words and, in an attempt to cheer her, suggested she apply to Wilhelm for help.

Samantha scoffed at his suggestion. "Since you are his host, you must know that we are in his black books. And I hardly see Wilhelm consenting to sponsor us anywhere but to York, or perhaps to Jericho," she said gloomily.

Sheffield, only too well acquainted with Wilhelm's opinions of his cousins, acknowledged his idea a poor one.

"But is there no one else you know here in London?"

"No one," Samantha said miserably.

"Except for Lady Alice North," Pamela piped up, all but forgotten by the others in the room. She colored slightly as Sheffield turned an inquiring eye toward her.

"Lady Alice North?" he inquired.

"Yes," Pamela hastened to explain. "She was Mama's great friend."

Samantha hunched an impatient shoulder. "We don't even know if Lady Alice is alive, Pammy. She may have died years ago."

"Oh, Lady Alice is very much alive," Sheffield said.

"Even so, she doesn't know us from Eve. And I shan't descend upon her with such a request." A flush crossed her face. "That ragmannered I'm not!"

"How true," Sheffield said affably. "You only descend upon me with such requests!" He laughed. "No, don't rip up. I fully realize how vexing this must be to you. But perhaps if we had a bite of something to eat, inspiration might strike one of us. Shall we go into the small dining room?" he asked. "Alphonse has promised me eels this noon."

Ten minutes later in the dining room the viscount glanced up to see his guest chewing valiantly on a piece of the promised delicacy, a look of mild revulsion on her pretty face. He could not resist a grin.

"Well?" he inquired as she swallowed hard.

"Do people really eat such things?" Samantha demanded after two gulps of water to clear her palate. "They taste horrid."

"You cannot reach such a judgment after just one bite," Sheffield chided. "Such cowardice! I would have wagered anything that you were pluck to the old backbone. Eels, I'll have you know, are a gourmet's delight. And there are some parts of the world where the people would sooner eat eels than beef or fowl." And he swallowed a large forkful to prove his point, occasioning a shudder in both of his guests.

Leaving the plate of eels to be enjoyed by Sheffield, the sisters turned their attention to the cheese wedges, strawberries, ham, and mince pies while their host regaled them with tales of the Americas and Africa.

"Did you really see the Pyramids?" Samantha asked raptly.

Sheffield smiled and nodded. "Why? Do you have a great interest in them?"

"I have a great interest in anywhere," Samantha said with a rueful laugh, explaining that the only two places she could remember seeing in her life were York and London. "Although Papa did tell us that we saw a good bit of the Continent when we were younger and he was trying to outrun his creditors."

A half hour later the meal came to a conclusion with the successful depletion of the entire bowl of strawberries, both sisters sharing Sheffield's own avowed weakness for the dish, which had them squabbling like schoolchildren for the remains. The three of them were just passing out of the dining room and into the entrance hall, where Samantha planned to take her leave, when Miss Horick, resplendent in a rose-colored dress and sable pelisse, suddenly sailed through the front door. On seeing Sheffield and his guests, she came to a rigid halt.

"Warren?" she quizzed.

"Good afternoon, Frieda," Sheffield said adroitly. "You remember Mrs. Langford and Miss Curtis, I should hope?"

"Of course I remember them!" the Beauty said acidly.

"Well, good," he said a trifle uncertainly. "They came to call on their cousin Wilhelm, who has been staying with me, and who unfortunately was not in. I persuaded them to take luncheon here in hopes he would show up. Have you eaten, Frieda?"

"I have already partaken of a noon meal," Miss Horick intoned magestically.

"What a pity," Sheffield murmured, "especially since the eels were quite delicious, were they not, Miss Curtis?" he asked affably.

"Quite the best I have ever tasted," Samantha said, trying to control the slight quake in her voice.

Miss Horick was not about to be waylaid into a discussion of sea creatures, edible or nonedible, and took over the conversation by reminding the viscount of their plans to go to Almacks later that evening.

"I need no reminder, Frieda," Sheffield replied. "Wednesday night at Almacks. Nothing could be simpler to remember."

"Good. For I am looking forward to it immensely. The Assembly is always delightful. The dancing, music, and lights! Don't you agree, Miss Curtis?"

Samantha replied that she had not as yet had the pleasure of attending Assembly. But she could not resist adding, "I hope to in the future."

"But of course you must," Miss Horick said, appalled at the idea of any lady not attending Assembly. "Shall we see you there tonight, perchance?"

Aware that she was treading on very thin ice, Samantha murmured that she could not say for certain, but that quite probably they would not take in this evening's Assembly.

"What a pity," Miss Horick replied, her gray eyes betraying a different emotion than her words. Her head dipped closer to Samantha. "But my dear, you *do* possess the vouchers, do you not?" she asked, then made a quick *moue*. "How *awful* for you if you did not. And really, what could I be doing, talking on this way about Almacks. The mortification you must be experiencing if you do not have the vouchers."

"Of course we have the vouchers," Samantha blurted out.

"You do?" Miss Horick pounced quickly on her answer. "How wonderful! Don't you agree, Warren?" She turned back to Samantha with a knowing smile curving her lips. "However did you manage to procure them in such a short time, Miss Curtis?"

Samantha was saved from stepping further into the Beauty's trap by the arrival of Wilhelm, an unlikely rescuer, all in all. Wilhelm, spotting his cousins in the entrance hall, advanced wrathfully toward Samantha.

"Now, now, Wilhelm, no violence, I pray you," Sheffield said, pulling him away by the arm.

"But I'm tired of living here," Wilhelm protested.

"Obliged to you and everything, Sheffield, and don't think me ungrateful, but I want my own bed. Stands to reason, after all; it is *my* residence," he reminded his friend.

"Yes of course it is," Sheffield soothed.

"And you shall have it soon enough, cousin," Samantha promised.

Wilhelm, however, was not about to be so easily placated.

"High-handed miss! Needs to be taught a lesson."

For a fleeting moment the viscount's eyes met Samantha's.

"I believe the lesson you desire shall shortly be under way, Wilhelm," he drawled.

~ *SIX* ~

"Samantha, have you gone mad?" Pamela demanded as she paced wildly in her sister's bedchamber in Cavendish Square. "Telling such an untruth. And in front of the viscount!"

"I know, Pammy," Samantha said wearily. "You are right. I have made a mull of things. But indeed, I couldn't help myself. She practically dared me to do it!"

"Miss Horick dared you to lie about having the vouchers for Almacks?" Pamela's voice rose an octave in disbelief. "What a rapper!"

Samantha sank down on the bed. "But she did. She was being so odiously superior to us, didn't you even notice? The way she burst into Sheffield's residence, as though she owned it!"

Pamela's eyebrows arched heavenward in mute supplication. "Miss Horick is practically betrothed to Lord Sheffield. No doubt she acts as though she owns the house because shortly she shall be its chatelaine!"

"That still doesn't give her the right to bullock me!"

"Yes, I know," Pamela murmured as she pushed her sister over on the bed to make room for her to sit. "It's just that this is such a coil! How do you think we shall get the vouchers for Miranda now?"

"I don't know," Samantha answered, thumping a goose down pillow with a fist. "She knew that I didn't have the vouchers! A real lady would not have gone on speaking about them in such a condescending fashion to me. She just wanted me to admit that I didn't have them so she could be odiously superior all over again, and I *couldn't*—"

"So you lied instead!" Pamela sighed. "I don't mean to pinch at you, Samantha, but don't you see that now we shall undoubtedly find ourselves snubbed by the Patronesses once they have heard that you presumed to say such an audacious thing. You realize Miss Horick shan't rest until the tale is all over the *ton*."

"I know," Samantha acknowledged.

"And that means we might as well do Cousin Wilhelm a favor and return to York immediately."

Samantha hurled the pillow onto the floor and sat up. "I shall not go back to York with my tail between my legs!"

"I say, is anything amiss?" Donald stood in the doorway, roused by the voices raised in heated discussion. He looked questioningly at his wife, but it was Samantha who answered his query.

"I have disgraced myself," she said gloomily.

"Disgrace?" Donald wrinkled his nose and laughed, accustomed to his sister-in-law's jests. "Surely you're roasting me, Samantha."

"No she isn't," Pamela answered dourly and explained what had happened at Berkeley Square.

"Vouchers to Almacks, I say," Donald said happily. "I didn't know you *had* the vouchers, Samantha."

"She doesn't!" Pamela said, put out of patience by her own spouse's stupidity. "She lied."

"It was the merest fib!" Samantha protested, before placing another pillow over her face.

"It amounts to the same thing," Pamela said trenchantly.

"I suppose so. But it can't be so difficult to get the vouchers, can it?" Donald asked, with what both women thought as another prime example of male stupidity.

"I hope not," Samantha said mildly. Donald, apparently satisfied that his wife and her sister were at least not murdering each other, withdrew. Pamela, however, lingered behind to ring a peal over Samantha for another five minutes.

Samantha accepted it all as her due. "I am sorry, Pammy," she said, emerging briefly from the pillow, "and I wish I could take the lie back, but I can't so it's past speaking of. You are right that Miss Horick shall not rest a moment in spreading the news about the *ton*. Odious female!"

"It appears to me that you are much too concerned about Miss Horick and what she thinks and does," Pamela said rather acutely, and on that Parthian shot left her sister to dwell further on her own misery.

Alone at last, Samantha stared gloomily at the walls. Although she hated to admit it, Pammy was right. She was a gudgeon to be so concerned about Miss Frieda Horick, and yet in truth she couldn't seem to help it. From the unlucky moment when she had first crossed paths with the Beauty, they had been at daggers drawn.

She propped her face up now on her fists. It wasn't merely that the Beauty was so beautiful, for Samantha had met other beauties before, and she wasn't usually prone to envy. Nor was it Miss Horick's enormous fortune! It was, Samantha decided, as she rolled over on her back, Miss Horick's air of self-importance and the way she perpetually held herself up to notice—*particularly* when the viscount was present.

"But that is only natural, since they are going to marry each other," Samantha reminded herself. A quick pang of pity for Sheffield struck her but then disappeared. This was not the time to waste thinking of the viscount's future problems with Miss Horick as a wife! Not when she had her own pressing problems to contend with.

And with that, Samantha placed the pillow over her face

once again, attempting to find there the solution to the perplexing problem of vouchers.

Several blocks away, the Viscount Sheffield was being ushered into a charming sitting room that bore the unmistakable touch of a female presence, attested to by many pillows of exquisite needlepoint.

"This is a fine how-do-you-do, Warren," Lady Alice North said, looking up in surprise at her afternoon caller. Her smile, however, gave the lie to her playful words. "I vow, I haven't seen you in an age."

"Several ages, I should think," Sheffield answered, with the smile he reserved for his closest chums.

Lady Alice patted the couch invitingly. "We shall have some sherry, and then you shall tell me all about yourself and what brings you by. I thought you were at Ascot, risking enormous sums on the horses."

Sheffield laughed. "Don't you know, Alice, that gentlemen must wager enormous sums on races? It is their lot in life, like visiting their tailor."

Chuckling, Lady Alice accepted the sherry from the tray her butler offered. Now thirty-four, she was still blessed with a crown of rich auburn hair, two clear hazel eyes, and a spirit that kept her in perpetual good humor despite having been left a widow at the untimely age of twenty-eight. A renown Beauty in her day, she still commanded a loyal flock of suitors, including two poets who were known to languish after her. But she was disinclined to accept any gentleman's offer of marriage, much less that of a poet!

"What does bring you by, Warren?" Lady Alice inquired, her eyes looking at him closely after a comfortable ten minutes listening to his tales of Ascot.

"To pass on some news and to ask a favor."

"Both at the same time?" she teased. "Well, which is it to be first?"

"I believe you know a young lady named Samantha Curtis."

Lady Alice had been listening to him with an indulgent smile, but now she put down her glass of sherry and fixed her eyes intently on his face. "To be sure I do. Her mama was the most delightful creature I knew, even though she was some years my senior. She married disastrously," she confided sadly. "Reggie Curtis. Both families dead set against the match, of course! But the two *would* elope, and that led to even more quarrels and disagreeableness. And Reggie proved to be nothing but a profligate, dying with his pockets to let, if what I understood of the situation is at all correct. And then Amanda died too. I was in Brussels at the time. But what is this about her daughter?"

"There are three daughters," Sheffield replied. "The eldest, Pamela, is married, but it is Samantha, the middle child, who has held the family together quite admirably since their mother's death. There is also another sister, Miranda, eighteen and a diamond of the first water."

"How come you by your information, Warren?" Lady Alice quizzed. "You were not acquainted with their family, and from what I understood of the Curtis girls, they lived somewhere in the North Country."

"So they did," he agreed. "But they have removed to London for the Season. Miss Curtis inherited a legacy from a relative and has brought the lovely Miranda to town to become the rage of the Season and make the usual brilliant match."

Lady Alice looked thoughtful. "Is the youngest so beautiful?"

"Oh, yes," Sheffield said without hesitation. "Quite ravishing."

Lady Alice, who had never heard such words to pass his jaded lips before with regard to any mere female, was properly impressed. If Sheffield, whom she considered immune to female charms, spoke in such glowing terms, then Miss Miranda Curtis must be a Beauty indeed.

"If she is as you say, she might well make the brilliant match," she informed him. "How long has the family been in London?" she inquired.

"About a se'ennight," he answered. "For the time being they are staying in their Cousin Wilhelm's residence on Cavendish Square. Wilhelm, ever concerned with propriety, removed himself to stay with me."

Lady Alice rocked with gentle laughter. "They are

cousins," she said, having no patience with such hair splitting. "And I must see them soon. I haven't laid eyes on Samantha since she was fourteen, and even then she was mostly elbows and knees!"

"Presumably she still possesses these joints, but you shall find her well turned out. Not as beautiful as the youngest, but more than passably good looking."

Lady Alice lifted an exasperated face toward her visitor. "Spoken like a gentleman who had at one time half the females in the *ton* laying in wait for him to throw the handkerchief. What, pray, do you mean by 'more than passably good looking'?"

"In Miss Curtis's case it means a heart-shaped face, two green eyes, a slight upturned nose, a rather audacious little chin, and a mound of sandy-colored curls."

Lady Alice threw him a saucy look. "So observant, Warren?"

He bowed ironically and smiled.

"If this is the news you have brought me, I am indebted to you. But you also spoke of a favor."

"It has to do with the Curtises," he explained, putting his glass of sherry down. "Miss Curtis is quite anxious to launch her sister into the *ton* and speaks longingly of vouchers for Almacks."

Lady Alice nodded. "If the sister is the Beauty you profess her to be, it *would* have to be Almacks."

"The favor I ask is simple enough, Alice. Would you sponsor a small dinner party for them? Nothing so grand, just a few of your friends and mine. I shall stand the cost myself and attempt to persuade Lady Jersey to attend. I am hoping that she shall be so enchanted by the lovely Miranda that the problem of vouchers shan't arise."

"A party shall liven things up here," Lady Alice agreed. "But you needn't advance me any sums, Warren. I may be a widow, but I'm not destitute yet." She laughed. "And I owe it to their mother to sponsor such a party. But if it's vouchers they are after, you should invite Maria Sefton along with Sally Jersey."

"If you think it best," Sheffield acquiesced at once. "But

mind, the Curtises are not to know that I asked you to undertake the party."

"It is not like you to hide your light under a bush, Warren," Lady Alice said with some curiosity.

The viscount grimaced. "Miss Curtis already believes I take too free a hand in her affairs."

"And do you?" she quizzed.

"I suppose so," he admitted. "But it stands to reason. They are green, and I feel some responsibility, since they descended on Cavendish Square thinking Wilhelm would be there and found me instead. And if Miss Curtis knew I were behind this party of yours, she might decline to attend it. She is the stubbornest creature!"

"How odd," Lady Alice said with a chuckle, "for I had thought you were the stubbornest creature I knew. I shan't say anything to her about your coming to me with the idea. But how is it that you concern yourself with them?"

"Because of Frieda," Sheffield answered.

Lady Alice's surprise sparked a fit of the hiccoughs. "*Frieda*? She . . . wants you to launch . . . Miss Curtis . . . in the *ton*?" she demanded somewhat incoherently between hiccoughs. "Now I know you have lost your wits, Warren!"

"No I haven't!" he contradicted. "And Frieda is not to know about my putting you up to this party!"

"There appear to be a good many people who are not to know about things," Lady Alice complained after she had vanquished her hiccoughs with a sip of sherry. "Has Frieda met Samantha?"

"They had a pulling of the caps," he went on, "the sort of thing Frieda is prone to do when she is irritated. And this morning it all came to a head. She questioned Miss Curtis on whether she had vouchers for Almacks, and for some unfathomable reason that chit said she did have them, which I'll go bail is a lie."

Lady Alice looked alarmed. "Good gracious, Warren, if what you say is true and the Patronesses get wind of it—"

"No one shall hear of it until Miss Curtis has the vouchers for Almacks for certain," Sheffield assured her. "I shall make it a point of telling Lady Jersey about it myself. She likes audacity so much she may well make it the *on dit* of the Season. She also dotes on me."

"Yes, I know that," Lady Alice replied. But despite her friend being a prime favorite of the Patroness, she still reserved some doubts. "We must have this party as soon as possible. Shall we say Friday evening? In the meantime, someone must stop Frieda's tongue from wagging."

"You may leave Frieda to me," Sheffield said blithely.

A half hour later Sheffield strolled into Miss Horick's residence on Grosvenor Square, carrying with him the ruby necklace that had won her approbation earlier in the week at Rundell and Bridges.

Miss Horick's face lit up with pleasure when she saw the gift. "For me, Warren? You must put them on me," she said, turning and offering him her back.

Dutifully Sheffield clasped the necklace round her slender throat. "They are almost as beautiful as you, my dear Frieda," he murmured into her ear. The Beauty rewarded him with a kiss on his cheek, then turned to admire herself in a pier glass.

"It is too sweet of you, Warren!" she exclaimed. "And I vow, such a surprise. I shouldn't know what I could ever do to thank you."

"I'm glad you asked that, Frieda," he said adroitly. "That little set-to today with Miss Curtis. It would oblige me if you said nothing about the incident to anyone."

Miss Horick stiffened in the midst of her preening. "Miss Curtis? Pray, what does she have to do with you?" she asked arctically.

"Not a thing in the world! But I do feel some sense of obligation to her cousin, who is a guest in my house, after all."

"I was not aware that your friendship with Wilhelm superceded your bond with me."

"It doesn't," Sheffield said with aplomb. "But I should hate just the same for him or her cousins to be snubbed if word of the tale ever came out."

Miss Horick had tired somewhat of the topic of Miss Curtis and returned to the mirror to admire her jewels. "She doesn't have the vouchers, you must realize, Warren."

"I know. But all the same, there's no reason on earth why she should not. And a little harmless boasting never hurt anyone."

"Except herself," Miss Horick pointed out with some satisfaction. "Miss Curtis does not as yet know her place in polite society. That was evident from the first second I laid eyes on her. I'm sorry, Warren. I don't mean to be disobliging, and if it were anything else I could do—"

Sheffield had come prepared for this eventuality. "There is another necklace I saw today at Rundell's," he said in a deliberately offhand manner. "A twin to this, only of course in sapphires—which, if memory serves me correctly, would be a perfect mate to that blue satin gown of yours."

Miss Horick eyed him coldly. "Are you trying to induce me to keep silent, Warren?"

Instead of replying, Sheffield smiled and resolutely examined the gloss on his Hessians, leaving Miss Horick to struggle momentarily with herself and her fondness for jewelry. The lure of the sapphires was considerable, as Sheffield knew it would be.

"I suppose a country miss could be forgiven her forwardness," she said grudgingly. "Where did you say this other necklace could be had?"

"At Rundell and Bridges," Sheffield said promptly. "Why don't we go there and examine it together?"

As Sheffield and Miss Horick undertook their joint examination of the sapphire necklace, Samantha was feeling all the happiness of a reunion with Lady Alice, who had allowed no grass to grow under her feet. As soon as Sheffield had departed on his own errands Lady Alice had sped off to Cavendish Square, and now she stood blinking back sudden tears as she gazed at the slender girl who resembled her old friend.

"Pray don't think me a watering pot. It was just that you have the great look of Amanda."

"It is civil of you to say that," Samantha answered with a laugh, "for I know Mama was an acclaimed Beauty. But in truth it is my younger sister who has inherited the majority of Mama's looks. Pamela, my elder sister, has received her gentle heart, and I am left, so they tell me, with her wits!"

"Intelligence has its place and its powers," Lady Alice pointed out.

"I am well aware of that, ma'am," Samantha said cheerfully. "And I'm not pining. I'm only sorry that Pammy and Miranda are not here to greet you. They took Brutus out for a walk."

"Brutus?"

"A mongrel, ma'am," Samantha answered with a laugh. "One that Miranda found and would not be parted from whatever the cost. So we are now the owners of a rather monstrous hound."

"It appears to me that Miranda has a soft heart too."

Samantha poured some tea. "How did you know we were here in London, ma'am?"

"A mutual friend, Viscount Sheffield," Lady Alice replied, watching her closely.

Samantha did not disappoint her. She looked up at the older woman with surprise clearly writ on her face.

"The Viscount Sheffield?" she repeated. "Good heavens, why did he do such a thing? Not that it wasn't civil of him—and he's actually more Wilhelm's friend than mine!"

"Have you taken him in a dislike?" Lady Alice inquired, trying to satisfy herself on exactly what the relationship was between Sheffield and Samantha. "That does surprise me, for Warren's manners are usually most impeccable. And as a rule he is a great favorite with the ladies."

"I am certain that Viscount Sheffield is much admired on every account," Samantha replied. "And I don't really dislike him—although I must own he is high-handed and opinionated!"

Lady Alice hid a tiny smile. At length she inquired after what had happened to bring the family to London, and listened to the brief history that unfolded in the drawing room about the Curtises' years in York.

"And now you have come to London," Lady Alice said when the tale was nearing its completion.

"Yes, ma'am. Because I want better things for Miranda."

"If she is as beautiful as Sheffield claims, there can be no problem about that. My dear, he described her in terms that practically glowed, and such praise is hard to come by, especially from Sheffield. I should confess that in matters concerning females he is alleged to be something of an expert."

"Is he indeed?" Samantha asked, finding this a rather disagreeable facet to the viscount's character. "I daresay he has engaged in numerous affairs of the heart?"

Lady Alice chuckled. "That was only in his salad days, when he was nought but a green halfling. Not now, when he is all but engaged to Frieda Horick." She gazed out of the side of her eyes and was not at all surprised by the flush that suffused Samantha's face at the mention of the Beauty. "But that is quite enough about Warren!" she said briskly. "I mean to give a small ball to welcome you and your sisters to London. Shall we say this Friday evening? Nothing so grand, merely a few close friends of mine. You can attend, I hope?"

"With the greatest of pleasure!" Samantha exclaimed. "But ma'am, you haven't even met Miranda yet. Perhaps you should wait and see her to assure yourself that she shan't put you to the blush. Even though I can vouch for her."

"I have seen you, and that is enough," Lady Alice answered. "And it occurs to me that while you are in London, Miranda might not be the only Curtis female to contemplate matrimony."

Samantha looked at her in bewilderment that changed almost immediately to amusement. "Are you speaking of me? Good heavens, Lady Alice, I should warn you, I am twenty-three!"

"But hardly on your deathbed!" Lady Alice laughed. "My dear, you shall attract a score of men or I shall eat my hat—and I shall even make it one of those odious Oldenburg hats!"

"But I am not on the scramble for a husband," Samantha protested. "If only Miranda is properly mated, I shall be content."

Lady Alice said no more, and at the end of another ten

minutes she rose, promising to take care of all the details
of the ball on Friday. She was just leaving the drawing
room with Samantha when Miranda rushed in, accompanied by the newest addition to the Curtis household, a
rather shaggy hound.

"Samantha! Pammy's outside talking to Donald . . .
Oh!" She came to an abrupt halt when she caught sight of
Lady Alice.

"Come in, Miranda," Samantha said with a smile. "Lady
Alice, this is my sister, Miranda. Miranda, you remember
Lady Alice North, Mama's great friend."

Lady Alice shook hands with Miranda, pleased to find
that Sheffield had not exaggerated her beauty. Once again
she was put in mind of her old friend.

"Friday evening," she said softly to Samantha, and with
this as her farewell, departed in her landau.

"What's this about Friday?" Miranda demanded, as she
attempted to dissuade Brutus from becoming overly infatu-
ated with one of Cousin Wilhelm's prize Buhl tables.

"Lady Alice has agreed to sponsor a small ball for us,"
Samantha said. "This is our first step into the *ton*, Miranda." She hugged her. "You shall undoubtedly become
the rage."

"Must I, Samantha?" Miranda asked absently.

"Why of course, my dear. That's the whole point to our
trip to London. You have come to enjoy the Season. And
your Season is just about to start."

～ SEVEN ～

True to her word, Lady Alice dispatched invitations to
a select few of her closest friends inviting them to a small
soirée in honor of the daughters of a beloved friend on the

coming Friday. Among the recipients of the personally penned cards were Sheffield, who fully qualified as one of Lady Alice's intimates, and Miss Horick, who did not.

Had the matter been left in Lady Alice's hands she would have struck Miss Horick from her list entirely. But since the viscount was practically engaged to the creature, the priorities did have to be observed.

At Cavendish Square the days leading up to the ball passed in a flurry of excitement and hurried dance instruction. Samantha, leaving nothing to chance, had detected a slight flaw in Miranda's dancing during one of their practice sessions and had sent for a dancing master to bring them up to snuff on the quadrille and the waltz, although the latter, everyone knew, could not be danced first without the approval of the Patronesses.

All these preparations, though tedious, seemed worth the price when they arrived at Mount Street Friday evening.

Lady Alice had mentioned a small gathering of friends, but Samantha saw immediately that they would sit at least forty to dinner. She wondered what would constitute her hostess's notion of a large gathering.

With one hand gripping the delicate iron balustrade, she made her way up the stairs toward where Lady Alice waited.

"Lady Alice," she said at once. "How kind you are to invite us, and how beautiful you look."

Their hostess, who did look rather radiant in a shimmering white satin, smiled seraphically. "Thank you, my dear. And you are looking quite the thing yourself."

Samantha passed over this compliment lightly. But in truth the question of what they would wear to the ball had consumed the greater part of two days of indecision. At last she had hit on a festive green gauze over a soft satin underdress, while Pammy had chosen for herself an azure blue crepe. While no one could fault the attire of the elder Curtis sisters it was Miranda who drew most of the attention in a pale rose muslin with matching roses in her hair done *a la Anglaise*. Samantha's heart filled almost to the bursting point as she noticed the stunning effect of her sister's beauty on several of the gentlemen present.

The first person whom Samantha laid eyes on after leaving Lady Alice was Miss Horick, who looked resplendent this evening in a ball gown of vivid red, very *décolleté*, with a glittering ruby necklace highlighting her elegant throat.

"Just one of the many gifts Warren showers on me," she informed a rapt audience. "Would you believe, he insisted on buying another necklace like this, made of sapphires, merely to keep this one company in my jewel box?"

Samantha began to think more and more that Sheffield fully deserved to be saddled with an odious female like Miss Horick for life.

She led the way into the ball room with Pammy, Donald, and Miranda trailing behind, and within minutes witnessed the pleasureable sight of her sister being borne off by a tide of admirers.

A half hour later Lady Alice came up to Samantha to say that Lady Jersey had arrived and wished to meet her. Eager to make acquaintance of the august Patroness of whom she had heard so much, Samantha trod across the room toward a lady whom she recognized too late as the lady in the red turban from Sheffield's party. Had it been possible to slink out of sight Samantha would have made a valiant attempt, but she could not. With a coaxing smile, Lady Alice was already leading her toward the Patroness.

"I have met you before," Lady Jersey said, clucking her tongue and gazing at Samantha too closely for her comfort.

"Perhaps long ago, ma'am," she said as Lady Alice drifted away, leaving her alone with the Patroness.

"No, not long ago at all." Lady Jersey frowned. "In fact, I am convinced it was only of late." She gave her head a distracted shake. "Bah, I am getting old. But it shall come to me in a moment, just see if it doesn't. I know I have seen you someplace before."

"Cavendish Square, Tuesday last," a cool voice intoned, and Samantha turned round to find Sheffield at her elbow, looking quite top of the trees in evening dress. "Miss Curtis arrived in the midst of Frieda's ball, dear Sally; how could you forget?"

"How indeed, Warren?" Lady Jersey agreed, glad at having that mystery solved. She rapped him on the knuckles with an ivory fan. "After all, that little episode put you in Frieda's black books, did it not? But I daresay that ruby necklace you just bestowed on her shall help to right the matter."

"My dear Sally, perhaps you know what you are talking about but *I* do not," he drawled. He gazed over at Samantha. "My compliments, Miss Curtis. You are looking decidedly better this evening than on the occasion of Miss Horick's ball."

"Thank you, my lord," Samantha said, not feeling thankful at all at being the object of his quizzing in front of Lady Jersey. "You may credit Fanchon with my appearance."

"Oh? Here I thought it was all my doing," he said reproachfully.

"Yours!" she exclaimed in some surprise.

"Yes," he said with some calm. "I did advise you to wear the color green, if you recall."

"Now that you have occasion to bring it to my mind," Samantha said with some condescension, "I do recall a discourse we had on that topic. But that was not in my mind when I chose my gown for this evening."

"No, of course it wasn't," he said so archly that Samantha longed to box his ears.

"Now, Warren, do go away," Lady Jersey commanded, looking highly amused by this exchange. "I have just begun to make Miss Curtis's acquaintance. Why don't you go off and challenge someone to a duel or whatever it is that gentlemen do to pass the time."

"An intriguing suggestion, Sally," the viscount acknowledged, "but I see tamer action afoot: Captain Maybury, a naval friend. As a favor to me Alice invited him this evening, and I see he is looking more at sea than if he were afloat." With this, he sauntered off toward a figure in regimentals.

Left alone with Lady Jersey, Samantha soon discovered that the Patroness was not as fierce as she had heard but was instead a good-humored although inquisitive soul. She found herself contending with some of Lady Jersey's curiosity.

"For someone who has just met you, Sheffield takes an inordinate interest in you," Lady Jersey observed at one point.

"Do you think so, ma'am?" Samantha asked. "I had supposed him just to be civil to me and my sisters."

"Ah yes, your sisters. I have heard much of that lovely sister of yours. Where is she? I should like to meet her."

Within ten minutes of making Miranda's acquaintance, Lady Jersey's approval was won.

"You are both the type of females who should be frequenting Almacks," the Patroness said, deploring aloud the usual run of milk-and-water misses the club had been attracting of late. "Females without a grain of sense who do nothing but titter behind their fans, which of course drives the men to distraction and they decline to attend, and what is the use of the club without the men," she said, looking more than a little distracted herself.

Glancing now at Miranda, she inquired if she tittered. To which Miranda, being a sensible sort of person, replied that she did not.

"Good," Lady Jersey said as though this settled the question. "Now I shall have to find Maria. Let me see, she was admiring the lobster patties when I saw her last."

While Lady Jersey hunted for Lady Sefton amidst the lobster patties and Miranda returned post haste to her corner of beaux, Wilhelm, who had been lurking nearby waiting for an opportunity to speak to Samantha, pounced on her with a vengeance.

"Cousin Samantha, I wish to speak to you."

Startled, Samantha caught her breath. "Good heavens, Wilhelm. You gave me a fright."

"Oh, I say, I am sorry," he said, then realized to whom he was apologizing. "I must talk to you."

"Oh, dear, I hope it is not another unsatisfactory episode with a fish," Samantha lamented. "Perhaps you should take up another sport, cousin. They say that archery is soothing to the nerves."

"My nerves don't need soothing," Wilhelm said. "Or at least they wouldn't if I were back where I belonged in my own house! Cousin Samantha, you can't be aware of the time and effort I took to refurbish that place, to make it just what I wanted in a residence!"

"But of course I have noticed," Samantha said at once. "It is a splendid residence. I saw that at once. And your Horace is quite a paragon. I don't know how we would have managed without him."

"Then you must see why I need it—"

"Wilhelm, this is neither the time nor the place to discuss such family doings. Why don't you come round tomorrow in the afternoon. We shall have time then for a nice cose."

"A nice cose!" The veins of Wilhelm's forehead stood out visibly, and he looked as though for two pins he would tell her exactly what she could do with her nice cose. But abruptly he recalled himself to his surroundings and grudgingly agreed to settle for an afternoon call at Cavendish Square the following day. Samantha breathed a sigh of relief as he went off.

The dinner that soon followed would have satisfied even a starving man: succulent pheasants, baby lambs, a full side of beef, lobsters, quails, and ducklings. Dishes came and went. Samantha, eating heartily and surrounded by the gleam of candlelight off crystal, felt it to be the fulfillment of every dream she had ever nourished back in York.

Indeed, the only flaw to the evening that she could perceive were her somewhat prosy dinner partners. Mr. Theodore Bunting, on her right, was a gentleman whose youth was betrayed by the intricate neckcloth he had not yet mastered. Her partner on the other side, Lord Coodle, was a good-natured man of middle age who seemed nearly as horse-mad as Mr. Langford. Samantha soon discovered that the best way to cope with her dinner partners was to say little to either gentleman and to merely nod her head now and then. So successful was this tactic that both of them soon formed the opinion that a more animated, charming, intelligent, not to say good-looking female could not be found, and each made a move to apply for the opening set with her when the party moved back to the grand ball room.

Unfortunately for both Bunting and Coodle, by the time they made their way to Samantha's side she was already being accosted for the opening set by Sheffield, a circumstance that surprised Samantha herself as much as it did Coodle or Bunting.

"Oughtn't you to dance with Miss Horick?" she asked, casting an eye in the direction of the Beauty.

"Certainly not," Sheffield answered as he continued to stand with an outstretched palm. "Here in London, Miss Curtis, no female dances the first dance with the gentleman who escorts her to the party. Just one of our quaint London customs."

Well, I'm glad you told me," Samantha acknowledged, placing her hand in his, "otherwise I wouldn't have known. If you're certain Miss Horick shan't be upset?"

"Quite certain," he replied, then looked down at her as she drew her hand back. "Now what is it?" he demanded. "This missishness is not like you, Miss Curtis. And I assure you, you needn't fear I shall trod on your feet. I am alleged to be a tolerable dancer."

"It isn't that," she protested. "It's the dance. A waltz!"

"So it is," he said. "Rather daring for an opening, but not depraved, I assure you." He looked somewhat puzzled. "Am I to understand the waltz is not danced in York?"

"Of course it is. It's been danced for years. But you must know I can't dance it here, for I haven't been approved of yet."

His brow cleared. "Is that what has you in a pelter," he said, placing one hand under her elbow and leading her toward Lady Jersey sitting with Lady Alice. "Sally, I beg some assistance. Miss Curtis is turning cat in the pan at the idea of waltzing with me without your permission. What do you say?"

Lady Jersey, with a good-humored twinkle in her eye, bestowed permission on all of the Curtises to dance all the waltzes they wished.

"You see how easy it is?" Sheffield asked when they were finally dancing together.

"You certainly are at first oars with her," Samantha remarked.

He smiled. "It's my mother's doing. She and Lady Jersey are bosom bows, even though Mama now resides in Vienna. And I shouldn't worry about the vouchers," he added as they swirled lightly in time to the music. "Lady Jersey is quite taken with all of you. You are exactly the sort of females Almacks should attract. Heaven save any gentleman I know from the sort of schoolroom misses that overrun the place." He rolled his eyes toward the chandelier.

Samantha gurgled. "So I have heard. But I had not thought you a habitué of Almacks, my lord."

"Not anymore," he agreed, which brought Miss Horick and her claim to him back once more to Samantha's mind. It was at Almacks, she remembered, that Sheffield had first laid eyes on the lovely Miss Horick.

"It appears to me that the people in India do it better," the viscount said now.

Samantha looked at him, her face a perfect blank. "It?"

"Marriage," he explained. "Or courtship, if you will. They marry the couples off as children."

"How appalling!"

"Oh no. They don't live with each other until they are adults, but a wedding is performed that I believe is binding. Or perhaps we would do better to copy the Arabs, with their harems."

"I am not myself acquainted with any harems," Samantha replied, but she could not resist asking him a few questions on the topic. As he delighted in answering with one outrageous remark after another, she was not long in deducing that he had been roasting her all along and had not so much as set foot in a harem.

"A failing that I shall endeavor to correct on my next trip to the Arabias!"

The waltz came to an end, and Sheffield escorted her back to her chair. After another bow he vanished from sight, and when next she spied his tall elegant form it was leading Miss Horick, rubies and all, out into the next dance, a quadrille. But why shouldn't he lead her out, Samantha demanded angrily to herself; they were practically betrothed.

She turned from the sight of the viscount with Miss Horick looking herself so much like a thundercloud that Lord Coodle, who had been screwing up his courage to ask her to dance, thought the better of it and headed for the cardroom.

Mr. Bunting, however, did not notice anything untoward in Samantha's countenance, and she accepted his invitation to dance. A moment later she was regretting this generous impulse.

Mr. Bunting was not a keen dancer. In point of fact, he was not even a good walker, and had great difficulty in keeping time to music. Samantha bore with all these difficulties as best she could, excusing him each time he trod on her feet. Fortunately there was no necessity to carry on a conversation with him, since he found speaking and dancing at the same time ruinous to his concentration.

To Samantha's relief Pamela had noticed her difficulties and dispatched Donald to rescue her from Mr. Bunting before he could suggest another dance. Her brother-in-law was followed in turn by Captain Maybury, Sheffield's gray-haired naval friend, who asked a great many questions about Lady Alice. These Samantha endeavored to answer as best she could, given her only recent reacquaintanceship with that lady.

Samantha was not the only Curtis dancing the evening away. From the start of the first waltz Miranda had been beseiged with requests for her hand. She had already stood up with Lord Garroway, one of the names prominently displayed on Mr. Phelps's list of eligibles, and with the Earl of Compton. Among her other admirers this evening was one Roderick Monroe, a young gentleman of three-and-twenty and a distant connection of Sheffield's whom Lady Alice had encountered on Bond Street the previous day and impulsively invited to her *soirée*.

It had taken Mr. Monroe only one glance at Miranda to

topple head over heels in love, something Samantha deduced from the ardent way Mr. Monroe gazed at her sister. Indeed, one would have to be perfectly doltish not to see where he was trying to fix his interest. With Miranda's future in mind, Samantha thanked the captain after the dance had been completed, fobbed off Mr. Bunting's entreaty for another try on the floor, and went off to find Lady Alice and learn more about Miranda's ardent admirer.

"Oh, Roddy? He is nothing to worry about," Lady Alice exclaimed when Samantha appealed to her. "Even though," she laughed as she cast a bemused look at the gentleman in question, "he does resemble a moonling. But it is only calf love, of violent but mercifully short duration."

"You are certain?" Samantha asked, looking relieved.

"Positive! Oh, Roddy's a perfectly nice boy, Samantha, but scarcely a man of mode nor of an age to think seriously of marriage, despite being a connection of Sheffield's."

From all this Samantha deduced that Mr. Monroe's star was nothing when compared to that of Lord Garroway or the Earl of Compton. Leaving Lady Alice with Captain Maybury, a situation that did not displease either of them, she walked around the ballroom fully intending to drop a word of warning in Miranda's ear at the proper time. But she was too late.

Mr. Monroe was being rewarded for his patience and devotion with a dance—and a waltz, at that! As the young couple passed, Samantha caught a glimpse of shining faces, and a new rush of alarm swept through her. Two angels could not have been exchanging more soulful looks!

"If you are wise, you shall nip that affair in the bud," an authoritative voice murmured in her ear.

She turned, not a bit surprised to find Sheffield behind her.

"I do wish you would not skulk around, my lord! And there is no affair."

"Good. For Miranda wouldn't do for Roddy."

Somewhat incensed at the notion that her sister was not good enough for anyone, Samantha took considerable pains to point out that it was Mr. Monroe who was not good enough for her sister. "And," she added, "I hardly see why the matter concerns you."

"Hasn't Alice told you that Roddy is a connection of mine?" Sheffield demanded. "And while in London, he is my responsibility. Good heavens, would you have another look at the pair of them? Cupid could not have asked for two more likely victims. But it wouldn't do for either of them to form an attachment, and in case you don't wish to heed my warning, perhaps this will clinch the matter. Roddy doesn't have a *sou*." He paused and threw her a reproachful look. "You don't look grateful for the news."

"One can hardly be grateful for such news," she said acidly, "unless one were a fortune hunter, my lord!"

"And of course you are no such thing," he agreed, the ironic gleam quite pronounced in his brown eyes. "I daresay no lady ever is. You merely want Miss Miranda to contrive a suitable match. I have the same wish for Roddy when he is of an age to marry. We are agreed that this match shan't come off?"

"On that if nothing else, my lord, we are agreed," she said, then broke off as Miss Horick advanced toward them with one hand fondling her rubies.

Samantha had no wish to indulge in another exchange with the Beauty, particularly in front of the Patronesses. She excused herself, leaving the viscount to his soon-to-be-betrothed, who complained loudly to Sheffield and anyone else who listened about the atrocious manners of mere provincials.

However vociferously offered, her opinion was found to be in the minority. Samantha and Miranda were much feted and admired. Pamela and Donald Langford too were spoken of with favor and had made several new acquaintances among some of the married couples about the town.

The evening's pleasure for Samantha was crowned when Lady Jersey and Lady Sefton came forward to voice their approval of all the Curtises and to inform them that the vouchers would be sent to Cavendish Square the following day.

"I daresay having you and your sister at Almacks shall

liven things up during the Season," Lady Jersey said to Samantha as her eyes flicked knowingly toward Miss Horick and the viscount.

The Patronesses moved off and the sisters separated, Pamela to drag Miranda away from her bevy of beaux and to whisper the good news into her ear and Samantha to weave her way through the throng toward Lady Alice.

Midway toward her hostess Samantha found her way blocked by Mr. Bunting, who begged her to accompany him on a drive the following morning. Since he seemed fully determined to stay rooted to the floor in front of her, and it was all but impossible to climb over him, she acquiesced, thinking to herself that in all likelihood he could not drive as badly as he danced!

~ *EIGHT* ~

The day after a ball normally held nothing more arduous for the members of the *ton* than rest and recuperation, but at the ungodly hour of ten A.M. Lord Sheffield strode into his ivory saloon to confront his early morning visitor.

"Don't you know, my dear Edward," he complained, "that in town one doesn't even show one's face before eleven o'clock?" He peered at the timepiece on the mantel and rubbed the sleep from his eyes with an impatient hand. "What the devil are you doing *here*?"

"I came round to thank you for persuading Lady Alice to invite me to her ball last night," Captain Maybury answered.

Sheffield struggled to repress a yawn. "That was a mere trifle, my dear fellow. You did seem to get along famously with Alice now that I think of it, but no thanks are necessary, and I don't see why you must thank me at such an *hour*." He paused, perceiving correctly that the captain was not attending to any of these complaints. "It appears to me, Edward, that you caused something of a sensation yourself with Lady Alice."

"Do you really think so, Warren?" the captain asked eagerly.

The viscount lifted a hand. "Yes, but do have some pity, I beg of you! It's much too early in the day for *shouting*. Let's have some breakfast and then you may tell me what is really on your mind."

He led the way to the breakfast room where they sat amicably demolishing several slices of ham, muffins, eggs and cups of coffee. Nothing, or so the captain claimed, was really on his mind. Sheffield however had cut his wisdom teeth long ago, and he could not help but conclude that his friend was smitten by Lady Alice, particularly since every word from the captain had to do with Lady Alice, her beauty, her charm, her grace, her smiles, and her civility.

"Next you will be singing the praises of her sneezes and hiccoughs," he scoffed. "Good Jupiter, I've known Alice for years and have rarely seen anyone so taken with her as you, not even her late husband, and he *married* her!"

"Yes, I realize that," the captain said, looking suddenly pensive. "You know, Warren," he confided, "I shouldn't be at all surprised if *I'm* in love."

Sheffield laid down his fork, all pretense of a normal breakfast at an end. "I can stand a good many things at the breakfast table, Edward," he warned, "but not a lovesick Romeo—particularly one of your years. Why don't you press on to Mount Street and tell Alice all this yourself and leave me to my bed."

"But it's only ten-thirty, Warren," the captain said, looking shocked.

Sheffield hooted. "That is exactly my point, you chucklehead!"

"And it's the day after the ball," Captain Maybury continued, impervious to the viscount's insults. "Thought I'd at least wait until the afternoon before I descended on her. But I couldn't stay by myself or I'd go mad. The hours seemed to drag so."

Sheffield nodded, a look of perfect understanding on his face. "So instead you came here. And quite right to do so, for there is scarcely *anything* I like half as much as being roused from a sound sleep and breakfasting with one whose conversation is all romantic gibble-gabble." He blotted his mouth with a napkin and pushed his chair back, the better to observe his morning caller. "Who would have dreamed, Edward, that when you came to town you would fall victim to Cupid?"

The captain smiled. "No one, least of all myself! And had I had an inkling I should have taken pains to stay away. No parson's mousetrap for me, thank you. At least," he amended, "that's what I used to think."

"When may I wish you happy?"

"Oh, Lord, Alice hasn't accepted me yet!" The captain's cheerful face clouded suddenly. "Warren, do you think she *will* accept me? Heaven knows she was so much feted last night. I mean to sell out my commission, and I have some estates left to me in Derbyshire."

Groaning, Sheffield held his head in his hands. "Edward, Edward, you should be telling all this to Alice. But since she is undoubtedly asleep the way most *civilized* human beings are at this hour, and since you shall undoubtedly drive me to distraction if you remain here, I suggest a morning ride to clear both our heads."

This suggestion sat well with the captain, who had ventured forth to Berkeley Square on his own bay. Sheffield retired forthwith to his dressing room to change into a riding habit and gave the order for his gray to be brought round to the front door.

The morning was still cool and damp as the two men set out.

To the unobservant eye, Captain Maybury did not appear in any way altered in form or countenance. But the viscount could not mistake the sparkle in his eyes and the glow that suffused his face at any mention of Lady Alice. No one in the *ton* would have dared accuse Sheffield of anything so vulgar as envy, yet he himself could not help comparing his own countenance at the thought of Frieda to the captain's at the thought of Alice.

Angrily he touched his heels to the gray's flanks, and the horse obediently sprang forward. Sheffield did not wish to dwell either on Frieda or love—not that he had fancied himself in love with Frieda, even from the start.

Her beauty was all he required in a wife, he told himself as they cantered down New Bond Street. After all, he wanted a spouse not a soulmate, whatever the romantics said. And he would have wagered any sum that Frieda felt the same. Ordinarily this apparent harmony in goals would have pleased him. However, today, in light of Maybury's *tendre* for Lady Alice, it struck Sheffield as oddly wanting.

By the time they neared the Park his envy had dissipated, and he was chastising himself for feeling anything so shallow. As penance, he applied himself to the captain to learn more about the fascination Alice exerted on his friend. Glad for an audience, the captain willingly poured into Sheffield's ear the many charms he had deduced in one evening in Lady Alice's company, including the news that he had been smitten by her as soon as they had shaken hands—a record, Sheffield thought dubiously, that might possibly stand through the next decade of Montagues and Capulets.

He was just advising Edward on this point when they began a brisk canter on the riding paths. He was about to issue a challenge to race to his lovesick companion when they heard the rattle of carriage wheels approaching at a rapid clip on an intersecting path. Abruptly they reined in, and the vehicle shot past out of control. But not before he had spotted the ashen face of Miss Samantha Curtis perched on the passenger seat.

Some ten minutes earlier Samantha had entered the Park with Mr. Bunting, who was displaying all the skill of a ten-year-old in handling his cattle. In truth she had forgotten all about his invitation to her, since she was happily reliving her sister's triumphs in her dreams. Then Marie ruthlessly pulled aside the curtains of the bed and announced that Mr. Bunting was waiting impatiently belowstairs for her.

Now, as the horses shied and Mr. Bunting quaked, Samantha felt tempted to thrust him aside and take over the reins herself. Not that she knew anything about horses, but even her little knowledge was presumably more than Mr. Bunting possessed.

"Can't you quiet them?" she asked as one of the horses, the leader of the pair, looked ready to bolt.

"I am trying to do just that, Miss Curtis," Mr. Bunting said thickly, his happy goal of a pleasant morning drive with a beautiful lady now completely by the board. "They're a new pair I bought last week at Tattersall's," he explained. "I thought to try them out today."

"Perhaps we should turn back," Samantha suggested as the horses shied against a passing rider. "They seem a bit nervous."

"They are just stubborn," Mr. Bunting complained. "And I can cure them of that easily enough." So saying, he picked up his whip and lashed out with it, landing several sharp blows on the horses' backs before Samantha could utter a protest.

If young Mr. Bunting had desired to cause his team to bolt, he could not have chosen a surer mode of action. The horses on the receiving end of the whip darted forward, their movement causing Mr. Bunting, who had not anticipated such an instantaneous reaction, to drop both whip and reins. With nothing to hold them back, the animals took off in break-neck fashion, careening down the path.

Samantha, jolted out of her seat by the runaway, clung with both hands to the edge of the seat under her, calling for help as best she could over the roar of hoofbeats. Mr. Bunting made a feeble try at gathering in the reins, which had fallen between the two horses, but he soon gave that up as an act that required considerably more heroism than he possessed. He did not relish being trampled to death by his own team.

"We shall be killed," he screamed. The horses, taking a bend in the path, nearly toppled them both from the seat.

"No we shan't," Samantha answered. Then she abruptly thought better of that, for a much bigger curve than the last was looming up ahead. As the carriage headed for it, Mr. Bunting hid his face in his hands and began to moan.

"Dead, we shall be dead," he groaned.

"Mr. Bunting," Samantha shouted as the carriage swooped around the curve, "this is not the time to give in to hysteria!"

Mr. Bunting, however, had long passed hysteria and was now deep into panic, lamenting aloud all his past failings to the Deity watching over them with such fervor that, had Samantha been any less involved with her own troubles, she might have enjoyed eavesdropping.

"Help! Someone please, help!" she shouted as the carriage narrowly missed two men riding on horseback. "Help us," she shouted. But by then it was too late to determine if the riders had heard her or not.

Mr. Bunting, his prayers completed and his face now dreadfully white, clutched his cravat. "We shall be dead," he murmured.

"Nonsense," Samantha said, out of patience with such pessimism.

Hoofbeats sounded off to her right, and she shot a quick look over her shoulder, feeling a wild hope. Her heart leapt at the sight of the two riders they had passed only seconds ago. The two men were rounding a small path to cut the carriage off on the main road. One figure she recognized as Captain Maybury from Lady Alice's ball, but his companion had his face hidden by a high-crowned beaver. Whoever he was, Samantha noted, he did not lack for courage. He sprang his horse forward at the point where the two paths met and, bending down, snatched up the reins of the carriage, then rode alongside the two horses to calm them.

"Easy, easy," he commanded. The horses, hearing the voice of a master, slowed, first to a trot and then finally to a complete stop. Samantha released her breath in an audible woosh and looked down. She was stunned to find her Rescuer was Sheffield.

At the moment the dearest wish of her heart was to climb down from Mr. Bunting's carriage. But this plan was impeded by Bunting himself, who was looking even paler than normal. Unwilling to desert a sick companion, Samantha dug into her reticule, extracted her hartshorn, and applied it ruthlessly to each of his nostrils. Under this remedy Mr. Bunting soon revived enough to comprehend that the team had been stopped and that he had not gone to meet his Maker.

"I should have known that you would be mixed up in this, Miss Curtis," Sheffield said now, crossing his arms on his chest.

Samantha, taken aback by this unjust attack, abandoned her succor of Mr. Bunting and glared down at him.

"What are you doing here?" The viscount continued to speak in an autocratic manner. "I would have thought you still abed, after the rigors of Lady Alice's ball."

"I *was* in bed," Samantha said, eyeing him with no great affection. "But Mr. Bunting had cordially invited me on a morning drive with him today. And that explains my presence here. Naturally," she added civilly, "I am obliged to you for saving his team, and us as well, but that does not excuse you from trying to bite my head off."

"I don't mean to bite your head off," Sheffield retorted. "Have you no more sense, my girl, than to go off half cocked with a gentleman who could no more handle his team than could tie a simple cravat?"

"Now see here," Mr. Bunting started to protest as he found his reputation undergoing an attack right in front of his nose.

"Skip-brained chit," the viscount muttered. "Could have been killed. And it would have been entirely your own fault."

"Don't be absurd! When Mr. Bunting invited me to take this drive, neither of us anticipated such a mishap would occur or we wouldn't have undertaken it," Samantha returned coldly. "I may be skip-brained, but I'm not a dolt."

"It wasn't a mishap," Sheffield answered. "It was a plain case of bad driving. And no excuse for it," he continued, as the captain who had been hovering in the background noticed Mr. Bunting's fresh attack of apoplexy at these new aspersions on his driving skill. Sheffield did not notice the worried look the captain shot him.

"You should know better," the viscount chided Samantha. "The company you keep."

"Pray, how am I to know what type of whip a gentleman is without riding with him myself?" Samantha inquired, nearly stamping her foot in frustration before she realized that such an activity might cause the team to bolt again and that Sheffield might be obliged to rescue them again, an activity that would render him twice as sulky as he already was.

"How are you to know?" Sheffield asked. "Quite simply, my dear girl. You may ask me."

"Now look here, Sheffield," Mr. Bunting interrupted. Fully recovered from his faint, and forgetting his earnest prayers of a minute ago, he was nursing the considerable wound to his pride. "Can't have you saying such manner of things about me. And in front of a lady. Had a touch of rum luck with my cattle. New pair from Tattersall's. You make me out some April squire who can't control a team."

"You can't," Sheffield said witheringly. "And you ought to know better than to share your follies with a female. You may have other talents, Bunting, I'm sure, but as a whip you are sadly deficient."

Unable to sit still for any more of this, Mr. Bunting jumped down from his carriage, nearly causing Samantha to topple from the unexpected movement.

"You shall take that lie back, Sheffield," he warned, thrusting out a rather undistinguished jaw.

Sheffield had tired of his conversation with the younger man and was occupied in steadying the carriage seat with one hand and extending the other up to Samantha.

"Come down," he ordered.

"Why should I?" Samantha asked mutinously, although scarcely seconds ago she had in fact been eager to quit the carriage. She was not about to be ordered hither and thither by Sheffield, no matter what his grand station in the *ton* might be or how many Patronesses doted on him.

Sheffield sighed. "Don't be a goosecap, Miss Curtis. I can't let you risk your pretty neck a second time in that vehicle! What would I say to Alice if you broke your neck? She's only just launched you and your sister, remember?

Those horses have the look of a high-strung pair, and if you'll take my advice, Bunting," he darted a quick look at their owner, "you'll sell them. Rather poor buy all around."

Mr. Bunting looked more and more aggrieved. "First my driving and now my judgment on horseflesh. I demand another apology from you, Sheffield!"

"Demand all you like, my good fellow," Sheffield said testily. "And now, Miss Curtis, no more mutton-headed protests. Do step down. My horse is getting extremely cold from all this standing about, no doubt the captain's as well."

"But how shall I get home now?" Samantha inquired, climbing down from the carriage.

"On my gray," he said promptly.

"But then how will you get home?" she asked in surprise.

For answer he smiled at her. As the meaning of this smile sank in, Samantha halted with astonishment in her green eyes. "You can't really be seriously contemplating the two of us riding on one horse, sir!"

"Don't be an old woman. You had an accident, and I have merely rescued you from the worst of it, so you can't quibble on my form of transport, can you? Besides," he grinned, "it's not that far to Cavendish Square, and we shan't scandalize so many people; it's much too early for them to be up."

"I would think that you would be asleep yourself," Samantha murmured as he led her to the gray and helped her into the saddle.

"You may blame Edward for that," Sheffield said, pointing to the captain. "And don't for pity's sake start talking to him unless you wish to hear love-sick drivel."

Samantha smothered a giggle. "Perchance would it have anything to do with Lady Alice?" she asked cautiously.

"Why yes, it does," the captain said eagerly. "I say, Miss Curtis, perhaps *you* can advise me—"

"Now you've done it," Sheffield scolded.

"Lord Sheffield!" Mr. Bunting, puffed and red faced, stood in front of the viscount.

"What is it, Bunting?" Sheffield asked impatiently, turning just in time to receive a glove on his right cheek. "Don't be a fool, man," he warned.

But Mr. Bunting was past the point of right thinking. "I can't have you saying such things about me!" he declared. "You shall have your seconds call on me?"

"Don't be a fool," the captain quickly echoed Sheffield's sentiments. "No one is about, and you can hardly blame Sheffield for being concerned. Miss Curtis is a particular friend of his."

"That doesn't explain his aspersions on my reputation," Mr. Bunting said grandly. "But I hope I'm not an unreasonable gentleman. An apology shall suffice; otherwise I demand satisfaction."

An odd glint shone in Sheffield's eyes. "Satisfaction meaning a duel, Bunting?" he asked affably. "Or else I suppose I am to apologize for saying all those things, true as they may be, about you being a notoriously poor whip and those horses of yours being ill-tempered brutes. Thank you, but I don't care to do so. I suppose it shall be a duel." He paused meditatively to look at the captain. "Haven't had a duel in years, Edward, but I trust you are still acquainted with the form and will stand me second. And I think pistols rather than swords, which are so barbaric in this day and age."

He swung himself onto the horse with Samantha, who had been following the scene avidly. "I shall be returning Miss Curtis to her home, Bunting, but your seconds shall find me at Berkeley Square later this afternoon." With that, he touched his heels lightly to the gray and rode off.

"Don't you have any more sense than to become embroiled with a halfling like Bunting?" he asked Samantha as they exited the Park.

"I am not embroiled with him," she said at once. "He merely asked me to ride with him, and I saw nothing amiss in the invitation."

"Which is another piece of foolishness," he said, tightening his arms about her waist as the gray cantered forward. "The number of carriages young Bunting has overturned would fill a graveyard. Miracle is he hasn't broken his own neck by now. Am I right, Edward?"

Even the captain, who had spent most of his years at sea, was obliged to admit that Mr. Bunting's reputation as a very poor whip had preceded him.

"But pray, how am I to know all this?" Samantha demanded, trying to free herself from Sheffield's iron clasp and receiving for her efforts the curt command to sit still. "I've only just arrived in London," she reminded them both.

"You could ask me," Sheffield replied, his warm breath tickling her neck.

"Are you such a font of knowledge on everything in the *ton*, my lord?" she inquired, turning in the saddle to glare at him.

"On one or two topics I own to some ignorance," he demured.

Her laugh trilled quickly. "What fustian! You are the most arrogant man I've ever known, and I shan't add to your consequence by asking you anything, even though," she admitted, "I am curious as to your opinion of Mr. Foster and Lord Carlisle."

His dark eyes twinkled at her. "Suitors of yours?" he asked politely.

"It so happens they are not," she retorted. "They are dangling after Miranda."

"Ah yes, the lovely Miranda," the viscount nodded. "The sister you are so determined to marry off. The two you mention are nothing out of the way, although Foster is a bit long in the tooth. And pray, why are you fidgeting so?" he asked irascibly as she shifted her position again.

"I'm not comfortable," she informed him as the captain shot them both a quick look. "I daresay one always hears how romantic it would be for a female to be slung over a gentleman's saddle and borne off into the distance, but after these few minutes sharing your saddle, I cannot understand how any such female would arrive in any mood for romance!"

At these words both Sheffield and the captain laughed aloud.

"I suppose you would prefer to be lying on the ground with a broken neck?" the viscount asked, but not unkindly.

"That, I assure you, would be twice as uncomfortable! However, you might bear up, for we are fast approaching Albemarle Street."

At the Park Sheffield had airily predicted that no one would be present to see the peculiar sight they made together on one horse, but for once he was in error. Several leading members of the *ton* witnessed the curious sight of Miss Samantha Curtis sitting in front of Viscount Sheffield, sharing the same saddle, if you please, in broad daylight!

They reached Cavendish Square not a moment too soon as far as Samantha was concerned, and the captain helped her down from the saddle.

"I suppose I should thank you both for saving my life," she said, eyeing Sheffield still on his horse.

"That would be the proper behavior of a well-mannered young lady," Sheffield replied, "but you needn't put yourself to any trouble to do so. As long as you promise not to go riding with Mr. Bunting, I shall be satisfied."

Samantha, who had no intention of riding or dancing with Mr. Bunting ever again, had no qualms about issuing such a promise. She then impulsively invited them both to come inside for some refreshment.

"No, thank you," Sheffield declined the offer. "I must return to Berkeley Square. There are preparations to be made."

She looked blankly at him. "Preparations?"

He gazed quizzically down at her. "Why yes, Miss Curtis. I have a duel with Mr. Bunting, you must recall."

"Good heavens," Samantha exclaimed, conscience-stricken that she had forgotten all about the incident looming so large in his future. "The duel. But you mustn't, my lord. Indeed, you can't."

"Oh, I can't," he agreed, "but Mr. Bunting can and has. And there the matter sits." And with another bow and a flourish to her, he rode off, with the captain following closely behind on his bay.

⚓ *NINE* ⚓

Samantha, thinking it all but impossible for one female on foot to give chase to two men on horseback, crossed the threshold into her residence. She was immediately met by Horace, wearing a conspiratorial expression.

"Mr. Curtis is within," he warned as he took her gloves and riding hat.

The butler was only partly correct. Wilhelm was not only within but without.

"Without the comforts of *my* home, *my* servants, *my* bed, *my* chef," he growled as Samantha greeted him in the blue drawing room.

"Now, now, cousin," Samantha protested, seating herself on the Egyptian couch. "I grant you Henri's lobster patties are very tasty, but that hardly makes him indispensable to you."

Wilhelm scowled at her. "Well, he is. And his patties should be tasty, for I pay him enough, and you," he said with an emphatic nod of a double chin, "are not paying him a single groat."

"No," Samantha agreed. "But nothing could be easier than to pay your servants myself. However, in all probability I would pay them more than you do now and that wouldn't auger well when you return, for you might then have a rebellion on your hands. From what Marie tells me her wages are sadly deficient, cousin, and I think that since she has been looking after me so well, I shall give her a raise. What do you say?"

"I say that you have stayed here long enough," Wilhelm snorted, "and it's high time that you go."

"Good heavens, Wilhelm, don't be a nodcock," Samantha exclaimed. "I can't leave now. Where would I stay?"

"I don't know," came the stormy answer as Mr. Curtis burrowed even deeper into a gilded Hepplewhite chair. "But I want my own home back. I'm devilishly tired of Sheffield and Berkeley Square."

"Well, that doesn't surprise me, for I vow Sheffield can be quite vexatious. But surely you cannot be contemplating throwing me out of the bed I have been sleeping in, for I do think the *ton* shall frown on bodily eviction. And," she warned with a twinkle in her green eyes, "I shan't go quietly!"

Wilhelm ground his teeth. "Dash it all, Samantha. This is my home."

"Yes, I know," she soothed. "But for the time being it is ours. I don't mean to be disobliging, but you do see we can't suddenly quit Cavendish Square now when we have just begun to be noticed in the *ton*. People would think us freakish, and that would reflect badly on you. It is," she said, riding over his attempt to speak, "a delicate situation, coz. But I assure you you shall have your residence as soon as Miranda makes a match of it."

Wilhelm folded his hands on his stomach. "Match?" he barked. "Do you mean marriage?" His face turned thoughtful. "Is that what's behind your removal to London?"

"Of course! Why else would we come to London! And if you do want me out of here you shall help me find Miranda a suitable mate, for once she is engaged I shall consider my goal accomplished and return to York."

Wilhelm knew a bribe when it was tendered and hesitated only a moment. "What is it you want me to do?" he asked in a voice of abject surrender.

"For a start, you may peruse this list," Samantha commanded, drawing out from the small escritoire in the corner of the room the list Mr. Phelps had so thoughtfully drawn up for her. "My solicitor says these gentlemen are seriously contemplating marriage and that if Miranda were to attach any of them it would be a feather in her cap. What think you?"

"I think that Lord Ownby could be omitted, cousin," Wilhelm replied, looking over the names on the list. "He is rising fifty and you can't wish a man of his years for Miranda."

Samantha was persuaded to strike Lord Ownby from the list.

"And not Tompkins," Wilhelm scolded, entering fully into the task he had undertaken. "He is in Lady Jersey's black books. A bit of a to-do at one of her parties. Fellow had the bad luck to try and steal kisses from a chit who just happened to be one of Lady Jersey's nieces." A rumble of laughter shook him at the memory. "Did you say Phelps drew this up?"

Samantha nodded. "And while he did his best, I am sure he may have omitted one or two names. So if you would just keep your eyes and ears open, cousin, it would assist me in launching Miranda."

"If it will get my bed back I'll assist you in launching a monkey!" Wilhelm exclaimed. He glanced over at her. "Who else knows about your plans other than Phelps and your sisters?"

"Lady Alice and Sheffield," she replied. "I was obliged to ask his opinion this morning of Mr. Foster and Lord Carlisle. Miranda met them last night at Lady Alice's."

"You saw Sheffield this morning?" Wilhelm inquired.

"Yes. Actually, I encountered him while out with Mr. Bunting. His team, Bunting's I mean, ran away from him in the Park, and fortunately Sheffield and Captain Maybury were nearby and stopped it before it became fatal. Only of course, having done that, Sheffield *would* stand about saying cutting things about Mr. Bunting's ability to handle a whip, right in front of him. And no one, not even the captain, could get him to desist. Then what must Mr. Bunting do but cut up stiff over it, instead of being grateful for having been saved. And he challenged the viscount to a duel."

"A duel!" Wilhelm said, all interest in matchmaking at an end. He pushed the list impatiently back at his cousin. "Are you sure of it? I heard Sheffield once proclaim that he would not indulge in such idle sport again."

Samantha here acknowledged that Sheffield did not appear that enamoured by the idea, and that it was actually

Mr. Bunting who pressed the matter home so insistently that the viscount had no alternative but to accept.

"But I do hope someone shall convince him not to partake in the duel."

"A bit late for that," Wilhelm commented, which made Samantha peer more closely at him. Her cousin, after all, was staying under the viscount's own roof and would have opportunity to see and speak with him. But when she broached her suggestion, Wilhelm bridled.

"You are green to even think anyone could talk Sheffield out of anything his mind was set on. Bound to get on his high ropes if I even mentioned such a thing. No, he is set on blowing Mr. Bunting to bits, and I suggest we post off to Bunting's and bid him adieu."

"Is Sheffield considered that excellent a shot?" Samantha asked, impressed despite herself by the certainty with which Wilhelm spoke of Mr. Bunting's demise.

Wilhelm raised and then lowered his bushy brows and proceeded to relate with some relish several tales of Sheffield's prowess with a pistol, including the story of how he had once shot a hat off the head of a reluctant partner. "And it weren't a high-crowned beaver, neither!"

"Then Mr. Bunting is doomed!" Samantha wailed, feeling a pang of guilt for her part in the whole gloomy affair. Had she not accepted Mr. Bunting's invitation to drive with him the horses would not have bolted and Sheffield would not have saved them. But even as she reasoned along these lines, a more sensible voice from within advised her to eschew martyrdom, since there had been no way of determining beforehand Mr. Bunting's lamentable skill with a whip.

"If Sheffield cannot be dissuaded, perhaps some pressure could be brought to bear on Mr. Bunting," Samantha suggested.

"Shouldn't wonder at that," Wilhelm agreed. "Bit of a lamb, all around. Not prone to violence, as I recall, but I can't think why he would want to challenge someone like Sheffield."

* * *

Ordinarily Mr. Bunting might have been a lamb, but Sheffield's remarks had so incensed him that he had turned leonine in his wrath and nothing, he informed Wilhelm, could induce him to relent. His reputation had been sadly besmirched, and in front of a lady.

"By which he means you," Wilhelm reported back to Samantha, puffing a little as he had made the trek from Cavendish Square to Chesterfield Street, where Mr. Bunting lived, and back, in record time.

Still a bit flushed from his exertions, Wilhelm slumped into a chair, accepted the sherry Samantha offered, and supplied the information that the duel would take place at sunrise the day after the morrow at Paddington Green.

"Pistols at twenty paces," he intoned, and then, having finished his sherry, he took himself back to Berkeley Square.

Although put out of patience by the micefeet that gentlemen *would* make of an affair of honor, Samantha had hoped that the duel would blow over. But the following day, during a visit to Fanchon's with Miranda, she discovered that the duel was the talk of the *ton*.

Several ladies who had been animatedly discussing it fell abruptly silent when Samantha stepped into the shop to discuss their latest needs with the modiste.

Quickly she concluded her visit with Fanchon and herded a protesting Miranda out the door before she could suffer a snub. Once safely ensconced in the barouche, she ordered Kenrick to take them to Sheffield's. The duel, she was convinced, must be stopped immediately.

"What do you want with Lord Sheffield?" Miranda asked, looking at her sister with marked curiosity.

"I don't want anything with him," Samantha said with some vehemence, "except someone must dissuade him from this duel, and that task seems to have fallen on my shoulders. And you must help me, Miranda."

Her sister appeared utterly baffled. "Me, Samantha? How, pray, would I do that?"

"I don't know," Samantha answered as she tried to think. Sheffield would be immune to anything she herself might say, but perhaps be more amenable to Miranda.

"You must tell him that if he fights this duel your chances for making a brilliant match shall die aborning," she said decisively.

Miranda wrinkled her nose. "I don't see the sense of that," she complained.

"Because," Samantha improvised quickly, "people shall say I have something to do with the duel, and you, after all, are my sister."

"Well, if they do say such things, they are idiotish!" Miranda said in a practical vein. "And anyway, I don't care a rush about a brilliant match."

"Don't be a goose," Samantha said impatiently. "Every woman yearns for an excellent marriage."

"You don't," Miranda pointed out.

"Only because I am on the shelf, or as near to being there as it were possible, so it hardly matters what I do at this stage. But you are a different story, for we have barely begun to launch you."

Miranda, turning mulish, insisted that she didn't wish to be launched anywhere. The barouche arrived at Berkeley Square, and they were bustled into the house to find the viscount going over the preparations for the duel with Mr. Monroe and Captain Maybury in his ivory saloon. At the announcement of visitors, Sheffield looked up frowning, an expression that was in marked contrast to that of Mr. Monroe, who erupted in a radiant smile aimed at Miranda.

"Good morning, Miss Curtis, Miss Miranda," Sheffield said, leading them toward the chairs by the fire. "What a delightful surprise. I wonder what could have brought you by."

"An errand of mercy, my lord," Samantha responded, not about to peel eggs with him at such a time. "I'm determined to dissuade you from this idiotish scheme. You can't really mean to foist this duel on poor Mr. Bunting. With your superior skill with a pistol, he is certain to be killed."

"Far be it for me to slay any suitor of yours, Miss Curtis," Sheffield said affably. "You may rest assured that poor Mr. Bunting shall return breathing to your arms after the duel."

"He's not my suitor!" Samantha said crossly, and then as his words sank in she looked up in sudden hope. "Do you mean that you have reconsidered and are calling off the duel?"

"No." Sheffield nipped this hope in the bud. "I simply shall not kill him! That is all I promise for the moment." He smiled. "A wound, undoubtedly, probably a minor one. But there is no certainty of that, for in the heat of the moment my aim might falter. But I shall do my best to refrain from killing him."

"Even if you don't kill him, the disgrace shall be quite enough to cause an uproar. And we shall be affected as well. You know that! Please, do think of Miranda—" She broke off and glanced toward her sister, who upon hearing her name should have leapt in at once to shed copious tears. Unfortunately, Miranda appeared more absorbed in flirting with Mr. Monroe on the couch than in heeding her cues.

"Don't be such a ninnyhammer, Miss Curtis," Sheffield said, looking amused. "This duel has not the slightest thing to do with you or your family. And I assure you, Mr. Bunting shall come to no great grief over meeting me on the green tomorrow. But I cannot help noticing that you do not seem concerned over my possible demise."

"I hardly consider *that* a serious possibility, sir," Samantha said dismissively. "You are alleged to be so excellent a shot as to make that an improbability. Not that I would enjoy seeing you shot or killed."

"No, of course you would not," he murmured.

"For nothing is more tragic than to be cut down in the prime of one's life. But since I don't know exactly how many years you have . . ."

"I made thirty on my last birthday," he said blandly.

This fact surprised her, for she had thought him rather older. "Oh? Then it would be quite prime indeed, and of course it would be a pity if Mr. Bunting shot you, but I know he won't!"

"Do you read fortunes too?" Sheffield asked delicately, a look of unholy glee in his dark eyes.

Startled, Samantha glanced up. "Fortunes?" She choked on a laugh. "Are you calling me a gypsy, sir? I protest, I am no such thing. I do know you to be an excellent shot." She colored slightly as he raised an inquiring eyebrow. "Or so I have been told by Wilhelm. Only yesterday he told me a tale of how you had once shot the hat off of some unfortunate companion, and while some might cite your courage and skill for doing such a deed, I'd liefer find the man who allowed you to do such an idiotish thing."

"There is no need for you to look any further," Sheffield said with a laugh. "There you have him," and he gestured toward the captain.

"Aye, I remember it well," the captain said, grinning from ear to ear. "I was foxed, of course. I daresay we both were, eh, Warren? And there was some fool wager at stake, as I recall."

"There always seemed to be," Sheffield agreed.

With that the conversation soon veered into reminiscences of the various scrapes the captain and the viscount had been obliged to bail each other out of during their years of friendship, and although Samantha wished to turn the topic back to the impending duel with Mr. Bunting she was unable to do so. During one point in her visit she became aware that Miranda had been unnaturally quiet and, glancing in the corner, observed her sister's total absorption in Mr. Monroe. As quickly as possible she rose, pleading a thousand errands to be run, and cut short Miranda's protracted farewell of Mr. Monroe. She dragged her sister off, intending to point out the disadvantages of such an attachment.

They were just mounting the barouche, intent on the journey back to Cavendish Square, when a smart black tilbury halted in front of Sheffield's door, and Miss Horick descended. The Beauty gazed at them both for an auspicious moment but did not deign to speak. Then she sailed grandly into Sheffield's residence.

The same tongues whose wagging had caused Samantha such acute distress had found their way to the ears of Miss

Horick. Not unexpectedly, she was put into an immediate flame; the version reaching her had it that the viscount, a gentleman all but betrothed to her, was dueling Mr. Bunting over one Samantha Curtis. Nor did it help Miss Horick's disposition to find that woman just quitting his establishment on her arrival.

Observing Frieda's countenace as she entered his drawing room unannounced, Sheffield muttered a silent oath. Frieda was evidently in a mood, a thought that struck the captain and Mr. Monroe simultaneously. These gentlemen had no liking for the fireworks they suspected would be shortly emanating from the Beauty, and bade Sheffield a hasty adieu, practically bolting the room. Wishing that he might follow suit, Sheffield turned a cautious eye toward his remaining guest.

"Well, Frieda," he said heartily, "do sit down and have some sherry."

"It seems, Warren," Miss Horick replied, disdaining with a wave of her hand the offer of sherry, "that I have come at the end of an auspicious gathering. That was Miss Curtis and her sister I saw departing just now, was it not? And now the captain and Roddy? I'm a bit surprised to find you with visitors. Don't you usually spend every moment possible at Gentleman Jack's?"

Sheffield shrugged. "There can be no great harm in missing a session, Frieda. An addiction to too much sport can be fatal."

"So can duels," Miss Horick remarked.

The viscount did not bat an eyelash. "How did you hear?"

The Beauty's teeth flashed in a cold smile. "The *ton* is prattling of nothing else. At least three people today have quizzed me on the matter. I am the butt of all their jests!"

Sheffield had been following Miss Horick's explanation with tepid interest, but her concluding remark made him lift his head, baffled at what part she played in his duel.

"What do you have to do with the duel?" he asked now.

"Nothing," she replied in a tragic tone. "I could see if you were fighting the duel over me because someone had insulted me, but instead you choose to fight it over Miss Curtis. A mere provincial!"

The viscount struggled in vain to suppress his laughter, hardly the reaction Miss Horick had expected.

"You are laughing at me!" she accused.

"No, by Jove!" he protested, stifling the last vestige of his mirth. "It's only that your suggestion is so absurd. And how the devil things do manage to get twisted about I wish I knew."

Miss Horick's forehead narrowed into a frown. "You mean you aren't fighting a duel?" she demanded skeptically.

"Oh, I'm fighting it all right," he said, helping himself to the sherry she had declined. "Bound to do so, since that fool Bunting foisted the affair on me. But it's your idea of my battling over Miss Curtis. That is the nackiest notion I have ever heard. She doesn't enter the picture at all."

"I see, Warren," Miss Horick said languidly. "I suppose, too, that the information that you were seen riding down Bond Street with her yesterday on the same horse must be in error as well?"

"I can explain, Frieda," he said, thinking wryly that perhaps he should have gone on to Gentleman Jackson's, for it would have spared him this *tête à tête* with Miss Horick.

"It's not what you think, Frieda," he began.

"But of course not, Warren," Miss Horick said with overpowering graciousness. "That is why I came by specifically to hear your explanations. Explain to your heart's content."

"Miss Curtis went for a drive with Bunting, and his team bolted. Fortunately, Maybury and I were in the vicinity and were able to stop it. Naturally I couldn't allow her to return home in the vehicle, for the pair might bolt again. They looked to be a mean-spirited team, and Bunting is a notoriously poor whip."

Miss Horick waved away Mr. Bunting's inadequacy with a rein.

"So you did take her up on your mount with you, Warren."

"Yes," he replied, adding swiftly that there was nothing

wrong in the maneuver. "I couldn't allow her to walk from the Park, and I didn't feel up to walking myself, and I couldn't ask Edward to trod on foot either. Really, you make too much of it."

"I suppose so," Miss Horick said with such consummate sweetness that anyone acquainted with her would be on their guard. "But it's not every day that I am informed that the gentleman with whom I have an understanding has been seen sharing a saddle with a young lady and then shortly is to fight a duel caused in no little part by her."

"Rubbish!" Sheffield objected. "She didn't cause it at all." But he knew instinctively that the more strenuously he denied this falsehood the more Frieda would refuse to listen to him. His temper turned sulkier with every second and each new accusation from her. No female, not even one soon to be his wife, dictated to him how he should act.

Miss Horick, being unacquainted with the viscount's train of thought, settled herself more comfortably on the confidentiale and continued to harp on the supposed inadequacies of a pair of country yokels until Sheffield bluntly ordered her to keep her tongue still.

She glared at him in mute fury.

"You may say whatever you like about the Curtises elsewhere, Frieda, for I don't think I could stop you. But in this house you shall keep silent. Do you understand?"

"You champion their cause so splendidly, Warren," Miss Horick answered. "But I just wonder what Sally Jersey would say if I told her about their audacity regarding the vouchers."

"That threat has no teeth left to it," he answered. "I have already told Sally the truth, and she thought it a famous joke and a true indication of the Curtis spirit."

Miss Horick snorted. "I also wonder how many more duels you shall be obliged to fight because of Miss Curtis, Warren. Such a plain creature, with none of her sister's beauty. Her manners may be *de rigeur* back in Yorkshire, but she shall undoubtedly find herself in the briars with such free and easy ways."

"I find nothing untoward in her manners, behavior, or

speech," Sheffield snapped dangerously. "But perhaps you mean that she had not acquired the brittle artificiality of so many beauties in the *ton*. And if so, I can only thank heaven for that."

Miss Horick, as befitted a notoriously self-centered person, had the tendency to take any comment personally when it concerned a Beauty in the *ton*. She reacted to the viscount's last remark by rising and marching out of the room—a move Sheffield witnessed with relief.

But he soon found himself unable to tolerate the empty drawing room. Plagued more than he liked by Frieda's accusation, he rose, headed not for Gentleman Jack's but for Manton's Shooting Gallery. As he drove toward the gallery he wondered at what price Frieda would put an end to this latest quarrel. And then more peculiarly came the question of whether he would be willing to pay such a price!

～ TEN ～

The day of the duel dawned a sepulchral gray. The first rays of sunlight peeking through the overcast sky passed lightly through the filmy curtains surrounding Samantha's bed, causing no stirring from within. The hour was well past sunrise when she finally awoke with a guilty start.

A glance at the window told her that the duel might well be a *fait accompli* by now. Nevertheless she threw on her clothes and quitted her room at breakneck speed, only to pause midway down the stairs.

Since the duel was in all likelihood over, she could not go to Paddington Green now. But she was on tenterhooks to learn the outcome. Quickly she mulled over the possibilities open to her. Ought she to post over to Berkeley Square to inquire? She shook her head quickly. Miss Horick no doubt would be in vigil there, and an encounter with the Beauty at such a delicate moment was bound to put her on end.

Horace brought these musings to a stop with the news that Mr. Wilhelm Curtis was partaking of a meal in the breakfast room, and Samantha made quick work of the remaining stairs, all but dashing in to confront her cousin.

"Wilhelm, is the duel over?" she cried out, amazed to find him eating. But this, she decided, must be a good omen, for surely not even Wilhelm would be so ill bred as to eat while his friend and host lay slain or wounded.

"Did Sheffield kill Mr. Bunting?" she asked, sitting down in the chair next to him.

Absorbed as he was in helping himself to another muffin and a helping of eggs and ham, Wilhelm was unable to speak and he contented himself with a shake of his head. For a moment Samantha felt as though a cold hand had reached out to touch her heart.

"You can't mean that Mr. Bunting killed Sheffield!" she exclaimed. "Oh, Wilhelm," she said despairingly. "Do stop gorging yourself for a moment and speak to me."

Wilhelm swallowed hard. "Bunting didn't kill Sheffield," he reported at last. "Sheffield walked away from the Green as clear as day, although perhaps that ain't saying much, since it was coming on to rain. Thought I'd catch my death of cold out there."

Samantha, feeling perilously close to inflicting another mode of death on her cousin, demanded to be told who had won the duel.

"No one," Wilhelm muttered as he forked food into his mouth. He put the utensil down momentarily to avail himself of some of Henri's prize marmalade, and Samantha snatched the fork up, vowing not to return it until he had told her everything.

"But I am telling you!" he expostulated. "And you can't begrudge me a bite to eat, I should hope, since after all the food is mine to begin with," he reminded her. "And I'm half starving, since I rose well before dawn, and none of us had a bite to eat, since that would be unwelcome in case any blood were spilled."

"From what I can see," Samantha responded tartly, "a little less nourishment would do you no mortal injury, cousin. Now tell me, is it Bunting or Sheffield who is being attended to by the surgeon? Neither killed the other, I take it?"

"Oh, no," Wilhelm said, grinning.

"Wounded each other?"

His grin broadened. "Nope."

Samantha stared at him. "Cousin Wilhelm, wasn't there a duel today?"

"Of sorts, yes," Wilhelm chortled. "And a freakish thing it was, if you want my opinion. Sheffield told Bunting that since he had the right to pick the type of duel, he wanted a shooting match. Well, Bunting didn't like that by half and spluttered and protested, but it was too late. Sheffield, cool as you please, puts up his pistol and aims it at the captain's beaver felt and blows it off. The captain's hat, I mean, not his head."

Samantha sat back, her imagination boggling at the scene just described. "I suppose they had agreed upon it beforehand?" she asked. "The viscount and the captain, I mean?"

"Good Jupiter, no," Wilhelm replied, rumbling with laughter. "It took the captain as much by surprise as anyone—probably more come to think on it, for it quite ruined his hat. Sheffield promised to buy him another at Locke's."

"What happened next?"

"Then, still cool as a bird, Sheffield turns to Bunting and bids him do likewise with one of his own seconds."

"And they submitted to being so treated?" Samantha asked.

"Course not," Wilhelm roared. "Be bosky if they did, cousin. They turned cat in the pan, as any sensible fellow would. Of course Bunting didn't like that and roared that they weren't very good seconds. Then he comes up to ask the captain or Monroe if they would stand up for him, but neither liked that idea much. Damned puppy even asked me. I told him he was daft.

"After which," Wilhelm continued, "Sheffield said the duel seemed to have come to a halt, which didn't please Bunting. But I daresay he might have been relieved all in all to let the matter go, especially after Sheffield told him he wouldn't be a bad whip if he had the right teacher and volunteered to give him lessons."

Samantha dissolved into laughter. "Why didn't he think of that before!" she demanded. "Not that Mr. Bunting would have consented, for he was quite angry with the viscount. Is that all to the duel then, cousin?"

"Just about," Wilhelm agreed. "The captain went off to tell Lady Alice the news, as well as Miss Horick. The viscount and Bunting made for the Park for their first lesson, and Monroe and I posted back here to tell you the outcome."

"Except," Samantha pointed out, "that you have done nothing but eat a rather full breakfast." She handed him back the fork, with a frown. "You said Mr. Monroe was with you, Wilhelm?"

"He's in the blue saloon," Wilhelm answered, digging into his food like a starving man. "Not in the mood for food, or so he said after he saw Miranda. I daresay she's entertaining him well enough, cousin."

Aghast at the idea of her younger sister entertaining Mr. Monroe alone, Samantha started into the hall just in time to surprise the pair on their way out. They were bound, according to Miranda's hasty explanations, for an outing to Somerset House, Mr. Monroe having been so obliging as to invite her to see an exhibit of painting there.

"And Pammy has given me permission to go with him," she said, anxiously avoiding her sister's quizzical eyes.

"If of course you do not have an objection, Miss Curtis," Roddy said nervously.

In the face of the two expectant looks they threw her way, Samantha would have felt like the beast of the world if she said no, so she reluctantly agreed to the excursion. Whereupon Miranda, in an excess of glee, threw her arms about her sister's neck and then dashed madly up the stairs for her gloves, vowing that she would not be gone a moment.

Samantha smiled at Mr. Monroe. "It is civil of you to take Miranda to Somerset House. Are you fond of paintings?"

"Paintings?" he echoed. "Oh, yes, *paintings*. Well, I suppose I am in a way. I say, Miss Curtis, will you be attending Assembly on Wednesday at Almacks?"

Samantha nodded. The whole point of Lady Alice's party had been to secure the vouchers for the Assembly, and she was not about to miss that for the world.

"But all the same, I'll wager that Roddy shows up to dangle after Miranda in full view of the *ton*," Samantha complained to Pamela in the sitting room after Miranda and her suitor had departed. "And I do wish you would not encourage them."

This mild criticism drew Pamela's attention from her stitchery. "I see nothing amiss in allowing Miranda to view some paintings in his company, Samantha," she protested. "If I did, I would never have told her to go with him."

"Yes, I know! It's just that I do wish she would stop yearning after him in such an insipid way. And," she grumped, "he after her."

Pamela smiled. "Do you dislike him so much?"

"Good Jupiter, no," Samantha protested. "He seems quite well enough, in his own way, and he is a connection of Sheffield's, which must count for something in the *ton*. It's just that I don't wish Miranda to become overly fond of him, for what would be the use to dote on him. He is not as eligible a match as the Earl of Compton or even Garroway." She stopped, suddenly noticing a lovely bouquet of red roses on a pier table. "Where did these come from?" she asked at once.

"Compton," Pamela explained but sighed. "I'm afraid that Miranda did not pay him a jot of attention. Although I made sure she thanked him civilly for the flowers." She watched her sister drift toward the roses. "I rather think she has lost her heart to Mr. Monroe."

"Good heavens, Pammy, don't say such a thing!" Samantha chided. She inhaled the fragrance of the roses. "If you think I have transported her to London from York merely to have her fling herself in the arms of the first man who pays her the slightest attention—"

"She has not been acting that badly," Pamela protested.

"Not yet!" Samantha said, abandoning the flowers and sitting down on the chair opposite Pammy. "Has Miranda confided her feelings for Mr. Monroe to you?" she asked.

Pamela shook her dark head. "No, but I do have eyes to see with. She shows all the signs of nursing a *tendre* for him."

"Oh, Pammy! Don't say such a nonsensical thing," Samantha implored. "To be sure, I have nothing against him. He might do very well as a friend, or as someone to escort Miranda to Somerset House. But she has not even been to Almacks yet!" She fretted to herself for a moment, but made a quick recovery. "I know what it is. A mere schoolgirl crush, nothing more. It shall come to naught."

"I am not so certain," Pamela demurred. "And I think in this matter you might be in error, Samantha. After all, you have never been in love, and I am probably more acquainted with the true symptoms of love than you. And I do think it's love."

Her sister's words were gently spoken, but they caught Samantha off guard. There was nothing earthshaking in Pamela's utterance. Samantha herself had often proclaimed no interest in either love or matrimony. But to hear it put so baldly and from Pammy, was a distinct shock.

Excusing herself to Pammy, who noticed nothing untoward in her sister, she wandered into Wilhelm's library, ostensibly in search of a good book. But really she intended to ponder her problem in private. *Never been in love!* How appalling! How galling! But how true!

And there was no point in pretending that she had ever nursed the remotest *tendre* for any gentleman, for she certainly had not!

"Never been in love," she murmured to herself as she slumped lower in Wilhelm's chair. But of course that wasn't to say that she couldn't fall in love with someone in the future. This thought sparked new hope in her breast, and she sat up straighter. Indeed, she was quite certain that, with only a little application, she might find a gentleman in London, perhaps at Almacks, with whom she could shortly become enamoured. And once that occurred, she told herself with budding excitement, perhaps a grand passion and marriage—which she had always spurned before—might be in the offing!

While Samantha sat in Wilhelm's library contemplating the thorny dilemma of finding a suitable *amour*, Sheffield was stepping across the threshold of his establishment. He had by this noon hour survived not only his morning duel with Mr. Bunting but his first driving lesson with him as well.

Shuddering at the memory of the faces of coachmen they had encountered along the way, the viscount was halted almost at once by his butler with the news that Miss Horick was waiting in the ivory saloon. The message had startled Sheffield, since never in the two months they had known each other had Frieda displayed any great concern over his well-being. He was nonetheless touched at the idea of her keeping a vigil for him and hurried off to the ivory saloon.

Upon entering, he discovered that his first reading of Miss Horick's character had been the accurate one. The peevish face she turned his way displayed no signs of relief that he had emerged unscathed from his duel of honor with Bunting, but seemed intent on unleashing a thundering scold upon his head.

She was upset, he soon learned, by his effrontery in making Miss Curtis the recipient of the services of his groom and his barouche, a fact she had only lately been made aware of.

Sheffield yawned. "I think what I do with my groom is my own affair, Frieda," he said when she paused for breath. "I don't go about telling you what to do with your servants."

Miss Horick sniffed. "But I haven't given any of them to *that woman*. And if you did wish to loan Kenrick or the barouche to someone, why not me? I could use another town carriage."

"You already have two," Sheffield pointed out. "Both much more fashionable than my barouche, which you once described as stuffy and antiquated."

"I am sure I said no such thing," Miss Horick protested. "And if I did, it was a mere jest. You know what the quizzes and prattle boxes shall make of your gesture, Warren. On top of being seen riding with her the other day on one horse—and the duel!"

"I don't as a rule keep up with the prattle boxes, Frieda," Sheffield said mildly, "so I don't scruple to think what they might say. However, you have made your opinion plain. And I have only to remind you that I loaned Miss Curtis and her family the services of my groom and my barouche. Nothing, I am sure, that would scandalize anyone other than the most odiously starched-up sort."

Miss Horick's face twisted into a pout. "Are you calling *me* odiously starched up, Warren?" she asked petulantly.

"Don't be a shatterbrain. And I do beg pardon if I've gone and offended you again, for I seem to be making a mull of it. In plain truth I've had a devil of a morning, and I don't fancy being raked over the coals for something that amounts to a mere trifle. So if you have nothing further to score me about?"

Miss Horick reddened with fury. No one in her years in the *ton* had ever dared to address her in such a fashion. Except, an evil demon whispered from within, Miss Curtis herself. Sheffield would soon learn what it meant to cross her, she thought grimly.

"When I merely point out the impropriety that might attach itself to your actions, you flare up," she said now. "But I am certain that if *she* had entreated you to do anything at all, even jump into the Thames, you would be most obliging."

Sheffield stared at her as though seeing her for the first time. "If Miss Curtis had made such a henwitted request of me, Frieda, I should have lost not a moment in telling her she was queer in the old attic."

To which Miss Horick, still continuing to bridle, replied that being called queer in the attic was still possibly better than being odiously starched up.

Sheffield tried another swallow of the Madeira. Obviously in this quarrel, as with every quarrel he ever had with Frieda—and he had had quite a number of them—he was destined to lose. Not that their quarrels had ever been over anything major. On the contrary, Frieda could fly into a pet over the merest trifle. At first this had amused him, but of late he had lost his tolerance for it. And he was not about to beg her pardon with yet another trinket that had caught her eye at Messrs. Rundell and Bridges.

Brusquely, he rose to his feet, cutting short her tirade with the pointed explanation that he had not eaten a bite since he had awakened several hours ago.

"But I shall be at your service Wednesday night, of course, to escort you to Assembly."

"Pray don't put yourself out on my account, Warren!" Miss Horick said stiffly. "Perhaps Miss Curtis may have some need for your services that evening. And," she smiled coldly, "while you might be her only friend in the *ton*, you are not *my* only friend." And with this warning that hinted of other fish to fry, she departed.

Sheffield watched her go, his lip curling slightly. Now she would be in the boughs for days, or at the very least until Wednesday night. For some reason, this did not irk him as much as it used to. She was quite shatterbrained to talk continually of Miss Curtis to him. He had no interest in her whatever—did he?

⟶ *ELEVEN* ⟵

Almacks on King Street was known to the irreverent of the *ton* as the Marriage Mart, where eligible bachelors wooed and won marriageable young ladies. To those matrons with daughters still to marry off, Almacks stood as a combination of the Promised Land and the Holy Grail itself.

So much had Samantha heard of the illustrious Assembly rooms that when she finally ventured to step into them on Wednesday evening, she suffered a mild disappointment. In reality these rooms were not so much different from the apartments and ballrooms in York. In her opinion they were found to be a trifle small, an impression which may have had to do with the numbers of people gathered there.

Although the rooms themselves were unimpressive, boasting a bare minimum in the way of flowers and candles, the same could not be said of the guests. The gentlemen in evening dress with quizzing glasses in hand stood ready to pass judgment on each new female to pass their way, while their female counterparts, the Reigning Beauties were quick to spot a potential rival and make her the butt of their jests to their circle of admirers.

As a newcomer Samantha was treated to several blunt stares, but no one even among the dandy set could fault her appearance this evening. Determined to cut a swath through the *ton* and uncover a suitor or two with whom she might possibly fall in love with, Samantha had given more than her usual attention to her toilette, rejecting the azure dress with an embroidered hem as well as a pale pink muslin before settling on an ivory satin with brilliants tucked about the bodice, and she felt the real undeniable pleasure of a lady who knew herself to be in first looks.

Lady Jersey and Lady Sefton greeted the Curtises kindly, making them known at once to the other Patroness present, the Countess Lieven, whose youthfulness and Russian accent surprised Samantha. The countess's approval of the Curtises as charming, unaffected females, was relayed to Samantha later that evening by Lady Jersey, who sported a new lime green turban.

"Not that she isn't curious about you after that to-do with Sheffield," Lady Jersey confided, tapping Samantha on the knuckles with her fan. "And I must own that Warren never struck me as the sort who would scruple to duel over anything. Although," she acknowledged, "the settlement of the hostilities, from what your cousin informs me, was a trifle odd."

She dipped her head a fraction closer to Samantha. "Just how does the land lay between the two of you?"

The color rose unchecked in Samantha's cheeks at the older woman's quizzical look. "Indeed, ma'am, Lord Sheffield is a friend, nothing more," she said, astonished that anyone would think otherwise. "And," she went on emphatically, "I'm sure he would not wish anything else. Nor would I."

The upshot of this was that within minutes Samantha found herself applied to for each of the dances forming, an opportunity she did not mean to waste. More than anything this evening she meant to find someone with whom she could flirt and fall in love, thus proving to one and all that she did know what love was all about!

Intent as she was on this task, Samantha felt all the pleasure of making a splash—albeit a modest one—in the waters of the *ton* with admirers, including the dashing Mr. Philip Hancock. Despite the gratification of waltzing with Mr. Hancock, an agreeably handsome young man with easy manners, Samantha could not keep her gaze from straying willy-nilly toward Miranda and Roddy Monroe.

Before the evening had even commenced Samantha had warned Miranda about the folly of devoting too much attention to young Mr. Monroe, and she had been relieved to see Miranda stand up with several of her other admirers. This emotion, however, was short lived, for Miranda danced with all the animation of one doomed to the gallows.

As for Roddy himself, he showed no inclination to dance with any other lady and instead followed Miranda's every movement with such stormy eyes that Samantha would have been in stitches had it been anyone other than her sister whom he was pursuing. As it was, she could hardly keep from stalking over to where he stood sulking in one corner, to order him forthwith to stop being such a moonling!

What would the viscount say to the lamentable sight of his connection languishing so publicly after her sister,

Samantha wondered—a thought grim enough to occasion a quick survey of the gentlemen present. She was relieved and yet at the same time oddly disappointed to find Sheffield missing this evening. But his beloved Miss Horick was present, and in fine fettle.

Frieda Horick had in fact been one of the earliest arrivals at Almacks, a circumstance prompted by her desire to recapture the position as the most courted female of the *ton*, a position she had relinquished by her alliance with Sheffield. She would show him just whom he had treated in such an abominable fashion. She took up command in one corner of the Assembly rooms, a dazzling sight in a turquoise gown with matching earrings that one of her admirers, Sir Cyril Chauncy, had bestowed on her earlier in the year. Since she was all but betrothed to Sheffield, Sir Cyril, a noted dandy in his own right, was surprised to find the Beauty wearing his jewels. And he was more than gratified at the way she flirted with him from behind her charming Chinese fan.

Miss Horick's flirtations that evening were not limited to Sir Cyril, and her behavior generated no little talk in the ballroom. The more discerning members of the *ton* deduced a quarrel somewhere in the works between the Beauty and the absent viscount.

Samantha took no hand in this speculation. She was too engrossed as the evening wore on in fending off Mr. Bunting's invitation for another morning drive in his carriage, an invitation she declined with every show of reluctance. Hot on the heels of that triumph came Lord Coodle, who accosted her to waltz with him and then pressed home this advantage by inquiring if he could possibly call on her the following morning at Cavendish Square. While Samantha could not refuse his request, at the same time she did not find herself cast in alt by the prospect of finding Coodle in her drawing room.

Nor, if the truth be known, was she cast into transports by any of the gentlemen she had encountered so far at Almacks. Not one Corinthian or Tulip had sparked the wildest flurry of interest in her breast or the faintest palpitation of her pulse. Where love ought to have been coursing through her veins, she felt only a lingering dissatisfaction with every gentleman she met. Midway into the evening she finally identified her dissatisfaction accurately: boredom. Whatever she had expected of her first encounter with love, it was *not* to be bored.

Without fail the gentlemen were amiable, civil, and of pleasing countenance. She wondered reluctantly if she was turning into one of those odious females who set themselves above being pleased, but she certainly did not think she was being too nice in her requirements.

She was not moved by the flattery, much of it insincere, of the Tulips, preferring a gentleman of sense, one who might challenge her opinions at times, who could spark fire in her mind and interest in her heart. Was that so impossible?

"But of course not," answered a voice from within. "There is still Sheffield!"

At this Samantha nearly laughed aloud. *Sheffield!* He, to be sure, would challenge her opinions if he were here, furnishing, she supposed, a full dozen of his for every one of hers. Nothing excessively civil about him, either. On the contrary, a more high-handed gentleman she had yet to meet. And she had been coming to cuffs with him almost from the start of the first evening they had met. All in all, she did not think Sheffield the answer to her dreams of romance.

Brusquely she shook her head and ordered herself not to be so gooseish. The evening was still young, and perhaps someone new and interesting might yet enter the rooms.

She turned her attention back now to Mr. Hancock, coming toward her with two glasses of lemonade. She supposed she could do worse than to nurse a *tendre* for him. A pity her heart did not pound wildly the way Miranda claimed hers did at the very sight of Roddy, but perhaps with a little application that might yet happen.

Mr. Hancock's attentions to Samantha during the evening had drawn notice from several, including Miss Horick, who took a singular interest in the young gentleman who had started the evening as a member of her flock and then drifted away, a practice that to her bordered on treason. Determined to scotch such behavior, she rose now and advanced toward the straying sheep.

"Good evening, Miss Curtis," Frieda said, her eyes glittering dangerously.

"Good evening, Miss Horick," Samantha answered with wary composure, for she did not believe for a second that the Beauty had come by to pay her any respects.

Although Miss Horick boasted a score of admirers in the corner only too willing to fetch her a glass of lemonade, she confessed now to an overwhelming thirst and glanced so pointedly at Mr. Hancock that he rose to the occasion and nimbly offered her the glass in his hand, explaining that not a drop had as yet touched his lips.

Vexed that she had not after all sent him scurrying to the refreshment room in full view of the *ton*, Miss Horick was forced to swallow the lemonade with an expression every bit as tart as the drink itself.

"We are such good friends, Philip and I," Miss Horick informed Samantha with a fatuous smile at the flabbergasted Mr. Hancock, who darted a quick look behind to see if perchance another Philip lurked in the vicinity.

"Do you know our families have nearby estates in Devonshire?"

"No," Samantha answered. "But I daresay a good many families do have estates there?"

Miss Horick nodded. "But ours were so close to the other that we were used to spend all our time together, were we not, Philip? Practically bosom bows."

Mr. Hancock looked more and more harrassed under this unprecedented campaign, for his bosom bow was more accustomed to treating him in town as nothing more than a country yokel. He admitted now that they had at times seen each other.

"Inevitable, you know," he gurgled, "in the country."

Frieda chuckled. "You are too modest, Philip. Nearly every day would be nearer the mark. We were practically in and out of the other's pockets."

"How wonderful for you," Samantha said with an appreciative gleam in her green eyes. "And I know as bosom bows you must be longing for a comfortable cose, so I shall leave you two together to indulge yourself. I see my Cousin Wilhelm looking for me." With that she made for the opposite end of the room.

Wilhelm, who had not been seeking Samantha at all but was instead trying to fix his interest on a pretty brunette in a yellow ball gown, adjured his cousin to go away.

"You always seem to be telling me to go away," Samantha complained. "But I can't. I've all but told Miss Horick you wished to speak to me."

"Miss Horick, is it?" he said, glancing up. "Hmmph. It seems she's cut you out with young Philip, coz."

Samantha laughed. "You are probably not the only one who thinks that, Wilhelm. But now that she does have him back in hand, she appears to be deserting him," she noted as Miss Horick, having made her point about her power to entice a sheep back into the fold, returned to her corner entourage, leaving Mr. Hancock free to coax Miranda into dancing a quadrille with him.

As Wilhelm resumed his flirtation with young Miss Kitty Walker, Samantha wove her way toward Roddy's side. But her attempt at civil discourse with him met with no resounding success. Mr. Monroe could never have been described as rude, but the conversation did lag, as he answered each of her comments with but a syllable or two and seemed content in gazing after Miranda like a simpleton.

And, Samantha thought to herself in disgust, if love reduces everyone to such a dismal state, she, for one, had misgivings about being Cupid's victim.

As eleven o'clock, the hour designated by the Patronesses after which no one, not even Wellington himself, would be allowed entrance, fast approached, Miss Horick's agitation increased noticeably.

"That's because of Warren," Captain Maybury said shrewdly to Lady Alice and Samantha. "Not much sense in being the Prime Beauty here if he ain't at hand to witness her peacocking."

"I think it a pity that those in love would resort to such trickery," Samantha replied.

Lady Alice and her captain exchanged speaking looks.

"My dear child, what are you about?" Lady Alice asked. "The match, if it comes off between Warren and Miss Horick, is no love match."

"I know they don't have a *grande passion* for each other," Samantha acknowledged, "but surely they must feel some affection for each other. A mild *tendre,* perhaps."

Lady Alice was not so convinced. "I have never been able to discern even the most tepid *tendre* in either of them."

Samantha was shocked. "And they mean to marry? How heartless it sounds."

Lady Alice's lips curved upward in a surprised smile. "Too harsh, Samantha. Have you not been telling me of the necessity of removing Miranda from her attachment to Roddy?"

"Yes," Samantha admitted, "but that's hardly the same thing. For I don't desire that she marry *without* love. I just wish she'd fall in love with someone more suitable than Roddy."

The debate over these differences was interrupted momentarily by Mr. Hancock, who drew forward to tell Samantha that he had been designated Miss Horick's escort into the supper room later that evening.

"Although I can't think why she's chosen me," he said with a sheepish grin. "Never used to pay me a mite of attention before tonight."

Samantha smiled and advised him to enjoy the Beauty's favors while they lasted. It was apparent to her now, if not to Mr. Hancock, that Miss Horick was determined to drive home her point and annihilate any possible rival. Since Samantha had never for an instant considered her beauty on an equal footing with Miss Horick's, she felt a dizzying gratification at being singled out as a rival.

While she was still chuckling to herself over this extraordinary turn of events, the eleven o'clock hour began to sound. At the tenth stroke of the gong, an imperturbable figure appeared at the top of the stairs, gazing nonchalantly about the Assembly Room. It could only be Sheffield!

With no unnecessary haste he walked down the stairs, making at once for Captain Maybury's side.

"I vow, if your carriage had been a second later you would not have been allowed in," the captain twitted his friend.

"Good evening, Alice, Miss Curtis, Edward," the viscount replied blandly.

"Now, Warren, that won't do," Lady Alice scolded, making no attempt to hide her curiosity. "You cut it a trifle fine, even for you. Just where have you been?"

"Will it disappoint you to learn I merely overslept?" Sheffield asked with a smile. "I know I ought to have dreamed up something more adventurous for an excuse—a scuffle with a highwayman at the very least. But you know my lamentable lack of imagination. The dull truth is, I was curled up for an hour with my Walter Scott in the library. It never ceases to amaze me how that fellow can put a person to sleep. When I finally woke, it was nearly a quarter past ten, and I rushed to get here." Having finished with these explanations, he dealt a kindly smile at Samantha. "A pretty rig, Miss Curtis. In spite of it not being green, it becomes you greatly."

"Thank you, my lord," Samantha said, smiling back at him with real pleasure. But his next words took the wind out of her sails.

"Frieda here?"

The captain nodded gingerly toward the corner where Miss Horick held court.

"I'd best be off to pay her my respects," he said, and moved toward the cluster of men, who parted obligingly to allow him access to the Beauty.

As Samantha watched his cool figure move toward Frieda, and noted the ease with which he kissed her hand, chatting with all the familiarity of an intimate, she grew conscious of a pulse hammering in her throat. It was just like him, she thought moodily as she rose to accompany the Earl of Compton out onto the floor, to arrive at the last possible second, toss off compliments to whomever he chanced to see, and then saunter off.

If Samantha had been less occupied in following the earl's difficult lead in the quadrille, she might have noticed that Sheffield, far from dangling after Miss Horick, spent only a few minutes with her and then returned almost at once to Captain Maybury and Lady Alice, to evidence surprise at Samantha's absence.

"She can't always be where you expect her to be!" Lady Alice said tartly. "If you must know, she's dancing with Compton."

"Compton, is it?" Sheffield said, putting up his glass and admiring Samantha's light graceful figure, which was almost comically mismatched with the earl's woeful lead. When the quadrille came to an end, he sauntered forth to solicit the honor of the next dance with her.

"I'm afraid that Lord Coodle has that honor, my lord," Samantha replied frigidly, emphasizing the mood by turning her back to the viscount and greeting Coodle with every show of pleasure.

The captain chuckled at the viscount's discomfiture. "You look dumbfounded, Warren."

"How the devil does a person dance with her?" Sheffield demanded, not used to being spurned by any female.

"Come earlier," Lady Alice said succinctly. But her captain took pity on his old friend and graciously surrendered the next waltz that he just happened to have with Miss Curtis.

"Obliged to you, Edward," Sheffield said. "But I'm beginning to wonder if she'll even dance it with me. There was no mistaking that glare in her eyes just now. Do either of you know why I am in her black books?"

"I should think that would be obvious even to a three-year-old," Lady Alice said, quizzing him lightly. "But perhaps as you turn the matter over in your brain you might sort it out."

Although other young ladies cast lures his way, the viscount was not tempted to lead anyone else out. He bade his time until the musicians struck up a waltz, and then approached Samantha with his hand outstretched.

"I believe you are free for this waltz, Miss Curtis?"

Samantha drew back stiffly. "You err, sir," she said coldly. "Captain Maybury has bespoken this dance with me."

It was Sheffield's turn to be arch. "The captain is waltzing with Lady Alice. I persuaded him to allow me this dance with you, in order to delve into the mystery of just why you should be so angry with me."

"I am not angry with you," she denied.

"Oh no?" he asked affably. "Well, so much the better. But I still fancy the waltz." And without waiting for a reply, he pulled her to her feet, slid an arm about her waist, and led her out. She could not break free without causing a scene, something she was loth to do on this, her first occasion at Almacks.

In silence she suffered herself to be led onto the floor, oblivious to the charming spectacle she made with him as a partner, their figures so excellently suited in height and gracefulness as to spark compliments from several onlookers. However well matched they might have been as a dancing pair, their feelings were mildly disjointed. The viscount, put off more than one would have supposed by the Medusa face Samantha had chosen to wear, was genuinely puzzled as to why she showed hackle with him. Samantha, for her part, was determined not to be treated like any tottyheaded female, liable to swoon if by chance the illustrious viscount deigned to speak a word to her, or rendered mute by the sheer ecstacy of dancing with him.

This latter notion prompted her at once to break the silence, less he think she had been stricken dumb by the honor of the waltz.

"Thank you for not slaying Mr. Bunting." She said the first thing that came to mind, realizing that this could hardly be counted as a dazzling display of conversational wit.

"You are very welcome," Sheffield replied. "Not that I did so merely to elicit your favors. For it would have been bad *ton* to have any notoriety attached to my name."

"Recalling the stories Captain Maybury told me the other day in your drawing room, my lord, I would not have thought notoriety to be so unfamiliar to your name in the past."

His smile acknowledged her hit. "Those escapades took place in my salad days, Miss Curtis. I am prone toward much tamer sport now. It is important," he said blandly, "for a gentleman to be respectable as he nears his dotage!"

In spite of her best intentions, Samantha laughed. "I would not think you had any problem with respectability, my lord. Pride, conceit, arrogance, yes, but hardly respectability."

"You do lay heavy burdens on me, Miss Curtis," he said with a laugh as he spun her expertly about the room. "I hope you don't judge my flaws to be so fixed as to be irreversible!"

"Perhaps not to a woman of Miss Horick's derring-do," she answered. "But I confess I would consider such an attempt much too fatiguing."

He cocked his head quizzically at her. "That is doing it much too brown. Do you think me, then, so arrogant that I could not perchance reform, in say a year or two?"

"Only a year or two, my lord? Impossible. I greatly fear that reforming you would take a lifetime. I am perfectly sure you were autocratic and high-handed from the cradle and shall no doubt go to your grave crotcheting and fussing over the burial arrangements!"

"What a delightful picture you sketch of me," Sheffield drawled. "I could of course respond in kind, but I am too much the gentleman."

"And I too much a lady to do anything but pretend I heeded that!" she retorted, realizing that here was the first conversation she had enjoyed all evening. But no sooner had this thought flown into her mind than it was banished. Sheffield found a new bone of contention: Roddy and Miranda.

"That affair is still brewing in the nursery," he complained to her as they passed the young couple sitting together, gazing adoringly into each other's eyes. "I thought I told you to put a stop to it."

His manner caused Samantha to stiffen at once. "I understood your words to me on the topic were in the nature of a suggestion, my lord. I am not a servant of yours!"

"Don't peel eggs with me. I don't like the romance. And neither do you."

"Yes, I know," she said faintly, "and I have tried—"

"Not diligently enough, it would appear."

She could not let this pass uncontested. "I have been doing nothing but treating Miranda daily to all the reasons she should *not* be so besotted by Roddy. But she has eyes only for him!"

"Don't expect me to believe that drivel," Sheffield said bracingly. "Roddy is a mere sprig, lacking polish and town bronze. You should be able to talk more sense into the pair of them."

"They are in love," she pointed out. "People in love do not choose to listen to sense!"

"Very true," he said, so quietly that she wondered if he had fallen in love with any frequency himself during his years about the *ton*. But that, she reminded herself at once, had not a thing to do with her.

"If the romance troubles you so," she said now, "you might have said something to Mr. Monroe. He holds you in great esteem."

"I do not live with Roddy. My opportunities to speak with him are limited. You, however, are in daily touch with Miss Miranda."

"Why do you oppose the match?" Samantha asked curiously. "Do you believe her still to be so unworthy of him?"

Sheffield sighed. "Don't be a bacon brain. I have every belief that any of you Curtises would be well suited to marry a duke, if it came to that! And it shan't, because there aren't that many eligible dukes left for any of you to set your caps at. My objections are more basic. If your sister marries Roddy she will starve to death, for he receives only a modest allowance from his father's estate and shan't come into his full inheritance until he reaches twenty-five. Those are the conditions of the will."

Reading her silence correctly as dismay, he went on. "Roddy is now twenty-three. That means Miss Miranda shall have two years of hardship to look forward to."

"I can add, my lord," Samantha said with some asperity. "But why would his father leave such a will?"

Sheffield shrugged. "I suppose to save Roddy from wasting the ready while he was still a green head. It happens to more than a few of the gentlemen in the *ton*. They get into mischief as soon as they inherit. And Roddy has managed to get into some scrapes by himself, despite his lack of funds. I've bailed him out at least a half dozen times."

"Good heavens," Samantha murmured, glad that Sheffield had set her to rights on Roddy's predicament and more determined than ever to end the attachment between her sister and the young man. A life of genteel poverty spent outrunning the creditors was not what she wished for Miranda.

"I shall speak to my sister again," she said softly.

"Good. And don't look so sad. We are doing the right thing by them."

Samantha shook her head. "They shan't think so."

"That can't be helped," he pointed out. "Now smile, before Alice thinks I've browbeaten you. I know, a little supper shall make you feel better. In fact, I shall take you in myself."

Somewhat taken aback by this mode of inviting a lady to sup with him—if indeed invitation it was!—Samantha was on the verge of issuing a prompt refusal when the waltz ended. They were caught immediately in the crush of couples, and almost at once they were intercepted by Miss Horick.

Smiling graciously at the viscount and wholly ignoring Samantha, the Beauty explained that Mr. Hancock, with whom she had been dancing, had previously solicited the honor of escorting her into supper.

"But that was before I knew you were to be here, Warren! And of course—"

"Don't be silly, Frieda," Sheffield said bracingly. "Doesn't do to bestow too many favors on me for one night. It's entirely my own fault for coming so late. Go in and sup with Philip. Miss Curtis has been kind enough to accept my last-minute escort."

Miss Horick, her face a vivid red at this sudden reversal of her plan to bring the viscount to heel publicly, turned now and stalked off, with the unfortunate Mr. Hancock trailing in her wake. Sheffield watched them go, an enigmatic expression on his face.

The incident, brief though it was, proved illuminating to

Samantha. For it explained in a flash his improbable invitation to her seconds earlier. No doubt he had anticipated such a move by Miss Horick and thought to squelch it, and her, as a way of revenging himself for the audacity she had displayed at Almacks. While Samantha did not pity the Beauty, who deserved being squelched, she did not like to be used as a pawn in the game between Sheffield and Miss Horick.

"What is it?" Sheffield asked abruptly, his voice breaking into her reverie. "You are gawking at me as though my cravat were askew, or as though I were a villain."

"Am I?" Samantha asked with more lightheartedness in her voice than she really felt. "Then give me leave to say at once that your neckcloth is impeccable as always. As for your villainy, I daresay you would know better about it than me."

The brown eyes did not leave her face. "In any other female I would dismiss that as mere prattle," he observed, "but with you I'm inclined to believe otherwise. Something is bothering you, Miss Curtis. You've been acting dashed peculiar since I've arrived, and I shall take it upon myself to call on Cavendish Square tomorrow at eleven to get to the bottom of it all."

Then, still oblivious to her protests, he herded her down the stairs toward the crowd in the supper room.

~ TWELVE ~

Just as he had promised, Sheffield presented himself at Cavendish Square at eleven the following morning. He arrived just in time to witness Lord Coodle's rapid exit of the establishment with an expression of pure fright on his portly face.

"Monstrous beast!" he exclaimed before breaking into a dead run for his curricle.

Intrigued as to what Miss Curtis might have done to earn herself this charming epithet, Sheffield entered the house. An attack was launched immediately on his buff pantaloons and high-glossed Hessians by Brutus, the Curtis hound.

Miranda, tsking and scolding, dragged the dog away from the viscount's boots, explaining to him that Brutus was only trying to be friendly. "I tried to tell Lord Coodle that, but the silly man wouldn't even attend to me. He was put into a dead fright by Brutus."

"I had the opportunity to witness Lord Coodle's fright first hand," Sheffield told her, "and you have, I fear, lost a suitor. It shall be a warm day in January before he sets foot in this establishment again."

Miranda did not appear too disturbed by such a prediction. "He's not dangling after me, my lord, but Samantha. And I don't think she shall really care if he doesn't come back for it's not as though he were someone dashing like Mr. Hancock, after all."

Sheffield squatted on his haunches and patted Brutus on the back. "Is young Hancock one of your favorites?" he asked.

Miranda giggled. "Good heavens no. He thinks me frivolous, but I don't care."

"Perhaps you should," Sheffield said cryptically. "Is your sister in?"

"Only for a moment," Samantha herself said crisply as she descended the stairs in a blue morning dress and a sable pelisse. She paused at the foot of the stairs taking in the dubious sight of Sheffield nose to nose with the hound.

"Odd, I thought Horace told me it was Lord Coodle belowstairs. It's not like him to make such a mistake."

"Lord Coodle left," Miranda explained. "Brutus tried to make friends with him."

Samantha could not repress a smile. "Good heavens, the poor man. I shall have to beg his pardon the next time we meet."

"If I were he," Sheffield answered, "I'd give you a wide

berth the next time I crossed your path. You are going out?"

"On some errands," she told him as she drew on her gloves. "So I am sorry, I shan't have the opportunity to stay and chat with you and Miranda."

"I shall be happy to drive you wherever you are bound," Sheffield said promptly. "I'm a pretty fair whip."

"That's civil of you, but my errand shall undoubtedly take me into the City. I'm sure you must have other plans for your morning."

"Not one that I can recall at the moment," Sheffield said, amused at her efforts to fob him off and more determined than ever to stick to her side. He reclaimed his hat from Horace and led the way out of the door. "Business in the City? Not that solicitor of yours?"

"Yes," she divulged reluctantly, stepping out into the cool morning air and toward the high-perched phaeton, a form of vehicle she had never ridden in before.

"Don't be frightened," Sheffield soothed.

"I'm not," she replied, surprised at him for even thinking such a thing. "But I don't care to think what Mr. Bunting shall say to either of us if you overturn your carriage."

Chuckling, he helped her into the seat and within minutes had touched the reins to the backs of his well-matched grays. The team stepped off lightly. After the first giddy minute spent adjusting herself to the unaccustomed heights as Sheffield turned his team smartly around a corner, Samantha relaxed.

"What do you want with Mr. Phelps?" the viscount asked.

"I haven't the foggiest clue," she said. "He sent a message to me to call on urgent business."

Sheffield frowned. "Your Aunt Kendall's estate, perhaps? I don't suppose you can have wasted the ready so quickly?"

Samantha could not help thinking guiltily of the bills mounting in the offices of *modistes*, milliners, shoemakers, and other shopkeepers. "Things are more expensive here than in York," she acknowledged. "But I should have to be a ninnyhammer to spend ten thousand pounds in just two weeks."

They had started down New Bond Street as she said this, and Sheffield turned to her in astonishment. "Has it only been a fortnight since your arrival here?" he said quietly. "How peculiar. I should have sworn it was much longer. I feel as though I have known you forever."

Samantha began to laugh. "By that you mean it's been an interminable period for you. And don't scruple to deny it, for I'm certain it can't have been comfortable with Wilhelm complaining to you about us at all hours of the day."

"Oh, Wilhelm has grown more cheerful over his lot of late," Sheffield said offhandedly. "But if it has only been a fortnight, you cannot have gone through your inheritance so quickly—unless you or perhaps one of your sisters is a secret gamester."

Samantha shook her head firmly. "We learned that lesson too well from poor Papa."

"I see. I commend you, then, and wonder even more at the urgency of your solicitor's message."

Samantha too wondered about it as the carriage continued to roll along up past the Strand and into the heart of the City. When the phaeton halted in front of the solicitor's office, she thanked Sheffield for the ride and cautioned him not to wait, since Mr. Phelps, being a solicitor, would take a good deal of time to make but a single point, and he, Sheffield, must undoubtedly have other plans for the morning.

"Under penalty of having you think me a frippery fellow, Miss Curtis," he drawled, "I am forced to repeat again that I have no pressing plans for the morning." He then jumped down from the carriage and lifted a hand to help her down, moving with her toward the entrance of the solicitor's office.

Samantha halted immediately. "Now see here, my lord Sheffield. You can't come in with me to my solicitor's."

"Oh no? Why not, pray tell?" he quizzed. "Am I not properly dressed for the occasion?"

This, as Samantha took pains to point out, was a perfectly demented question, for he was as always exquisitely attired, despite his encounter with Brutus.

"We shall be discussing highly personal affairs. Matters that do not concern *you*," she insisted.

"I assure you, I am no gabblemonger," the viscount replied. "As my best friends shall attest, I am true blue and shall never stain. I'll keep your secrets. And might I add that I have been involved within this last week in your affairs entirely against my will, what with that scrape of a duel with young Bunting, so I don't think you need to stand on ceremony with me."

"Oh, very well," Samantha surrendered. "But the matter lies strictly between me and my solicitor, is that clear?"

The matter might have been clear as crystal to Sheffield, but Mr. Phelps was not so enlightened. He greeted the viscount with an obvious display of warmth, requesting him to sit next to Miss Curtis and looking so pleased to see him that Samantha felt more than a little annoyed.

As Mr. Phelps delved discreetly into the welfare of the viscount's mama, learning that her ladyship was enjoying a comfortable summer in Vienna with a host of her old friends, Samantha could hold her tongue no more. Briskly she informed her solicitor that Sheffield was here merely as a companion, having been civil enough to offer her a ride into the City.

"So I would be obliged if you stopped toadeating him! He is not your client," she reminded them both. "I am. And as such, I should like to know why you sent your message asking to see me this morning on urgent business."

Mr. Phelps crossed his fingers on his mahogany desk.

"My dear Miss Curtis, we have a calamity to face."

Samantha looked up quickly, but Sheffield had already taken command, desiring the solicitor to be rather less melodramatic and let them have the news at once.

"It's Lady Battiscue!"

Since Sheffield was unfamiliar with this relation of Samantha's, it was not to be expected that he would be greatly enlightened by this answer.

"Who the devil is Lady Battiscue?" he demanded.

"My cousin," Samantha answered almost absentmind-edly. "But what of her, Mr. Phelps?"

"She has learned that you have inherited your Aunt Kendall's estate," Mr. Phelps explained. "She appears to be thinking of contesting the will."

Samantha looked bleak. "Contest the will? What nonsense is this. You told me back in York that Aunt Kendall's will was perfectly sound."

"It was and is," Mr. Phelps asserted calmly. "Nothing shall come out of any lawsuit. From my understanding of the matter, it is just a threat to cause trouble for you. She is, I believe, your third cousin once removed, is she not?"

"Something like that," Samantha said dismissively, for she had never paid much mind to her family tree and was not about to delve into the complexities of that relationship now.

"Have you seen this Lady Battiscue yourself?" Sheffield asked, taking advantage of a lull in the room.

Mr. Phelps shook his head. "No, my lord. But I got wind of what she was up to through certain sources of mine in Devon. She's believed bound for London at any time to raise as much fuss and botheration as possible."

"Let her," Sheffield declared. "What harm can an old woman do?"

"You don't know her," Samantha said irritably, "or you wouldn't ask such a question! She was used to consider herself something of a theatrical actress and played a host of parts in the amateur theatricals in Devon. A grand tragedy is not beyond her range," she said gloomily.

"Oh, an actress, is she?" Sheffield said, latching onto this detail in Lady Battiscue's character. "How delightful. Reminds me a trifle of my Aunt Gertrude. She considered herself a *grande dame* in the amateur theatricals in her parts. Wouldn't wonder if the two of them knew each other!"

Samantha had no interest in Sheffield's aunt and said so. "You are certain there is no possibility of her overturning the will, Mr. Phelps?"

The solicitor shook his head emphatically. "No chance

in the world, Miss Curtis. And yet her actions may grow vexing, which is why I decided to speak plainly to you on the matter. Family quarrels over legal affairs have a tendency to become nasty. I recollect one case I handled years ago concerning twin brothers who thereafter would not deign to speak to each other when they met in their club."

"Well, I don't mind never speaking to Lady Battiscue," Samantha confessed, "or never seeing her, either. But I suppose I shall be doing both before too long." A new problem suddenly struck her: "Miranda! If Lady Battiscue does cause mischief, how can I ever hope to launch Miranda?"

"It appears to me that the lovely Miranda is already launched," Sheffield said airily. "She had at the very least a dozen men dangling after her at Almacks last night, not counting my idiotish relation."

"Last night, yes," Samantha agreed. "But if word of trouble gets out, the gentlemen might scatter to the wind."

"You have a rather low opinion of those of my sex," Sheffield said. "But you may be partly right about the Tulips and Pinks running from trouble, even trouble that is only suspect. If you want my thoughts on the matter, I would suggest buying her off."

"Buying her off!" Samantha scoffed. "You are all about in your head to think of such a thing. Besides, she has more money than I have. I assure you, she is no pauper. And I do think it is uncivil of her to begrudge me what little I have been lucky enough to inherit from Aunt Kendall."

"Perhaps she's not as you first knew her to be," Sheffield said, his optimism unabated. "People do change as they get on in years. Take my Aunt Gertrude. She used to be a veritable tartar. But as she got older she turned into a regular trump. No one in the family would believe it. Butter wouldn't melt in her mouth."

"If you say another syllable about your Aunt Gertrude, Sheffield," Samantha said distractedly.

"Oh, Aunt Gertrude deserves more than another syllable. But I'll give that over, since your interest in her appears to be on the wane." He stroked his chin with a finger.

"If your Lady Battiscue is so plump in the pocket, why does she need your small fortune?"

"Because she is a deplorable purse squeeze!" Samantha answered blightingly. "She was one in the days that Papa would try and borrow from her, or anyone else, if it came to that. I daresay the idea of anyone else in the family inheriting money that conceivably might fatten *her* coffers would be enough to bring on an attack of the apoplexy."

"If so, perhaps she shan't survive the trip to London!"

Samantha blinked. "I don't want her dead, my lord! Just back in Devonshire where she belongs."

"Then we shall have to hope for a *mild* attack of apoplexy," Sheffield said with aplomb.

"I don't wish for anything of the sort," Samantha retorted. She turned back toward Mr. Phelps, who had been avidly following this exchange. "When did you say she was coming to London?"

"My informants tell me in perhaps a week or two," Mr. Phelps prophesied. "And that gives us some time to prepare."

But prepare for what, Samantha wondered, even after they had left the City and she was back in the phaeton with Sheffield.

Sheffield, noticing his companion's abstract mood, held his tongue and thought of how he might cheer her up. Lady Battiscue, tartar or no tartar, had not even set foot in London, and he would be dashed if she would ruin the day for them. Even now the sky was clearing, a rarity in London, and he gave in to the impulse to take a brisk turn into the Park. Almost immediately he felt better.

Samantha had not been so involved over her impending problems with Lady Battiscue that she failed to notice they had turned into the Park. Before she could bring herself to ask why he had chosen this roundabout route home, another carriage bore down on them, and suddenly she had her answer. The vehicle approaching them was a dashing tilbury driven by one Sir Cyril Chauncy, and his companion this morning was none other than Frieda Horick.

Now Samantha fully understood why Sheffield had strayed into the Park. He was still intent on his odious game of revenge with his soon-to-be betrothed. *That* was why he had insisted on taking Samantha up in his phaeton and had even gone out of his way to the City returning to the Park in time to be seen by Miss Horick. Aunt Gertrude, indeed!

As the two carriages drew near, Samantha composed herself.

"Warren?" Miss Horick cried out gaily. "What a surprise! I didn't think it could be you, although that team of yours is so distinctive. You are an early riser, my dear. I would not have thought it of you."

"Nor I of you, Frieda," the viscount said amiably from his high perch. "But I suppose there are a good many things we don't know about the other." As she made a *moue* and looked arch, he turned to her companion. "Good morning, Cyril. Is that a new arrangement of your neckcloth?"

The dandy gave a good-natured nod. "An invention of my own, Sheffield. I call it Chauncy's Fall. What do you think?"

"Very pretty! But possibly too intricate for my fingers," the viscount answered, and he gave the Welsh-breds their heads again, chuckling aloud over the dandy's latest idiocy. "If you could only have seen the other arrangements he has come up with during the years. Chauncy's Fall indeed. More of Chauncy's Folly if you ask me!" He noticed that his companion failed to share his mirth and glanced sideways at her, stunned to see the expression of a thundercloud on her face. What in the name of Jupiter was wrong with her.

"Are you feeling at all the thing, Miss Curtis?" he demanded point blank.

"Certainly, my lord," she said arcticly.

"There's no certainly about it," he said rudely. "For I can see that something is wrong with you."

"You err, sir," Samantha said. He might play her for a fool but he would never know it from her lips!

Sheffield pushed back his high-crowned beaver. "Don't try and flummery me. Last night you looked deuced out of sorts, and this freakish whim you have fallen into this morning only proves it again."

"I am not in a freakish whim," Samantha replied as the carriage pulled up at Cavendish Square. "Thank you for the ride, my lord."

He made no attempt to heed this obvious dismissal but followed her into the house on her heels.

"If you don't tell me at once what bee has flown into your bonnet or what I have done to earn your obvious contempt, I shall remain here til you do so," he warned.

"And I should think that the coincidence of our meeting Miss Horick in the Park should be an explanation in itself!"

Sheffield stared at her as she turned to bolt from his grasp. But she could not escape him so easily. "What type of oaf do you think I am, Miss Curtis?" he asked, following her. "You can't honestly be thinking that I *knew* Frieda would be in the Park with Chauncy? Good God, that is it, isn't it? You do think such a thing. In fact you believe I would play such a schoolboy's trick on you."

"Oh, no, my lord!" Her reply was cold. "I am determined to think it a coincidence. A coincidence that you merely happened out with me. I wish you would find some other female addled enough to be used as a pawn in that most odious game you are playing with Miss Horick. You need not look very far. So many young ladies are all agog over you, as you probably know!"

"Don't talk drivel!" he snapped, advancing into the drawing room on her heels. The two of them came to a sudden embarrassed halt at the sight of Pamela, Lady Alice, and Captain Maybury seated there with the evidence on all three faces of having heard every word of the argument.

"Coming to cuffs at such an hour, Warren?" Lady Alice quizzed as she rose to take Samantha by the hand. "I've never known you to show such violence in the morning. Generally you reserve your displays of temper for the afternoon and evening. Samantha, you must sit here, out of his line of fire. When he is angry he can be as cross as crabs! And I speak with the authority of one who has known him in short coats."

Sheffield scowled, demanding to know what they were doing at Cavendish Square.

"We came by to tell Miss Curtis that Lady Alice has accepted my offer of marriage," the captain answered. "We had gone over to Berkeley Square as well, Warren, but you were out. Alice had an inclination that the two of you might be together."

"An inclination?" Sheffield asked dangerously.

"Yes, call it an intuition, if you will," Lady Alice said blithely. "My grandmother was Scottish and said to be quite fey."

"Marriage!" Samantha exclaimed, brushing aside Lady Alice's Scottish grandmother. "But how wonderful for you both. I do wish you happy!"

Lady Alice patted her cheek. "Thank you, my dear. Really, the captain and I have you to thank for it all."

"Me?" Samantha exclaimed in shock. "How, pray, did I set this romance in action?"

Lady Alice gave a throaty laugh. "If you had not arrived in London, dear Samantha, I would not have had occasion to throw that little party for you, and Sheffield would not have asked me to invite the captain! Then we should never have met."

"I must say, you haven't let the grass grow under your feet, Edward," Sheffield said to the captain. "Hasn't even been a se'enight since Alice's party!"

"I don't believe in allowing anyone else to steal a march on me," the captain grinned. "And I for one don't believe in long engagements, much as you might, Warren." He directed a meaningful look at the viscount, who scowled at him.

"Will you go back to sea, Captain?" Samantha asked, her quarrel with Sheffield momentarily forgotten.

The captain shook his head. "I mean to stay firmly at Lady Alice's side. No cicisbeo for her!"

"Very proper," Sheffield said, hiding a smile.

Lady Alice launched into a description of their impending nuptials, which they were listening to with every sign of pleasure when the door to the establishment suddenly slammed. Miranda's soprano could be heard bursting out with laughter and disclaiming: "Roddy, you mustn't!"

Mr. Monroe, apparently not heeding this order, could be heard next inquiring, who said so.

The two convulsed in giggles turned the corner into the drawing room, coming to an immediate halt under five pairs of questioning eyes.

"Good God!" Roddy ejaculated. "I beg your pardons."

"And so you should, Roderick," Sheffield said scornfully. "Is this your customary mode of entering a lady's drawing room?"

"Yes. No, I mean, of course not," Roddy answered, confused and flushing now darkly under the bite of his cousin's setdown. "Had I known, of course . . ."

"Had you known," Sheffield spoke with a terrible languor, "you might have acted with more decorum. As it is, your manners are insufferable! And I can only wonder at them and you!"

"It is not Roddy's fault!" Miranda flew instantly to his defense. "We were out riding," she said. "And anyway, Lord Sheffield, you have no right to rake Roddy over the coals. You're not his father!"

"Miranda, hush!" Samantha commanded.

The viscount, however, did not appear greatly offended by Miranda's words.

"You are quite correct, Miss Miranda. I am not Roderick's father, for which I can only be grateful. His father has been dead these past five years. But I am his nearest relation in London, and while he continues to live here he shall conduct his flirtations with more discretion!"

"Flirtations!" Miranda trembled visibly at the words. "It is more than a flirtation, Lord Sheffield," she exclaimed hotly. "Roddy and I are in love. He loves me and I him. Tell them so, Roddy, immediately!"

Mr. Monroe, no doubt feeling that his beloved might have chosen a less public method of making this announcement, nonetheless gathered his wits together to acknowledge the truth of her statement.

"I know you dislike it, Warren," he said to Sheffield.

"You think I'm naught but a green head. But I have fallen in love with Miranda and she with me, and despite your opposition, we shall wed!"

"Wed to starve for two years?" Sheffield reminded him. "Cupid hasn't caused you to forget the terms of your father's will, I should hope?"

"Of course Roddy knows that," Miranda interrupted. "And so do I. He explained it all to me days ago. But I shan't mind. And I don't care if we do starve."

"That merely proves how little removed from a nursery you are," Sheffield said acidly. "I expected better of you, Roderick. It's plain to me that I must take a hand in this, much as I hate to. Miss Curtis." He flicked a negligent glance over at Samantha. "I leave your sister to you." And with that he bullocked Roddy out of the drawing room with him.

～ THIRTEEN ～

"Oh, what an odious, odious man!" Miranda declared after Sheffield had departed with Roddy in tow. "I can't think of anyone half so disagreeable in the world!"

Samantha's own thoughts had moved along these same lines during her drive back from the Park, but now she found herself in the position of having to defend him.

"He has been extremely civil to us all, Miranda," she reminded her sister. "And there has really been no reason for him to be so kind. And I am in complete agreement with him on this matter. Marriage between you and Roddy is out of the question. Really, how could you have been so unheeding as to have made such a public declaration! Such a sad want of conduct!"

"I don't care," Miranda said, tossing her blond head

back. "I'm in love. I want the whole world to know it."

"The whole world shall think you a goose!" Samantha said dampeningly. "Had I known that you would fling yourself at the first gentleman who paid you any attention, I would never have brought you from York. Roddy may be pleasant and amiable, but he is *not* the husband I envisioned for you, my dear!"

"You can't make me marry anyone else, Samantha!" Miranda cried out. "I'll die first, I swear it." Whereupon she burst into tears.

Pamela, who had been sitting by nervously watching her sisters skirmish, felt dutybound now to intervene. Chiding Samantha mildly for putting Miranda into an emotional state, she excused herself to coax Miranda upstairs to her bed.

"As though I am the villain of this piece," Samantha said despairingly to Lady Alice and the captain.

Lady Alice gave a sympathetic cluck. "All the same, Pamela may be right, Samantha. It would do no good to ring a peal over Miranda now, for she is in a volatile mood. Being in love has caused her to speak rather more foolishly than she should have."

"She is not in love," Samantha declared. "She merely thinks she is. And I do wish Cupid would choose his victims with a little more discrimination. Not," she added quickly, "that I am not pleased over *your* romance!"

Lady Alice laughed. "I know." She then sighed. "However, Miranda's attachment to Roderick might be a lasting one. One never knows. And when he does reach twenty-five, he shall have that fortune you desire for her so much."

"If they are still alive to enjoy it," Samantha answered. Sheffield was right. Starvation might well be upon Roddy and Miranda within months of their wedding. And she did not want her sister doomed to a life of outrunning the creditors.

Fortified by this thought, she saw Lady Alice out with the captain and then mounted the stairs, steeling herself for the battle ahead. When she entered Miranda's bedchamber she found her sister alone, nursing what she claimed to be a violent migraine.

Usually solicitous of any symptom of ill health in either of her two sisters, Samantha was not hoodwinked now, particularly since Miranda sat back against the pillows staring daggers at her.

"And surely," she said affably, "you could not do that if the migraine were really upon you."

Miranda gave up all pretense of being sick. "How can you be so unfeeling, Samantha?" she demanded. "I love Roddy, and he loves me. Surely that is all that is required for marriage."

"Miranda, if only it *were* that simple," Samantha replied. "But you must try and look at the larger picture. Listen to me. Roddy's income now is barely enough to support himself with the habits he has. Not that I mean to imply that he is a profligate, but young men his age are prone to getting into debt. And if he is hard pressed now, what will be his state when he is married and must support you!"

"We'll manage somehow," Miranda said. "After all, look how we managed in Yorkshire after Mama died."

Samantha scowled. "We did that by selling most of our belongings. And until Aunt Kendall's inheritance fell into our laps I had nothing but worries about what we should do in our future. And while her legacy seemed enormous to me at the time, I'm obliged to think that it may not be so large after all. Indeed, when the bills are paid for the Season, there may only be something like five thousand pounds left. And Donald had been anxious to invest in Arabians for his estate, and I had a thought I might help them. And even if I have something left to give you—"

"I don't want your money, Samantha," Miranda said vehemently. "I don't need mere money as long as I have Roddy. And I should rather starve with Roddy than gorge myself at table with any other husband."

From this Samantha correctly deduced that her sister was not of a mind to be sensible. She went off to her own bedchamber, where she was accosted some minutes later by Pamela, intent on fostering Miranda's cause.

"It's not that I wish to interfere," she said gently, "but they are so much in love."

"I have heard Cupid blamed for entirely too much for one day!" Samantha warned, growing more and more exasperated by all this talk of love. She peered up at her sister. "Good heavens, Pammy, I had hoped for some sense from you. Have you even stopped to think what Miranda's future with Roddy shall be like? She might not remember how it was with Papa—in the Funds one day and out of it the next—but I do, and so should you!" She clenched her hands into fists. "I would not wish such a life on my worst enemy, let alone on Miranda, whom I love!"

"I know, but—"

"There is nothing romantic about poverty!" Samantha went on. "They are nothing but nursery brats, and we must show them the error of their attachment. If Miranda would just pay a moment's attention to anyone other than Mr. Monroe, she might notice that several quite eligible men were trying to fix their attentions on her, and she might fall in love with one of them."

Pamela looked agitated. "But she is already in love with Roddy. And he with her!"

"Fiddle! Roddy's whims for females is notorious," Samantha replied.

Pamela raised her delicate eyebrows. "Notorious, Samantha?"

"Yes! I did not like to say so in front of Miranda, but Lady Alice told me that night of her party how Roddy is always tumbling into love and then out of it. Calf love."

Pamela paused, obviously shocked by this assessment of Mr. Monroe's volatility. "It doesn't seem like calf love to me," she mused, "and I think I know what love is."

"And I suppose I don't?" Samantha asked, ripping up at this insinuation again.

Pamela paled. "My dear Samantha! I didn't mean to suggest that you—" She fluttered a protest. "Heavens. My dear—"

"Never mind, Pammy," Samantha said, instantly contrite. "It is just that my mind is in a whirl. I know you didn't mean to call me an old maid, even though I am molding on the shelf!"

"Samantha!"

"Let it pass, I beg you," Samantha said, her fit of pique over. "I have had a devil of a morning, what with Mr. Phelps telling me Lady Battiscue is sure to descend upon us and then that odious Viscount Sheffield using me as a pawn in his game with Miss Horick and now Miranda and Roddy making a Cheltenham tragedy out of their lives. It's enough to give *me* a migraine."

Pamela frowned and inquired what Lady Battiscue had to do with anything.

Samantha sat her down on the day bed and quickly told her the news from Mr. Phelps. "And you must see that if she does come and throws one of her wretched scenes, poor Miranda's chances shall go by the board."

"I don't believe that Miranda gives a rush about her chances," Pamela replied. "And Roddy certainly shall not care about what Lady Battiscue says."

"Miranda may not marry Roddy!" Samantha pointed out. Then, seeing in her sister's eyes a warning that she was about to launch into another spirited defense of the young pair, she begged off, claiming that Horace was waiting to speak to her.

Since this tale was an utter fabrication, Samantha was somewhat daunted to find that the butler indeed had been looking for her, to impart the news that Mr. Hancock had called in the small drawing room. Samantha was pleased to see the young man and surprised to receive from him an invitation to the Opera for herself and her sisters on Friday next. Since Pamela and Donald had already spoken of dining with some new friends that evening, she declined the invitation for Pamela but accepted for herself and Miranda.

"If you are sure you want us and not Miss Horick!" she could not resist teasing.

A faint blush overcame Mr. Hancock's cheeks. "Quite sure, Miss Curtis. In fact Frieda has given me my *congé*, and that does relieve me, for I had no idea why she would wish to attach me in the first place. Known her all my life, and she's not the sort of wife either I or my mother would choose."

Samantha, who had heard several provocative tidbits already concerning Mr. Hancock's mother and her precise list of do's and don'ts for any bride of her handsome son, ventured to ask curiously what sort of wife he did fancy, thinking that she might glean something useful from him that might apply to Miranda. Mr. Hancock was compliant in answering, so compliant that the visit passed for her into tedium, with her visitor listing all the virtues any wife of his must possess.

As Samantha sunk into ennui, Lord Sheffield was bullying his cousin into the sitting room of his Berkeley Square establishment, oblivious to the flood of protests emanating from the younger man.

"I've done nothing to be ashamed of, Warren!" Roddy insisted stoutly.

The viscount eyed him with acute displeasure. "Then you are even more of a slow top than I imagined. And pray don't part with any more of that nauseating drivel about your love for the fair Miranda. I've had as much twaddle on *that* as I can stand!"

Roddy smoothed the folds of his cravat with one hand. "I thought you wanted me to find the right female and fall in love," he demanded. "You're the very one who used to rake me over the coals for dallying with opera dancers!"

"Miss Miranda is no opera dancer."

"Lord, I know that!" Mr. Monroe exclaimed. "It seems that there is no pleasing you, Warren. You don't like my flirtations with females of the less virtuous sort, and then you play the ugly when I pay court to the proper type of female with the quite honorable intention of marrying her. Perhaps you'd rather I go to my grave a bachelor like you!"

"Don't be a gudgeon!" Sheffield barked. "And do sit down!" He waited until Roddy had complied with his command. "Your father's will precludes any opinions I might have. And I do think it is answer itself to the dilemma you face. Think, for heaven's sake! You receive barely enough from it to support yourself now. And you have such deplorable habits of losing at both White's and Watiers! How in the name of Jupiter do you think you shall support a wife and maybe even a child for two years!"

"We shall manage," Roddy said thickly.

Sheffield's reply was a blunt echo of Samantha's to her sister. "You shall starve. Miss Curtis and I may not agree on a great deal, but we are resolved on this point. Miss Miranda has barely had time to see anyone else in the *ton*. No, don't speak! I am not interested in your opinions. You must allow her the time and opportunity to meet other gentlemen and to compare them with you. And you needn't poker up, for I'm not speaking about allowing her to be seduced! However, she might go for drives with her beaux—excursions, picnics, and that sort of harmless thing. If that *tendre* you claim she has for you is really love, it shall survive such an easy test, don't you think?"

"Of course it shall," Roddy spoke through gritted teeth.

"I know it's difficult," the viscount began.

"You know nothing!" Roddy retorted. "How could you! You've never been in love."

"Perhaps not," Sheffield said coolly.

Roddy snorted. "I love Miranda. And I shall marry her. And I don't care if she sees a dozen earls and counts, eventually she shall marry me. And our marriage shall be a dashed sight better, even if we may be as poor as churchmice, than your cold-blooded alliance with Frieda Horick!"

Sheffield's jaw tightened a fraction. "Miss Horick is my concern, Roddy, not yours. I advise you to remember that. Now, you'll do what I ask about Miss Miranda?"

"Very well," Roddy replied grudgingly. "But I need to see her too, Warren!"

Sheffield threw his hands up to the ceiling. "Of course you shall see her. You shall pay your customary visits to Cavendish Square. But mind you don't glower when you find her engaged with some other!"

In the days that followed, Samantha discovered that some of Sheffield's words of wisdom and her own appeared to have sunk in. Roddy continued to call almost daily, but his behavior was exemplary. He did not even gnash his teeth when Horace on one occasion informed him that the Earl of Compton had taken Miss Miranda for a drive about the Park.

From Miranda's excursion to the Park came the news that Miss Horick had also been there with Sir Cyril. Indeed, the baronet had grown so attentive of late that the earl had laughingly remarked that an actress and opera dancer the dandy used to patronize had both departed London in a huff.

"I can't think what the earl must be about to refer to Sir Cyril's *chères amies* in your presence!" Samantha scolded.

Miranda tossed her head. "I'm not an infant, Samantha, even though you do persist in thinking me one. Every female knows that a gentleman has bits of muslin. Even Roddy himself," she said large-mindedly. "But that was before me."

Since Miranda had been behaving quite civilly to her other callers, Samantha was reluctant to scold her about such a trifle. Aside from uttering the hope that she would refrain from talking about barques of frailty to the gentlemen, she commended her sister for not pining over Mr. Monroe.

Samantha's feelings of goodwill toward Miranda and Roddy lasted only as long as Friday evening, when Mr. Hancock arrived to escort them to the Opera. As the two ladies descended the stairs, Samantha in a gown of white April satin with roses at the bodice and Miranda in a pink muslin, they discovered two gentlemen waiting belowstairs, Mr. Hancock along with Mr. Monroe.

"I invited Roddy to join our party," Mr. Hancock said, smiling as he shook hands with Samantha. "I knew you wouldn't mind."

Since Mr. Hancock was the host of the party, Samantha did not have the heart to tell him how he had been so sadly duped, but she vowed to herself to keep Roddy as far from Miranda as were humanly possible. This plan, however noble, was foiled almost from the start by Mr. Hancock, who insisted on sitting next to Samantha in the carriage and in his box at the Royal Opera House, leaving Miranda and Roddy free to exchange some private words.

Since she could not separate Miranda bodily from Roddy, Samantha gave up the attempt to keep them apart and did her best to enjoy what was left of the evening. The excellent position of Mr. Hancock's box afforded them an unobstructed view of the stage as well as of other boxes, including that of Sir Cyril Chauncy, now holding court for the evening with Miss Horick.

"Frieda's bringing Cyril to heel rapidly," Mr. Hancock said, following Samantha's gaze. "Not that it matters so much. Sheffield has a lock on that match, I daresay. She shall take him. If I were a female I know I would."

"How fortunate, then, for all of us that you are not a female," Samantha drawled, laughing at the idea of the lithe and handsome Mr. Hancock swathed in petticoats. "Does Sheffield frequent the opera?"

"Oh, he pops in now and then," Mr. Hancock replied. "But he's not much of a music lover." He pointed out the viscount's box, in use this evening by Captain Maybury and Lady Alice, who acknowledged with a quick wave the smile Samantha sent them. She could not help wondering if Sheffield would join them perhaps later in the evening.

As the curtain fell at the end of the act Miranda applied for leave to visit Lady Alice with Mr. Monroe, and Samantha readily consented, thinking that she would visit them during one of the later interludes herself.

"Have you known Roddy long?" she asked Mr. Hancock, who had spent most of the first act of the opera snoring lightly. He now roused himself to say they usually met once or twice a week at the club.

"Ran into him yesterday on St. James Street. In a pelter to see the performance tonight, not that I can comprehend *that*, for Catalani ain't singing, after all. So I invited him along. Didn't fancy him an opera lover."

"One never does know," Samantha said diplomatically as she gazed across at Lady Alice and the captain, who were speaking with Roddy and Miranda. Her eyes shifted toward Sir Cyril's box. Surprisingly, Miss Horick was not there.

The mystery of the Beauty's disappearance resolved itself a few moments later when she strolled into Mr. Hancock's box.

"Good evening, Philip," she said, offering her hand to him. "I wonder if you would be so obliging as to go and see Cyril. There is something he is longing to speak to you about. You needn't worry about deserting Miss Curtis. I shall contrive to keep her amused during your absence."

Mr. Hancock threw a questioning look at Samantha, who bade him see what the baronet wanted.

"Philip is an obedient sort of fellow, isn't he?" Miss Horick asked, settling into the chair he had just vacated. "His mother's influence, I daresay."

"I have not had the pleasure of his mother's acquaintance," Samantha replied, "so I cannot speak to that point. However, I have always found him to be amiable. Do you as a rule count obedience as one of the attributes a gentleman should possess, Miss Horick?"

Miss Horick plied a languid fan. "On the contrary. Take Sheffield, for instance. There is no point in any female trying to bring him to heel, for he can be so uncoaxable. I confess that he and I are often at cross-points with one another. But in spite of all that, a bond exists between us."

A little giddy at being thrust into the unexpected role of Miss Horick's confidante, Samantha inquired politely what Sir Cyril's role in this bond might be.

Miss Horick tittered. "Cyril? He is a pet, of course, and he is the dearest of friends. I hope, Miss Curtis, that you do not think that Sheffield and I are planning a marriage based on a grand passion!"

Miss Horick's eyes drifted lazily over the other woman's face. "Since you hail from the country, I thought perhaps you might have that antiquated notion that love is a necessary requirement for marriage. Here in London we are more sensible about such things. All that is really required is a similarity in station, mind, and fortune." She laid a peculiar emphasis on the last of these three.

"I see," Samantha replied.

"I'm so glad. Sheffield, after all, is of an age to marry. His mother was always so eager to see him wed. And I naturally am willing to be married to one of his standing, so nothing could be more suitable. He shall continue to enjoy himself with his *chères amies*, and I shall have Cyril and my other cicisbeos." She frowned. "Oh dear, I hope I haven't shocked you again. You are country reared. I keep forgetting that. How you must frown on our town manners!"

"Good manners in town and country are not so dissimilar," Samantha replied coolly. "And I do felicitate you on your excellent match with Lord Sheffield."

"Thank you," the Beauty said. "And I hope you do as well with dear Philip. Of course his fortune is nowhere near that of Sheffield's. But he is the faithful sort and shall probably not be scared off by rumors of your legal problems."

Her last words were punctuated with an arch smile, and Samantha's breath quickened. How had the Beauty learned of pending legal problems? Only three people had been entrusted with that secret: Mr. Phelps, whose discretion she would trust with her life, Pammy, whose path rarely crossed that of the Beauty, and Sheffield . . . *Sheffield!* She did not need to look further! He was the culprit! So much for his promise to be true blue and never stain. She became aware that Miss Horick was offering profuse apologies.

"I have such a wretched tongue. And I had come over with the sole purpose of assuring you that no one would hear a peep out of me on your unfortunate problem."

"You are very kind," Samantha said. Mr. Hancock's return to the box forestalled any further discourse, and the Beauty departed wearing the radiant smile of one who had done precisely what she had set out to do.

Samantha sat still in the full flush of anger directed against a certain peer who had the arrogance to divulge confidences in matters that did not concern him.

"It was naught but a wild goose chase!"

Mr. Hancock's mild complaint broke into Samantha's thoughts.

"I beg your pardon?" she inquired.

"That business with Chauncy," Mr. Hancock repeated. "He didn't want to see me in his box. Just a hoax." He wiped his brow with a linen handkerchief. "Did Frieda behave herself?"

"Of course," Samantha replied.

"Good. I say, where are your sister and Roddy, Miss Curtis? They'll miss the start of the next act."

While Samantha did not think missing the next act would be that grievous a sacrifice, she darted a quick look at the viscount's box, startled to find only Lady Alice and Captain Maybury there.

"They are probably on their way back here," she said to Mr. Hancock.

But when five additional minutes had passed without a reappearance by the young couple, she grew concerned enough to suggest to Mr. Hancock that they might conduct a search of the corridors. Just as the second act commenced they exited the box, traversing a few yards together headed toward the great stairs. Mr. Hancock, who had been a step in front of Samantha, came to a rigid halt.

Absorbed in her thoughts, Samantha nearly walked into him.

"Good heavens, Mr. Hancock," she said, stopping just in time and somewhat exasperated by his actions. She started to step around him.

"I don't think you should go any farther, Miss Curtis," he said in a strangled tone.

"Not go?" Samantha asked, bewildered. She stepped around him and then came to a dead stop herself. There on the stairway in front of them, oblivious to whoever in the *ton* might see them, stood her sister and young Roddy, locked in a soulful embrace and exchanging what looked to be a passionate kiss.

~ *FOURTEEN* ~

The charming tableau of Roddy and Miranda frozen on the Opera House stairs held Samantha spellbound for a moment. Then the fog lifted, and she stepped forward, hissing, "Miranda!"

The lovers sprang apart, guilt written plainly on their two faces.

"Samantha!" Miranda exclaimed, blushing wildly. "Oh, heavens! It is not what you think, I swear it!"

"What I think is of no importance," Samantha replied in a voice so cold that a shiver ran down the spine of Mr. Hancock. "I had hoped that you would show some particle of sense, but you haven't! And that is merely one reason why I frown on this marriage. As for you, Mr. Monroe, I shall thank you not to call on Cavendish Square hereafter, for my sister shan't be at home to you!"

"Samantha, you can't mean that!" Miranda wailed and burst into tears.

"Miss Curtis, please," Roddy managed to speak as he comforted Miranda. "I can explain."

Well aware that they were within seconds of attracting the attention of others in the Opera House, Samantha pleaded a headache to Mr. Hancock—a perfectly understandable excuse given the circumstances—and swept Miranda down the stairs, impervious to a fresh attack of the vapors that afflicted her sister. Turning a deaf ear to Roddy's continual pleas to explain, she thrust Miranda bodily into Mr. Hancock's carriage.

"You shall excuse us," she told Roddy, "if we do not take you up into the vehicle with us." And as soon as Mr. Hancock had taken his seat the carriage rolled away, leaving Mr. Monroe stranded as he watched his beloved being borne away.

"*I hate you! I hate you! I hate you!*" Miranda, rallying from her attack of the vapors, managed to launch a spirited attack on Samantha. "How could you treat me like a schoolroom miss! Roddy and I did nothing wrong."

"You did too much as it is," Samantha said sharply. "Skulking about the stairs like a parlor maid and a footman, and in full view of whomever might be passing by."

"We didn't skulk!" Miranda protested, sinking back against the velvet squabs. "We were coming back to the box from seeing Lady Alice, and it just happened. He was overcome by my beauty!"

"Oh, hush!" Samantha said despairingly.

"I wish I were a parlormaid," Miranda said, "and Roddy a footman, for then we could marry and no one would stand in our way. You are probably jealous, Samantha! No gentleman I know has ever tried to kiss you. So what can you know of such things?"

"Nothing at all, apparently," Samantha replied, managing not without difficulty to shrug off her sister's thoughtless words. "But unacquainted though I may be with the full particulars of love, I do have some semblance of good conduct. You obviously have none! And since you do not know how to conduct yourself in public, henceforth, whenever you do go out it shall be with me or Pamela at your side!"

As Miranda railed at the injustice of such a sentence, Mr. Hancock, who had been the unwilling witness to the family squabble, shouldered some of the blame for the evening's events.

"Feel as though I shouldn't have brought young Roddy with me."

"You are not to blame," Samantha said to him. "You were probably duped by them both. Miranda very likely told him she was going to the opera tonight with you, and he set about wrangling an invitation from you."

"He did not!" Miranda lifted her head to protest. "At least," she amended as Mr. Hancock looked quizzically at her, "he didn't do it in the odious way you suggest. And there's nothing wrong about Roddy trying to see me. He loves me and I love him!"

With dwindling patience, Samantha reminded Miranda that she had heard variations on this theme almost daily for the past week. "And you are becoming a dead bore on the topic!"

To the relief of everyone, particularly Mr. Hancock, who as an only child had no great experience with family quarrels, the carriage was fast approaching Cavendish Square. Samantha bustled out the still recalcitrant Miranda, thanked her host for an interesting evening, and dragged her sister past a surprised Horace.

"My sister is unwell," she informed the butler, a declaration that Miranda immediately gave the lie to by retorting that she was not. To prove her point further, she wrenched free of Samantha's grasp and dashed up the stairs. A second later came the slam of a door from an upstairs room.

Sighing, Samantha caught Horace's sympathetic eye and wondered if she should follow. Finally she decided against it for she had borne with enough *sturm und drang* for one evening.

"I shall be in the library, Horace," she told the butler and withdrew to Wilhelm's bookroom, staring into the kindling wood in the fire, feeling uncharacteristically tired, lonely, and—*devil take it*—unloved!

At least, she thought wryly, twisting her lips together, Miranda and Pamela were agreed on one point: she knew nothing whatever about love.

An hour later she looked up as the door to the library opened and Pamela peeped her head in. "Horace told us you'd be here."

"Come in, Pammy," Samantha invited, but so wearily that Pamela was concerned.

"Good God, Samantha. You look burnt to the socket," Donald said, following his wife into the room. "What the devil happened?"

Briefly Samantha told them what had transpired on the stairs of the Opera House.

"Kissing on the stairs!" Pamela was horrified. "Oh, no! Not even Miranda would be so foolish! I suppose you were very angry with her?"

"I was livid," Samantha replied. "Such behavior is intolerable, Pammy. I have half a mind to send her back to York tomorrow. But that might spoil any chances she may have of making a match with anyone other than Roddy. And besides, there was all the expense of coming here." She shook her head. "I don't really know what I shall do. But one thing is certain: if she steps out of this house one of us must accompany her."

While Pamela felt this a harsh punishment, she knew from the look in Samantha's eyes not to quarrel with it now. After five minutes she took herself off, intent on consoling Miranda's mangled emotions.

Her spouse, however, remained behind, holding out a glass of sherry to his sister-in-law.

"Restoratives, Samantha," he said encouragingly. "It appears to me that you could use it."

"Dear Donald!" She heaved a sigh and took the glass. "You are a prince."

Blushing, he insisted stoutly that he was no such thing and bade her drink up the sherry and tell him all about this frightful mull.

Much to her surprise, she found herself doing just that. Although Donald listened attentively and sympathetically, he offered no real help to her. Nor did she expect any from that quarter. Donald simply was not the sort of gentleman to seize trouble by the throat and throttle it.

Although grateful for her brother-in-law's company and the ear into which she realized she had poured more complaints than she ought to have, she could not help wishing that he were a different sort of gentleman. Someone more like . . . Sheffield, for instance.

But no sooner had she thought that than she dismissed it out of hand. The viscount had shown his true colors earlier in the evening!

Thoughts of Miranda continued to occupy the uppermost regions of Samantha's mind as the days passed. On Monday she sat perusing the bills for Quarter Day when Horace approached with the news that a female giving the name of Lady Battiscue had demanded and been given entree into the blue saloon.

"Perhaps I shouldn't have, Miss," he said apologetically, "but she did say she was a relation."

"And you have tangled once before with visitors claiming to be relations, have you not, Horace," Samantha teased as she pushed aside a ledger book. She stood up. "The blue saloon, you said?"

"Yes, Miss."

As Samantha moved toward the drawing room she wished that she had remembered earlier to tell her butler that on no account must Lady Battiscue be allowed into Wilhelm's establishment. Now, however, it was too late. Straightening her shoulders, she sailed into the drawing room and came to a halt as she observed an elderly figure hunched on the couch, an ebony cane beating impatiently on an Oriental rug.

The lean, almost gaunt face looked to be rouged and painted in the style of a much earlier generation. The hair, Samantha was certain, was a wig, and the form itself was swathed in layers of garments, as though to fend off a chill that might prove fatal to someone of advanced years.

"Lady Battiscue?" Samantha inquired, looking at the woman, who appeared now more garish than decrepit.

The beady eyes narrowed. "Aye, that I am. Reggie's girl, are you?"

"Yes," Samantha said, not liking such easy familiarity but determined to see the interview through. "I am Samantha Curtis. I believe you wished to see me? On business, my butler said."

"I wish to see you on a matter not of business but justice," the woman replied.

Samantha sat down warily. "Justice?" she asked, making the word a challenge. "How peculiar. Perhaps you had better petition to Bow Street then, ma'am."

Lady Battiscue snorted. "You may have pulled the wool over Jane's eyes—bound to have, since she left the money to you after promising me for years that I should have it. It's clear that you tricked her out of what should have been mine!"

"Yours?" Samantha asked with forced civility. "How extraordinary that sounds, ma'am. Perhaps you have some proof of Aunt Jane's promise to you?"

"Indeed I have," Lady Battiscue said as alarm flickered through Samantha's breast. "My proof is the word of a gentlewoman, and I am not accustomed to having it doubted, even in a court of law. Jane promised me the money years ago. Next thing I hear she's dead, and you've every cent!" The cane shook in a gloved fist. "You tricked her, is what. You and that solicitor between you!"

"Indeed, ma'am," Samantha spoke frigidly, "you slander both me and my solicitor. I did not trick Aunt Jane out of so much as a groat. She was too needlewitted for that, I think you shall agree, and would have seen through a ruse immediately."

"The mind plays foolish tricks with age," Lady Battiscue maintained.

"You would know more of that than I," Samantha said sweetly.

Lady Battiscue flashed a malevolent grin. "We shall see who has the last laugh, Miss Curtis. You fancied without my turning up. But I've friends in London. Very important friends, and I shan't rest until what is mine is returned to me."

From this stirring speech Samantha concluded that Lady Battiscue's taste for the melodramatic was unabated. She found herself falling into her visitor's mood, responding that "what is mine is mine!"

"A court of law may alter that, Miss," Lady Battiscue warned.

"Do you mean to threaten me with a lawsuit, ma'am?" Samantha asked. "I would strongly advise against it. You shall only render yourself foolish. And I advise you to return to Devonshire."

"Foolish, is it?" Lady Battiscue tightened her lips. "We shall see just who is the fool. Not," she said grudgingly, "that I mean to be totally unreasonable. Jane did promise me all her money, but I shan't ask for it all. I might be satisfied with half."

Samantha eyed her in disbelief. "*Half!*" she exclaimed. "You might as well ask for *all* of it, ma'am, and have done with it," she broke off upon seeing Sheffield hovering at the door to the drawing room.

"Am I intruding, Miss Curtis?" he asked urbanely.

"Not at all, my lord," she replied with a fervor that brought an ironic smile to his lips. "Lady Battiscue was just leaving."

Lady Battiscue rose, an ominous figure reeking of lavender scent.

"We shall talk more later, Miss Curtis. This business between us is far from finished."

"You may talk, Lady Battiscue, and I shall listen," Samantha said politely, "but any business between us has already been concluded."

"Very prettily said," Sheffield commended as Lady Battiscue exited in high dudgeon. "How long was she here?"

"Too long," Samantha said succinctly. She sank back in her chair, feeling suddenly weary. "Oh, devil take it, Sheffield. Why did she come now? I could read mischief in that face of hers!"

"Could you, really?" Sheffield inquired blandly. "I'm not at all surprised. There was enough rouge on that face to write any number of words!"

Samantha choked. "This is no time for jokes," she said exasperatedly. "She wanted half of Aunt Kendall's money."

"You're not contemplating giving in to such a ridiculous demand?" he asked.

She shook her head. "No, truly I am not. I could not give up half my estate to her. And yet she claims Aunt Jane promised her the money, and I daresay neither Mr. Phelps nor I thought of that possibility. It could have happened."

"And it could be a Banbury tale, which I consider far more likely," Sheffield pointed out as he took a pinch of snuff. "Lady Battiscue is trying to bully you out of what is rightfully yours, and you're letting her! The thing to do is to fob her off for the time being and send out discreet inquiries of your own concerning her."

This advice appeared sound enough to merit Samantha's approbation, but she suddenly recalled in the nick of time that she was on the outs with him. After all, he had divulged her pending legal difficulties to Miss Horick. This thought made her stiffen her back again.

"Your suggestions are unnecessary, my lord," she said coldly. "My solicitor and I shall handle this problem without any help from you."

Sheffield looked puzzled. "What an aggravating creature you are to be sure! One minute you fall on me like a long-lost brother and the next you are in the hips. Spurn my help, will you?" he asked acutely. "And not for the first time, if I recall correctly. Well, never mind. How was the opera?"

Samantha was caught off guard. "Opera? It was quite tolerable."

"Really. Then it must not have been one of those Italian nights? Did you stay for all of it?"

She could not help darting a quick suspicious look at his innocent expression.

"We left after the first act, my lord," she said thickly. "My sister was not feeling at all the thing."

"Neither was my relation," he replied. "I believe it must be one of those new illnesses. Devilishly catching, it appears to be."

"Oh do stop shamming!" she exclaimed. "How did you know?"

He laughed. "Roddy himself. He came round Friday night after he had been dumped so unceremoniously, as he put it, outside the Opera House."

Samantha felt a momentary qualm. "Perhaps you think it uncivil of us."

"Not at all," Sheffield demurred. "The lad is in excellent health, the night was a fair one, and he managed to catch a ride with Captain Maybury, who dropped him off at my establishment. There he proceeded to complain in a dull-winded fashion that you had kidnapped his beloved from under his nose. I was obliged to point out that you were merely trying to marry her off, not kidnap her."

"Good heavens, what a simpleton!"

"Well, he *is* in love," Sheffield explained. "And as such he begged me, even going so far as to threaten bodily harm if I didn't come round to see you sometime this week and find out how the lovely Miranda was faring." A gleam of amusement danced in his eyes. "He seemed convinced you had her locked in a tower and would make her subsist on nothing but bread and water or something similarly *un-nourishing*. I believe he must have mistaken you for Richard the second."

Samantha could not help laughing herself. "I can't believe he is a relation of yours, Sheffield!"

"Yes, I know. But he is, rest assured. Now then, you aren't beating Miranda?"

"Good God, no," Samantha exclaimed. "Although perhaps I *should,* but it is much too late for that. Whatever the two of them may say or think, I am not such a beast."

Something in her voice gave Sheffield pause, and he glanced up at the face across from him. Her features were unchanged, but she did look a trifle out of sorts, no doubt from the abuse her sister had been hurling at her head.

"I can well imagine what you have gone through," he said softly. "I went through much the same thing with Roddy. I believe he called me an interfering, meddlesome old peacock. But my skin is no doubt thicker than yours. They are nursery brats, you must remember, prone to getting their way and throwing tantrums when they are thwarted."

"I know," Samantha said, grateful just the same for his sympathy. "So I beg you to tell Roddy that I am not forcing Miranda to live on bread and water. Nor am I beating her senseless."

Sheffield smiled. "Will you let him see her?"

"Perhaps. But not every day, and never alone!"

He nodded. "Quite right to be careful. I'll tell Roddy. I daresay half a loaf is better than none to a man as lovesick as he. Now then, have you told your solicitor about Lady Battiscue? If not, I advise you to do so at once."

"I haven't had the chance!" Samantha said in surprise. "She only just descended on me, and you came on her heels."

"Then allow me to drive you to the City. I know the way."

His words brought to mind their last trip together to Mr. Phelps's office, a trip that had ended, Samantha recalled, with an encounter with Miss Horick in the Park.

"Well?" Sheffield prompted.

"Will Miss Horick be riding out today with Sir Cyril?" Samantha blurted out.

"How the devil should I know?" Sheffield replied. "Is that a roundabout way of saying yes?"

"No, my lord. It is a roundabout way of declining. I'd

much rather talk to Mr. Phelps alone. There are some things best kept between a solicitor and a client."

"That sounds suspiciously as though you don't trust me," Sheffield said bluntly.

"Why shouldn't I trust you?" she asked sweetly.

"I don't know," Sheffield replied grimly. "But I shall make it my business to find out!"

⟨∼ *FIFTEEN* ∼⟩

After alerting Mr. Phelps to Lady Battiscue's presence in London and requesting him to set the wheels of a discreet investigation into motion, Samantha returned to Cavendish Square, where she found Wilhelm overseeing the removal of several coats, pantaloons, shirts, and other necessaries from an upstairs bedroom.

She felt a totally unexpected pang of conscience at the sight of her cousin. Not only had she usurped his establishment, but she had also turned his life upside down. Wilhelm, however, was having none of the belated apologies she offered him. He had news of his own.

"You did tell me that as soon as Miranda were engaged I might return, did you not?" he quizzed Samantha.

"Yes. But she's not engaged as yet. And if you think I shall allow her to accept Roddy Monroe, you are sadly mistaken."

Wilhelm's jowls shook with glee. "It's not young Roddy I had in mind to pop her the question. It's Compton!" He nodded as Samantha shot him a questioning glance. "Getting ready to do the deed or I'll go bail. Saw him myself this morning at White's, and all he would do would be to prattle on about my beautiful cousin Miranda."

Samantha digested this tidbit carefully. The Earl of

Compton intending to offer for Miranda? It was the culmination of every hope she had nursed back in York. It was a brilliant match, without question: a gentleman of undisputable rank, well pursed, with estates in Hereford and Hampshire. He was also disposed to being kind. So why, now that her goal for Miranda was suddenly within grasp, was she remembering her sister locked in Roddy's arms on the Opera House stairs?

Wilhelm was looking at her, mildly aggrieved. "Dash it, coz! You don't appear in alt. I hope you haven't gone and changed your mind again about my establishment."

Laughing, Samantha shook her head. "Poor Wilhelm. No! It doesn't mean any such thing. Your news merely came as a shock to me. And you shall undoubtedly get your residence back if Miranda does accept Compton—which I'm not so certain she shall." A tiny frown appeared and then vanished from her brow. "She is just so taken with Roddy, despite everything I may say to her. And I dare say very little to her at this point, for she already thinks me a veritable monster as is for attempting to loosen the attachment. What a coil! And to make matters worse, there is Lady Battiscue to be reckoned with!"

Wilhelm, who had been puzzling over his cousin's remarks, took her now by the hand and led her over to a chair in the hallway. "Must take it slow on the festivities, coz," he adjured. "Too many parties and all this dashing about on the Season addles the brain. You aren't prattling about old Lady Battiscue from Devonshire, the one with the dozens of mutts she lets run tame through her house?"

"I wish I weren't," Samantha answered. "But she's in London and planning mischief. She claims I stole Aunt Jane's money, and she wants half of it."

Wilhelm stepped back, looking dumbfounded. "Does she, by Jove. What a purse squeeze! If I don't begrudge the money to you, why should she? Don't give it to her!"

"If I don't, she has promised the most ghastly of lawsuits."

Wilhelm stroked his chin. "Court action, eh? That might scare off Compton."

"I know," Samantha said sadly. But at the same time, if the earl were frightened off by such a trifle, perhaps it would be better if Miranda did not wed him.

Wilhelm left. Samantha debated whether or not to tell Miranda about her impending offer from Compton, then decided to remain silent on the matter. Although she was grateful to Wilhelm for the news, he might have mistaken some of the earl's offhand remarks for a more serious declaration, and, Samantha reasoned further, the less Miranda knew of the offer to come, the less of a Cheltenham tragedy the rest of the household would have to endure.

Samantha had been forewarned of an offer of marriage for Miranda, but she was not expecting any for herself. Her shock, then, was considerable that afternoon when she realized that Mr. Philip Hancock, visiting in the blue drawing room, was actually making her a proposal! For a fleeting moment she wondered if he could be foxed. But his handsome countenance showed no symptom of drink.

"Are you offering *me* marriage, sir?" she inquired as Mr. Hancock sat looking expectantly at her.

His genial face creased into a shy smile.

"Well, yes. Pending my mama's approval of you, of course. But I don't think she will dislike you. And why do you look so surprised? We are good friends, after all."

"Yes, indeed. Good friends," Samantha murmured, still in a fog as her brain attempted to adjust to her sudden change of circumstance. Mr. Hancock was actually offering for *her*.

"After all," he went on, "just the other day in this very room you quizzed me about the virtues I'd require in a wife." He emitted a soft chuckle. "A fellow would have to be a slow top not to see the way the wind was blowing then!"

"Mr. Hancock!" Samantha cried out, aghast. "I assure you I had not the slightest intention of—"

He silenced her protests by kissing her hand lightly. "There is no sense in denying it, Samantha. What is the harm of casting out a lure or two? We gentlemen might otherwise be wholly in the dark in determining if a female returned our interest. And I hope you shall call me Philip. Are you wondering what my mama shall say to all this?"

"Good God, no!" Samantha blurted out without thinking then blushed. "I mean . . ."

He laughed indulgently. "You are very excited. Quite understandable. Let me assure you, Mama shall be pleased and surprised."

"Hardly as surprised as I am," Samantha murmured. Glancing down, she noticed her hand still clasped lightly in his and withdrew it at once, murmuring how gratified she was at his kind offer.

"But I really had no expectation of such a thing occurring! And I assure you, I was not casting out lures to you the other day." She pushed her hair distractedly back from her forehead. "In fact that day I was merely trying to determine what a civil, amiable gentleman such as yourself would look for in a wife, thinking that with a little application my sister Miranda could contrive to foster such virtues, not," she said hastily, "that I wished to cast out lures for Miranda's sake either."

Mr. Hancock, having followed this unnecessarily complicated answer to his civil offer of marriage, now drew himself up as best he could, since he was seated on a couch—and asked if Miss Curtis were in fact Refusing His Offer.

"Yes, I do believe it comes to that," Samantha said, finding relief finally in speech. "Not that I am not honored, for I truly am. Much more than I could ever put into words. I have never had an offer tendered to me before, so I daresay I don't know just how one refuses properly. And I do hope I haven't been uncivil to you, although judging by that expression on your face, you must be put out."

Mr. Hancock, while inclined privately to agree with this assessment of his emotions, was too well bred to give vent to them now. He merely inquired stonily if her feelings were engaged with some other.

Samantha looked at him blankly for a confused moment. "Some other?" she repeated. "Oh, you mean some other gentleman! No. It's just that I really don't think of marriage, Mr. Hancock. And I am sorry for being *so* shatterbrained, but I cannot marry you. I do hope that we can remain the best of friends."

As her speech held the unmistakable note of dismissal, there was little left for Mr. Hancock to do but rise, bow, and exit the room. Alone at last, Samantha held her head between her two hands as though to quiet the thoughts whirling about her brain like a huge Catherine wheel. An offer from Mr. Philip Hancock—the dashing young man who, despite the handicap of a mother who carped and complained about the females he would bring home, would undoubtedly have been snapped up by any other young lady of the *ton*. And she had allowed him to pass through her fingers like so much water.

"You shall not get a better offer," she chided herself later as she lay on her bed thinking the matter over.

"Are your feelings engaged with some other?" Again and again during the afternoon this question returned to haunt her. Reviewing it at greater length, she was startled to find a yes bursting from the depths of her heart. Her feelings were engaged—more's the pity!—for they were engaged with *Sheffield,* of all people!

Reluctantly her brain acknowledged the truth her heart had known earlier. She was in love with Sheffield. Foolish, foolish girl! Nothing could be more disastrous. She had no expectation of an offer from him ever, not when he was bound hand and foot to Miss Horick, who was so beautiful and rich!

Yet not even the smoldering remnants of the anger she felt at his betrayal of her confidences to Miss Horick could smother the love that dwelled further within. There was something about Sheffield, something more than mere elegance, fortune, and figure. It was the feeling of comfort that fell upon her like a cloak whenever he was with her, as though there were no troubles he could not overcome.

And yet, despite all that, he had never given her any reason to feel anything but friendship for him. She was in fact a wet goose to even think of him in such a stupid, besotted way. For what man would choose her when he could have Frieda Horick!

As the futility of the impossible situation dawned more fully, Samantha buried her head in her pillow and quite uncharacteristically burst into tears.

In his library at Berkeley Square, Lord Sheffield was rapidly reaching the conclusion that Samantha Curtis had won the prize as the most aggravating female of his acquaintance—a statement that covered considerable territory for ever since his comeout he had been dutifully acquainted with the scores of young females fired off each Season.

All these beauties, he recalled now as he chomped on a cigar, had taken enormous pains to cater to any whim he uttered, so much so that he often thought if he voiced the desire to run through Whitehall unclothed they would fancy it a tremendous idea.

Not surprisingly, after ten years of such feminine wiles he had become a cynic with regard to women, feeling that his marriage when it came about would be an inevitable choice between a schoolroom miss of milk and water disposition or a jaded Beauty. Since he had never had much stomach for missish ways, he had settled on Miss Horick—until fate had sent Samantha to London.

Not for a second had she stood in awe of him, not even the night of her arrival at Cavendish Square, looking, if memory served him correctly, like something the cat would forebear to drag in! And throughout her stay in London she had treated him in a distinctly offhand manner, even at times attempting to dismiss him from her company when any other female would have been ecstatic to have him address a word or two her way. If she had been any other female, he would have taken her behavior as a ploy to attract him, but he knew instinctively that such tactics would be repugnant to her.

Frowning, Sheffield stretched his top boots out to the fire and puzzled over Samantha's sudden pet. The more he brooded over it, the more peculiar it seemed. He had merely offered with customary civility to drive her to the City, but she had chosen to throw Frieda back in his teeth. Was it her way of hinting none too delicately of the impropriety of driving one lady about the town when he was all but betrothed to another?

He leaned back in his chair, suddenly recalling now that Roddy had mentioned in passing a visit Frieda had paid to Samantha in Hancock's box the night of the opera. Had another pulling of caps occurred between the two ladies? Knowing Frieda, it was quite possible. Hoping to get to the bottom of Miss Curtis's sudden distrust of him, he finished his cigar and ordered his phaeton out. Ten minutes later he approached Grosvenor Square, just in time to see the Beauty departing in Sir Cyril Chauncy's tilbury.

Unnoticed by either of them, Sheffield watched the carriage draw away. Giving in to his curiosity, he followed them from a distance.

Since it was the fashionable hour he had thought them bound for the Park, but this theory went by the board as the tilbury passed the Park entrance. After another ten minutes surreptitiously following the tilbury, Sheffield received an answer. Chauncy's carriage pulled up at Pulteney's Hotel, and Frieda descended while Chauncy remained behind. This behavior was odd enough to intrigue Sheffield. He pulled his carriage up against the tilbury, startling the baronet, who turned, bent on imperiously quelling the disturber.

"Good heavens," he quaked visibly. "It's Sheffield!"

"Ah, Cyril! Good afternoon to you," the viscount responded, smiling at the dandy, whose face was a perfect match to the rose-colored waistcoast he wore. "Fancy encountering you here."

"Yes, well . . ." Chauncy darted a nervous glance over one shoulder.

Sheffield followed the gaze toward the hotel entrance. "Are you staying at Pulteney's, Cyril?"

The dandy paled. "No, nothing of the sort."

"Well, I hope not," Sheffield agreed. "Such places can be dashed uncomfortable, even Pulteney's. I hope the lovely Frieda won't be too long," he said without missing a beat.

Chauncy eyed him as best he could, a difficult task since the phaeton was a good head higher than the tilbury's.

"Have you resorted to spying on us, Sheffield?" he demanded.

"What? Cloak-and-dagger stuff? Really, Cyril. I would never stoop to anything so banal. I merely happened to be driving out and saw the two of you together. I gave in to a moment's curiosity."

"Do you object to my escorting Frieda about?" Chauncy asked, thrusting his chin out.

"Bless me, no! See as much of her as your heart desires —within reason of course, for we can't have you camping at her doorstep the way poor Caro Lamb did with Byron." He glanced toward the hotel entrance again. "Not that I would consider Frieda your style in females. Are you sure there isn't an actress or two lingering about?"

Cyril paled. "Wh-what do you mean?" he stammered.

Sheffield stared, surprised that Chauncy, whose affairs in the petticoat line were known about the *ton,* should be flustered by such frankness in speech.

"I'm sorry if I've been too candid," he said now, "but I had heard from someone that that *chère amie* of yours— what the devil was her name, Campbell? Carter? No Cartier—had left town in a pique over you. And I just wondered if she would be returning."

"I don't know," Cyril said coldly. "And anyway, it's none of your concern."

"Of course not," the viscount said smoothly. "No reason to get yourself worked up over it."

"I am not worked up," the baronet denied.

"Well, I'm sorry to contradict you, Cyril, but you are. Your face very nearly matches that waistcoat of yours. Miss her much?"

"Who?" Chauncy demanded, rather confused by his questions.

"That actress of yours. Or was she a ballerina? Never can tell the difference between the two." He paused as he saw Frieda exiting the hotel, looking like a cat that had just swallowed a very plump canary. The smile faded off her lips when she caught sight of the viscount with the dandy.

"Good afternoon, Warren," she said warily.

"Good afternoon, Frieda. I was keeping poor Cyril

company out here. Did you have a nice visit to Pulteney's?"

"Really, Warren, how you love to jest," Miss Horick said with a hollow laugh. "I merely came by to call on an old crony of my father's. He is suffering all the pains of an attack of gout."

"Visiting the sick, Frieda?" Sheffield inquired, swallowing his incredulity with difficulty. The day Frieda Horick would waste on an errand of mercy was the day he would enlist in the nearest monastery. "How kind of you. I suppose this is an example of Cyril's influence on you. And in only a matter of days too. You are to be commended, Cyril!" he said. The dandy, rather flustered, began to stammer again.

But Sheffield had already driven off, leaving Miss Horick to confer with some haste with the baronet on just what had and had not been said to the viscount.

～ SIXTEEN ～

To celebrate their betrothal, which had been duly announced in both the *Gazette* and *Morning Post,* Lady Alice and Captain Maybury threw a small evening squeeze to which Samantha and her sisters had been duly invited. Although in the midst of her own love affair, Lady Alice had not been blind to the others in progress about her, and having glimpsed a partiality for Mr. Hancock in Samantha, she invited him to the party.

But this charitable impulse, she saw at once, was unwise. No sooner had Mr. Hancock laid eyes on Samantha, dressed in pomona green with tiny hearts embroidered at the hem of her gown, than he flushed scarlet and moved off, the proverbial rejected suitor.

Realizing the awkward position in which she had inadvertently placed both of her guests, Lady Alice took command of Mr. Hancock, leading him off toward a small amiable gathering of young ladies who would, she knew, be immediately smitten by his charm. Within the quarter hour she was congratulating herself on doing the thing, for Mr. Hancock, looking rather more cheerful, was dancing with a blushing but agreeable-looking young girl.

Samantha was thankful for Lady Alice's intervention. She liked Mr. Hancock, much too much to see him in the doldrums. She had already promised herself not to breathe a word about his offer and her refusal to anyone, not even her two sisters.

Now, with a clear conscience, she swept off on the arm of Lord Coodle, noting that Miranda for once was behaving circumspectly and had even accepted several invitations to dance. Samantha was of course pleased, but she could not help a slight paroxysm of guilt at the black scowl emanating from Mr. Roderick Monroe.

No such guilty pangs afflicted her when she declined Sheffield's repeated entreaties to dance. She had made up her mind before arriving at Mount Street that she would avoid him whenever possible this evening.

The viscount, however, was not about to take no for an answer. After dispatching Colonel Simms off to the card-room on a fool's errand, he swept Samantha up into the waltz the colonel had spoken for, remarking that his dancing had never before scared off any female.

"I am not scared off!" Samantha retorted in spite of herself.

"Then why not tell me why you are in the hips with me."

She eyed the puzzled expression on his face with some disfavor. "I am not in the hips."

He shook his head and swung her round. "Now, that won't do. And I'm bound to find out anyway. So do tell me, for I've been trying to discover what foul deed I've committed of late. Aside from giving my valet a scold now and then and not writing to my mama as frequently as I should, I consider myself innocent. Do enlighten me."

"What would be the use, my lord," she said, "since you are such an innocent."

His eyes met hers for a moment. "Roddy tells me you had another pulling of the caps with Frieda the night of the opera."

"I am not in the habit of pulling caps with every female I know," Samantha retorted, vexed by the easy way he had inserted the Beauty into their conversation. "And," she continued, "since Mr. Monroe was trying to fix his attentions on my sister that evening, I hardly think he qualifies as a reliable witness."

"You are probably right," Sheffield agreed. "And yet I can't help feeling that she may have put you out of countenance. I know how she can be in one of her moods."

At this further proof of the easy relationship between Miss Horick and the viscount, Samantha gave in to her devil.

"Miss Horick did not upset me in the least, my lord. In fact her conversation proved enlightening."

"Enlightening!" Sheffield gaped at her. His own conversations with the Beauty consisted of nothing but prattle. "Can you be hoaxing me, my girl? Or are you all about in your head?"

"I am not your girl," Samantha said hotly. "And I am not all about in my head. Miss Horick enlightened me on several points, my lord, including my pending legal difficulties. Odd, don't you think, that she should know of it on the night of the opera, especially since up to then there were only three people in London acquainted with the particulars of my problem, namely yourself, Mr. Phelps, and Pamela. So it was not too difficult to deduce just how she came by her information!"

The viscount glared down at her, looking black but saying nothing.

Vexed, she prompted him. "Do you deny informing her of my affairs?"

"If I did deny it, would you scruple to listen to what I said?" he inquired coldly. "It seems you have tried and convicted me at one fell swoop. I have no idea how Frieda learned of your circumstances, but I see plainly that to say so would be a waste of my breath and time."

They finished the dance in silence. He escorted her stiffly back to her chair, then disappeared into the cardroom. Watching him go, Samantha was prey to the most conflicting of emotions. On the one hand she told herself she had every right to lay the burden of guilt on him for his despicable actions. On the other hand, he had cut up so stiff at her words that she wondered if she might have erred. But she shook away such doubts. Of course she hadn't erred. Sheffield had betrayed her trust. How else would Miss Horick know of her affairs.

So absorbed was Samantha in her thoughts that she failed to notice Miranda had already stood up twice with Roddy and was showing imminent signs of encouraging him to ask for a third. Recalled to this apparent lapse by Lady Alice, Samantha crossed to her sister's side, adjuring her not to be foolish.

"I have danced with those other gentlemen, Samantha," Miranda said mulishly, "and just because Roddy wishes to dance with me again—"

"Roddy has already danced with you twice. A third occasion would definitely be *de trop*. You promised to act sensibly tonight, did you not?"

"Yes, I know." Miranda said, giving way and accepting the Earl of Compton's entreaty for the quadrille.

As Compton led Miranda out, Wilhelm bustled over to introduce Samantha to Miss Kitty Walker, the pretty brunette he had been courting since last week's Assembly. It appeared to Samantha and Lady Alice that Wilhelm was more than usually besotted by the young girl.

"It is all the romance and music in the air," Lady Alice said, waving a slender hand. "I vow, it is enough to cause the most hardened bachelor to step into Parson's Mousetrap. But you seem strangely immune to it all, Samantha. And," she said immediately, "you needn't prattle about being on the shelf!"

Samantha laughed and insisted that she had had no expectations of marriage when she had arrived in London and had none now. Or at least, she amended to herself, none that truly counted.

Before Lady Alice had time to tax her on such an opinion, their attention was drawn to the couples on the floor. An angry scene had erupted. Miranda, Samantha realized, had dashed away from Compton and was exiting the ballroom in tears.

"Now what is the matter?" she asked herself as she hurried to Miranda's side, shouldering past several dancing couples who out of an exaggerated sense of propriety continued to dance.

"It is all my fault, Miss Curtis!" the earl accosted her as she neared. "Devil take it, who would have thought any female would burst into tears when a fellow made her an offer of marriage. Know I should have spoken to you first, but the music and the champagne quite went to my head."

Samantha accepted this flustered apology and hurried after Lady Alice, who had already intercepted Miranda and was leading her up the stairs and into a spare bedchamber. Samantha followed on their heels.

"You may rest here, Miranda," Lady Alice said soothingly. "I vow, Compton must have a pea brain to make an offer on a dance floor!"

But the merest mention of matrimony coupled with the earl's name was enough to cause Miranda to collapse, weeping, on the bed. Lady Alice turned despairing eyes to Samantha.

"I'll handle this, Lady Alice," she said quietly.

"I'll be downstairs," Lady Alice said, stepping aside.

"Now, Miranda! You must not cry," Samantha commanded, sitting down on the bed and stroking her sister's hair. "Your face shall get blotched, and you shall drench these pretty pillows." She saved some of Lady Alice's prized needlepoint from this fate by wrenching them free of her sister's grasp. "Do listen to me, goose! This isn't the end of the world! The earl has done you a great honor by offering for you!"

Miranda turned over and opened her eyes. "You shan't

make me marry him, Samantha! You shan't! I'll die first.
I'll run off and become a parlormaid to some horrid family. I swear I shall," she said, nearly choking in an effort to
speak.

Samantha sat back. Was this her sister's impression of
her, after all the years of looking after her?

"Miranda," she said with ill-disguised asperity, "I have
no intention of forcing you to wed anyone against your
will. If Compton is displeasing to you, say so and that shall
put an end to things. There is no reason to raise such a
hubble bubble over what would have cast any other
woman in alt."

"I am not any other female," Miranda said darkly. "And
I love Roddy."

"So you have told me time and again," Samantha
pointed out, nearing the end of her patience. "If you do
love him, you shall have to wait the two years until he has
inherited his fortune and can support you."

"I don't mind waiting a hundred years," Miranda announced tragically and then sat up quickly. "Do you mean
you shall allow me to marry Roddy?"

Samantha grimaced. "I suppose I must! I had hoped
your feelings for him would die down, but it appears they
shall stand the test of even someone like Compton!"

"Yes, indeed they shall!" Miranda exclaimed, her vapors
forgotten.

"It shan't be easy for you and Roddy," Samantha
warned.

"I don't care!"

"Well, I do," Samantha said with a wry smile. "And
since Roddy is not yet fixed enough to support you, I mean
to set some sums by for your portion. That may keep you
together if you have any economical bent—"

She got no further. Tears forgotten, Miranda threw her
arms about her sister's neck, babbling that she was without
a doubt the best of all possible sisters—a rapid trans-
formation from her previous position as the beast of the
world.

"Now, no more," she implored, holding her sister off,
"or you shall be crying tears of joy. That is equally damag-

ing to your face. Now we shall go downstairs to enjoy what is left of this party."

Together they departed the bedchamber, and were met at the bottom of the stairs by the earl, still suffering from the ignominy of having his form of address put a female into fright. Samantha, feeling that she could take care of the matter better than Miranda, took him off into a small anteroom for a moment of private conversation.

"Is she recovered, Miss Curtis?" Compton inquired. "Deuce take it. I never saw a female cry so much, not even my mother, who is vaporish. As though her heart was broken. Miss Miranda's, I mean, not my mama."

"Yes," Samantha said, distractedly wondering how to begin. "Lord Compton, I hope you shan't take this as a personal affront, but Miranda is not disposed to accepting your kind offer of marriage."

"I thought as much," the earl said without a blink. "I suppose it's Monroe?"

"Yes, as a matter of fact it is. The two of them have had a *tendre* for each other. A rather enduring one, it seems."

"Thought as much," the earl repeated. "Monroe always glowered so whenever anyone looked at her. Still, I had cherished some hopes. She is such a pretty little thing, and I did think we should suit."

She smiled at him gratefully. "Lord Compton, you have been most understanding! And I shall always be thankful for it. And now, I think we should go back to the ball."

Compton dutifully rose to help her up. His hand was still on her elbow when the door to the antechamber was flung open, and Sheffield walked in. His dark eyes raked them both from head to toe.

"What's going on here, Compton?" he demanded.

"Nothing!" Samantha interjected. She turned to the earl. "Lord Compton, I believe my sister is recovered enough to speak to you now."

"As you wish, Miss Curtis," he replied and bowed and left the room.

Sheffield turned from the door, his arms crossed over his chest. "What were you doing here with him?"

"As I have already stated once before, nothing!" Samantha replied. "Not that my actions concern you, Sheffield. You've no right to interrogate me!"

"I seem to have been premature in blaming Miss Miranda's hoydenish behavior on herself. It seems to have run in the family. Have you fallen so low that you now conduct your flirtations in back rooms? Or perhaps," he said goadingly, "it has gone beyond mere flirtation."

Samantha flamed immediately. "We were *not* flirting. The earl has been most civil to me. That, I assure you, is more than I can say about you, whose manners always give offense! And you've no right to chide me on this matter. I don't even know why I bother to stay in this room with you!" She moved at once to pass him, but he caught her wrist and pulled her close.

"Let me go!" she cried out.

"Not yet," he muttered grimly, and lowered his mouth to hers.

For one maddening moment Samantha surrendered to the passion that had been building within her, then she struggled free. The amusement in his dark eyes incensed her. Without hesitation, she brought one hand up swiftly and slapped him as hard as she could across his cheek.

~ *SEVENTEEN* ~

For a moment Samantha stood frozen in place, the palm of her hand tingling from the shock of impact that had left a spot of color flooding the viscount's left cheekbone. His words, when they finally came, seemed to traverse a great and icy distance between them, though the reality that separated them was barely a foot.

"There is no need for violence, ma'am," he said acidly;

"since my attentions are so distressing to you, I shall leave!"

She watched him go without a word, feeling powerless to follow and struggling to catch her breath. Oh why had she ever hit him? But why had he kissed her? Before she could form an intelligible answer to these questions, Lady Alice appeared, a worried look on her pretty face.

"Here you are, Samantha," she said with obvious relief. "My dear, whatever happened? Sheffield has just departed looking as though he shall undoubtedly murder someone on his way back to Berkeley Square, and while it might be the sums of money they tell me he dropped in the card-room, he never cared a rush before whatever his losses. And the earl, Compton that is, thought it might have something to do with you in here——" She broke off, perceiving her guest was obviously agitated.

"It is nothing," Samantha said, forcing a smile to her lips. "Merely a row. Nothing to signify, I do assure you."

"Well, I should think it would signify a good deal," Lady Alice replied, looking at her closely. "For whatever the row might be, it has certainly distressed you and put Sheffield in a thunderous humor." She walked the younger woman over to the couch. "My dear, do you care at all to talk about it? I don't mean to be the prying sort, but I have grown uncommonly fond of you in the brief time you have been here in London. And I suppose I have always been fond of Warren, even though without a doubt he is the most vexatious man I know!"

Samantha choked, but whether on a laugh or a sob she could not really determine herself. "I don't see why he would be so odious as to flirt with me."

"Was he flirting with you?" Lady Alice asked, giving in to her curiosity. "How excessively odd of him. Not that a great many gentlemen would not want to flirt with you, because of course they would. But Sheffield has rarely indulged in such antics, even before his attachment to Frieda."

"He meant nothing by it," Samantha said in a small voice.

Lady Alice, however, was not so convinced. "With Warren one never can tell," she advised. But seeing that nothing more could be discerned from her guest, she gently guided her back to the ballroom.

Within minutes Samantha was once again mingling with the other guests in the great ballroom. But despite the laughter that rang out, the intoxicating music, and the compliments that came her way, she found no respite from the cold, rebuking voice she still heard in her head. *"If my attentions are distressing to you . . ."* But were they?

Even back at Cavendish Square she found no answer to her torment, and what little sleep she got that night was punctuated by much tossing and turning. She woke more fatigued than when she had retired. Dressing slowly in a French muslin frock, she went out of her bedchamber and was intercepted at once by Pammy and Miranda, who were embarking on an excursion to the Bartholomew Fair with Donald and Roddy. She was quickly invited to join the expedition, but she felt in no mood for such frivolity and declined, resigning herself instead to a breakfast alone.

As she nibbled on a muffin, she reviewed the previous night's events. True, she had been taken unawares by Sheffield's embrace, but was it necessary to have struck him so hard? No sooner had the question been posed than she answered it with an emphatic yes. For once in his life Sheffield had mistaken himself, and she had no regrets—especially as she thought of him sharing the incident with Miss Horick. Rethinking the matter now in the light of morning, she only wished she had dealt him a blow twice as hard!

Feeling much better now that her mind was settled on that point, she left the breakfast room for the sitting room and was soon engrossed in the complexities of half stitches. Her isolation was broken by Wilhelm, who came in a half hour later looking so pleased with himself that one would think he had pulled a coup on the Exchange.

"Bah, what is money?" Wilhelm asked cheerfully in answer to this query. "This is not the occasion to speak to me of finances, coz, not when something greater is afoot."

"Indeed? And what pray would that be."

"*Love,* of course!" Wilhelm answered, puffing out his chest. "Miss Walker in particular. Good gracious, cousin, you must have seen last night how she was favoring me with such sweet smiles that I was in alt. I've sent Horace upstairs to find my pale magenta waistcoat. Miss Walker informed me that that was the color best suited for my eyes."

Samantha's own eyes danced with mischief. "You must be roasting me, cousin."

"Why should I roast you about my waistcoat?" Wilhelm asked with a puzzled expression on his portly face.

"Not the waistcoat, but love!"

"Good Jupiter, I'm not funning about love! I cannot recall ever seeing a more ravishing female than Kitty. Cheeks like peaches. Eyes as big as plums, and," he paused delicately, "there is her ten thousand pounds for a dowry. Not that I am so concerned over that, for even if she hadn't a feather to fly with I'd marry her in a trice."

Samantha had been listening to Wilhelm with every show of interest, but at the mention of marriage her head snapped up.

"Marriage, Wilhelm?" she gasped. "Can this be the avowed bachelor of the family speaking of marriage?"

Wilhelm looked momentarily abashed until he saw that she was still roasting him. "Oh, very well, laugh as much as you wish. I own I have it coming, for I've said some harsh words about the marital state," he conceded. "But after all, a man is entitled to change his mind, Cousin Samantha."

"And here I thought such indecision the perogative of my sex," she retorted. "But if what you say is true, why are you not applying forthwith to Miss Walker's father?"

For the first time, Wilhelm looked downcast. "I can't. He's not even in town. Oh, there's an aunt, but she's a mighty skittish creature, and I think it wisest to apply to the father myself. Kitty says he dotes on her and loves trout fishing."

"A bond that should stand you in excellent stead," Samantha pointed out.

Wilhelm's head bobbed up and down in agreement. "The thing is, coz, with my mind set on marriage, I shall be needing the return of my establishment. Not that I mean to marry tomorrow, for I still have to apply to the father and then put an announcement in the papers, but still—"

"I quite understand, Wilhelm!" Samantha exclaimed. "After all, you cannot entertain your bride's family under Sheffield's roof. And I told you that I planned to stay here only long enough to get Miranda attached, and that shall soon be accomplished."

The puzzled look returned to Wilhelm's face. "Has Miranda changed her mind, then, and agreed to take Compton? Thought she turned him down flat—not that I blame her, for a more ragmannered proposal I never heard of. Declaring himself during a quadrille. Was it his fortune that turned the tide?"

"Miranda is not the least bit interested in the earl's income. She is, however, quite intrigued with Mr. Monroe, despite his lack of one, and so determined to have him that I have consented."

Wilhelm blinked. "Even if Sheffield objects?"

"Even then," she said stoutly. "I just hope he doesn't dislike it too much. But that is neither here nor there, since Roddy is of an age to marry if he wishes too."

"So Monroe shall win the fair Miranda," Wilhelm said. "I wish them happy. And I suppose Compton shan't repine for long. Always struck me as a flighty sort. Same as Hancock. I would have wagered anything that he was gearing up to pop you the question."

"He did," Samantha said without thinking and then immediately regretted this lapse of judgment.

"He did what?" Wilhelm asked, eyes widening.

"He made me an offer, only I turned him down. And since there is nothing so unflattering for a gentleman, I am resolved that it shall be our secret. So I charge you not to speak of it to anyone, Wilhelm, for I like him too much to make him the target of *on dits*."

"I shall be as silent as a grave," Wilhelm promised, and as Horace entered with the magenta waistcoat recommended by Miss Kitty Walker, she thought no more of the matter.

* * *

Contrary to Lady Alice's gloomy expectations, Sheffield did not murder anyone upon quitting her ball. He had gone off straight to White's, then adjourned to his bed, where he lay awake reliving the kiss he had shared so briefly with Samantha as well as the blow he had received immediately afterward. But the kiss had been well worth the facer.

He woke in a cantankerous mood, a fact attested to by his valet, who was ordered to leave him alone to dress in peace, and by his butler, whose offer of a nourishing breakfast was summarily dismissed out of hand.

As he took the last of a dextrous series of turns of his neckcloth, the viscount recalled the charge Samantha had laid at his door before the incident in the anteroom, namely the betrayal of her confidences to Miss Horick. As befitting a gentleman of honor, Sheffield never betrayed a trust, and her accusation rankled.

Thoughts of Miss Horick brought a grimmer set to his mouth as he peered into a looking glass, satisfied finally with his appearance. As a rule he had the masculine distaste for scenes, but there was no way around the inevitable. He would have to see Frieda—not only to discover how she came by her information concerning Lady Battiscue, but also to break off his involvement with her.

Samantha's kiss had sealed his fate. Despite what she thought of him, he was top over tail in love with her. Frowning, he slipped his glass through its riband. Perhaps if he helped her with the problem of Lady Battiscue that would return him to her good graces. Thinking along these lines made him feel much better, and he dispatched word belowstairs to have his Welsh-breds readied for a morning run.

Twenty minutes later he pulled up at Grosvenor Square and, pushing aside the protests of Thomas, Miss Horick's butler, bounded into her private drawing room unannounced. So stirring and unexpected a figure did he cut, swathed in his great driving cape, that the two people engaged in ardently embracing each other on the couch broke apart on the instant of his entrance.

"How now, Warren! Must you barge into my private rooms?" Miss Horick demanded, patting her hair back into place and conveniently forgetting the many occasions when she had run tame through Berkeley Square.

"I beg pardon, Frieda, Cyril," Sheffield said calmly, having understood at once that crying off would be easier than he had feared. "I told Thomas he needn't bother to announce me. The fellow did protest, and I see why now." His glance fell on the baronet, and he inquired politely if that were another new neckcloth.

The dandy, who had been struggling to restore the magnificent folds of cravat that Miss Horick's passion had inevitably creased, looked up in confusion. "Yes. No." Finally he lapsed into silence.

"Just what is it you want, Warren?" Miss Horick asked, picking up the threads of her inquisition. "I'm all amazement to see you abroad before ten-thirty."

"I do beg pardon, Frieda. I merely came to ask a favor, and then the two of you can get back to doing whatever it was you were doing before I intruded. The name of your father's crony at Pulteney's, if you please."

"My father's crony?" Miss Horick's countenance was twisted in incredulity. "Sheffield, you're foxed. And I am in no mood to tolerate it."

"It is just like you to forget your good deeds once they are behind you, Frieda. Perhaps Cyril will be able to refresh your memory." He flicked an eye at the baronet, who opened and then closed his mouth. "You do recall the afternoon when I encountered the two of you at Pulteney's Hotel? You were just coming from a visit to one of your late father's friends, who was suffering all the pangs of the gout."

Miss Horick shrugged. "I fail to see your interest in the matter."

"It's my mother," Sheffield said, looking unperturbed. "You know how her circle of friends and your father's overlaps. Since she is in Vienna, she shall comb my hair if she finds out some acquaintance of hers was ailing and I was too indolent to pay my respects to him."

"I'm afraid it's too late," Miss Horick said darkly.

"Dead, Frieda?"

"No, not dead," she snapped. "He merely left Pulteney's.

He was only planning to spend a day or two in London."

"What a pity," Sheffield murmured. "Just what was his name, Frieda? I should like to tell my mama when I write to her."

"Lord Caulding."

If Miss Horick had been more nimblewitted she might have made a better choice for Lord Caulding, as Sheffield now took pains to remind her, had broken his neck in a riding mishap some nine months ago, a fatality which precluded him suffering now from the gout.

"Well, someone like him," Miss Horick said desperately. "I have the most atrocious head for names."

"Yes, I know," Sheffield said affably. "I also know your head for mischief when it suits you. So I think we shall have to turn to Chauncy for edification. What do you know of Lady Battiscue, Cyril?" he asked in a stern voice.

Flustered by this wholly unexpected attack, the baronet gulped audibly and turned glazed eyes toward Miss Horick.

"Warren, you are all about in your head," Miss Horick said. "What needs must you come here to speak to us of gouty gentlemen and a totally unfamiliar female. I see no point to your questions, particularly this early in the day, and I find them vexing and ill mannered. And neither Cyril nor I shall answer any more."

"That saves you the bother of lying to me, doesn't it," Sheffield said as he looked from one face to the other. "I know something is underfoot, Frieda, and before the day is up I shall know everything, that I promise. By the by, Cyril, how is that actress friend of yours?"

"Oh, I say, Sheffield," Cyril burst out. "Just a joke. No harm in it, what?"

"Hold your tongue, Cyril!" Miss Horick commanded. "As for you, Warren, I have no intention of saying another syllable to you while you are in such a foul mood. You will oblige me by leaving."

"Certainly," Sheffield bowed. "But not before telling you that our understanding is at an end. I know it isn't *haut ton* to have the gentleman cry off, but ours was never much of an understanding, was it? You may put out whatever story you like as long as you don't blacken my reputation too badly." He strolled over to the door, stopping only to shoot one last glance at the baronet and the Beauty. "If Cyril does offer for you, Frieda, I'd advise you to accept. The two of you seem to deal so splendidly together."

Sir Cyril Chauncy could not have been called a gentleman of notable intellect, but he now perceived that fate had thrown a plum in his lap. As soon as the door closed, he dropped to his knees and implored for Miss Horick's hand in matrimony.

The beautiful Miss Horick, who had watched her best-laid plans for the viscount crumble to dust, toyed with Cyril for a knee-splitting five minutes and then duly accepted him. A quick betrothal would undoubtedly convince the *ton* that it was she who had thrown over Sheffield, instead of the reverse.

Driving away in his phaeton, Sheffield considered what little information he had gleaned. There was nothing substantial about the suspicions that had taken root in Grosvenor Square, but he was determined all the same to lay them in front of Samantha for her scrutiny.

His vehicle pulled into Cavendish Square just as Lady Battiscue descended from a chair. For an elderly woman, he noted, she moved with considerable grace, or at least she did until she observed his eyes on her; she then reverted to her previous decrepitude.

"Allow me, Lady Battiscue," he said, stepping forward like a knight of old to offer her an arm, which she clutched gratefully.

As they stepped across the threshold their progress was impeded by the furiously barking Brutus, a welcome that went unappreciated as far as Lady Battiscue was concerned. She clutched Sheffield's arm with a violence that would have smitten his tailor to the core and shrieked for someone to call off the dreaded hound before he devoured her for breakfast.

"Oh, I think Brutus has already had his breakfast," Sheffield said playfully. "He is just trying to be friendly.

Do open your eyes, Lady Battiscue, and you shall see for yourself."

His companion, however, was in no mood to acquiesce to his suggestion and with a fierce shudder let loose another shriek, which summoned Samantha from abovestairs. She stood for a moment, stunned at the sight of Sheffield, while Lady Battiscue uttered another unveiled oath concerning an animal allowed to run wild in the streets—a comment that caused the viscount to point out that while Miss Curtis's hallway at the moment was very congested, due to the presence of the three of them plus the still barking Brutus, it could not be mistaken for any thoroughfare of his knowledge.

Paying no heed to Sheffield's nonsense, Samantha ordered Horace to lead Brutus away, and then availed herself of the tiresome task of soothing Lady Battiscue's shattered nerves. She was assisted in this onerous chore by Sheffield, who proved to be a paragon, installing Lady Battiscue in the Windsor chair in the blue drawing room and fetching her some of Wilhelm's prize Malaga.

After ten minutes she was bound to admit that his effect on elderly females was nearly equal to that on schoolroom misses. Lady Battiscue had been coaxed into drinking the Malaga and had abandoned her vinaigrette to converse almost cordially with the viscount.

"Did you wish to see me about something, Lady Battiscue?" Samantha asked now, a bit nonplussed at being ignored by the other two in the room.

Lady Battiscue looked up in some surprise. "Well, yes," she admitted primly. "But it is of a personal, family nature."

"My dear Lady Battiscue," Sheffield said with a charming smile, "Miss Curtis and I are at first oars with each other. I assure you that you may speak freely in front of me."

"Perhaps, my lord," Samantha said arcticly, "since Lady Battiscue wishes to speak to me on a private matter, you should depart."

"I would, but I haven't finished my Malaga," he pointed

out. "That would be a shocking waste! Wilhelm would call me accountable for such an action. Lady Battiscue, I implore you to speak freely to Miss Curtis. I am one of her few confidantes."

"You were, my lord," Samantha replied, laying awful emphasis on the past tense as her green eyes flashed. "And I warn you, if you are not careful you shan't be anyone's confidante in the future."

"Are you threatening me with violence?" Sheffield asked sweetly. "Not to worry. You shan't hear a peep out of me."

Somewhat mollified by this statement, although not completely convinced, Samantha turned back to her elderly guest. "Now then, ma'am. Your purpose behind this call."

"Justice, Miss Curtis."

"Oh, not that again!"

"Yes, Miss Curtis, again. And as many times as is necessary to extract justice from you. I have come to reiterate my terms to you."

"What terms would that be?" Samantha asked coldly.

"How could you possibly forget," Sheffield chided. "How fortunate that I am here to refresh your memory. Lady Battiscue desires half the fortune left you by Lady Kendall, am I right, ma'am?"

"You have an excellent memory, my lord," Lady Battiscue said, beaming at him. He beamed back.

"However excellent his lordship's memory may be, it is of no interest to me," Samantha fumed. "I repeat, Lady Battiscue, that I have no intention of halving my fortune with you!"

Lady Battiscue put down her glass. "Then I shall see you in court!"

"As you wish," Samantha replied. "But I advise you against pursuing such a step." She paused a moment. "I am aware that you and Aunt Kendall were relations. I am not being unreasonable. I have a cheque for two hundred pounds. You are welcome to it. But that is all you shall receive." She held it out to the woman. But before Lady Battiscue could react, Sheffield had plucked it up.

"A mere two hundred pounds, Miss Curtis?" he chided,

shaking his head. "Quite unthinkable. Unacceptable, I call it—wouldn't you, Lady Battiscue?"

"Yes, indeed," Lady Battiscue said, rather confused but delighted to find the viscount an ally.

"What are you doing!" Samantha cried out as he crossed to the fire and dropped the cheque into the flame. "And just whose side are you on, Sheffield!"

"The side of justice," he intoned solemnly. "As I was saying only this morning to Sir Cyril Chauncy." He cocked his head at Lady Battiscue. "Are you acquainted with him, ma'am?"

"No, my lord."

"A great pity," Sheffield said, "for once you have met him I doubt you could rid yourself of the memory. Tall chap, very black hair."

"I have not met the dandy, my lord," Lady Battiscue sniffed.

Sheffield's eyes glinted. "I have not told you that he was a dandy, ma'am," he said softly. "Cyril might have been one of the stodgy set instead. So, you are acquainted with him?"

Lady Battiscue swallowed more of the Malaga. "I have heard the name mentioned before by others," she admitted grudgingly.

"Oh, I don't doubt that," Sheffield said with a pleasant laugh. "His name is bandied about in all circles of the *ton*. Have you perchance heard of his proclivities for females of the theatre? Ballerinas, opera dancers, not to mention mere actresses. You wished to say something, ma'am?"

Lady Battiscue had made a mild exclamation. "No, my lord." She sniffed loudly. "I fail to see what Sir Cyril has to do with Miss Curtis."

"Nothing at all," Sheffield agreed. "Merely that it is too amusing to watch Cyril and his bits of muslin. I see you blench. Do you frown on the free manner of speech of my generation? I think that Cyril's wife shall feel that an annoyance as well."

"Cyril's *wife!*" Lady Battiscue exclaimed. "He is not married, my lord."

"No," the viscount said affably. "But when I left him

this morning, not above an hour ago, he was in the process of offering and being accepted by one of Society's leading ladies."

Although Samantha was surprised by this news, her reaction was nothing as compared to Lady Battiscue's.

"That scoundrel!" she hissed, rising in fury from her chair. "Play me for a fool, would he? And while my back was turned . . ."

"Engaged himself to some other," Sheffield supplied helpfully as she gnashed her teeth. Then he said, in a hardening voice, "You have been found out, my dear."

She looked up in sudden alarm. "It wasn't my doing, my lord, but his. He pleaded with me, saying only one of my skill would be able to convince Miss Curtis. And when I think of what he was up to——"

"Yes, most disagreeable," Sheffield agreed. "Particularly, as the saying goes, because you have given him some of the best years of your life. But then, you have not known him a year, have you? Well, no matter, a month or weeks as the case may be. There is no accounting for the whims of a gentleman of fashion."

Lady Battiscue's eyes blazed. "I'll fashion him," she threatened in a voice that held no decrepitude. "Marriage, you said?"

Sheffield nodded. "Yes, definitely marriage."

This comment had the effect of causing Lady Battiscue to erupt into voluble French and then flounce out of the room, muttering dark gallic imprecations on the head of Sir Cyril Chauncy.

~ EIGHTEEN ~

"Did you understand any of that?" Sheffield demanded as the whirlwind that was Lady Battiscue disappeared out of the room.

Still staggered by the scene that had erupted in front of her, Samantha shook her head. "Not a word, my lord."

"Thank God," he murmured. He rose and walked over to the tray of Malaga, bringing back two glasses. "I think Wilhelm will forgive us for depleting his supply. You look as though you could use it, and I know I can."

Samantha took a generous swallow of Wilhelm's prize Malaga and found it very good indeed. "What was she saying?" Samantha asked.

"That," Sheffield said with a gleam in his eye, "is something a gentleman like myself would not dare repeat to a gently bred female of your tender sensibilities."

"What fustian! You must at least tell me who she is! I know she can't be Lady Battiscue!"

"Unfortunately," Sheffield demurred again, "that too is something a gentleman should not divulge to a gently reared female."

Samantha put down her glass, rather out of patience with this image of herself as a ticklish female prone to swooning at the first touch of reality.

"One would think me a veritable schoolroom miss, by your description!" Exasperation laced her words. "May I remind you I am on the shelf, practically an ape leader! So do give over prosing like one of those undeniably milky heroes in those library romances Miranda borrows from Hookam's, and tell me all."

Sheffield chuckled. "Very well, if you must know! That

female is one Mademoiselle Cartier, an actress of some local repute and one of Cyril's demireps."

"Is that why you quizzed her so strenuously about the dandy? Did you know she was an imposter?"

"I had no actual knowledge, only an intuition based on something Chauncy let drop this morning when I spoke with him. Actually, it was Brutus who clinched the matter for me. Mademoiselle Cartier's dislike of dogs is notorious."

"Is it?" Samantha asked with a pang. "I shouldn't have known that, of course. But I should have remembered how the real Lady Battiscue dotes on dogs. I should have seen through the ruse at once."

"Perhaps not," he said charitably. "You have not seen your relation in years, and Mademoiselle Cartier is a very good actress."

Samantha sat back, still pondering the discovery. "But why should she do such a thing?"

Sheffield rolled the Malaga on the tip of his tongue. "To please Cyril, of course," he said finally.

"But that is even more absurd! Why should Sir Cyril wish me any harm?" Samantha asked, completely baffled. "He scarcely knows me, and I don't think him so hard pressed for five thousand pounds as to resort to such a scheme."

"No," Sheffield acknowledged with a smile. "I rather think his interest was in pleasing Frieda. What a mull people do make of things when they attempt to please others, don't you think?"

"Please Frieda!" Samantha exclaimed. "I should have known! She has disliked me ever since the day we met and no doubt would think it great sport to hoax a country provincial."

"Yes, it was an odious plan all around," Sheffield agreed. "Made even more odious because poor Mademoiselle Cartier shall be out in the cold at Cyril's winning over Frieda."

"Winning over Frieda!" Samantha was incredulous. "But how can that be? She and you——"

"My understanding with Miss Horick ended at approximately ten-thirty this morning," Sheffield said, putting the

Malaga aside to dip two fingers into the mixture in his snuffbox.

"At an end," Samantha said in a startled voice. "I am sorry to hear that."

The viscount lifted a brow. "That is coming it too strong, Miss Curtis. You are not sorry in the least."

In their brief but turbulent acquaintanceship Samantha had been on the receiving end of several of his lordship's bluntest rejoinders, but this latest remark struck her as the rudest of all. But her anger was tempered with alarm. Had he perchance deduced her true feelings for him last night in the anteroom?

"I assure you, Lord Sheffield, I am sorry," she said, speaking calmly and trying to avoid the mocking glint in his eye. "To break off any understanding must needs be disagreeable to all parties, and while perhaps I did not think you and Miss Horick suited in every way, it is unjust to imagine I am in alt at the ending of your attachment. I do hope it wasn't on my account."

The quizzical eyes turned again her way, withering the words on her tongue. She turned pink.

"On *your* account, Miss Curtis?" he queried lightly.

Samantha made a valiant effort to restore a little dignity to the moment. "What I mean, my lord, is that I am well aware of Miss Horick's feelings for me. And I know how you were sometimes obliged to help us during our time here in London, on account of your friendship with Wilhelm. I am quite aware that Miss Horick frowned on this. I am also aware that perhaps I may have said provoking things to her unwittingly—"

"Unwittingly!"

"Well, perhaps not unwittingly!" she acknowledged, wishing that he would not gaze at her in such an imperturbable fashion. "But anything I did say, she deserved! I still would dislike it to have been the cause of your breach."

"My dear child," Sheffield said, amused, "this display of guilt is charmingly made but utterly misplaced. The breach between myself and Miss Horick was inevitable, given certain differences in temperament. You were not the cause, believe me!"

His words had been uttered merely as a reassurance, but Samantha took it as further proof—as though she needed it!—that he did not give her a moment's thought.

"I fully realize how odious Frieda and Cyril's scheme was," Sheffield went on. "And while they deserve to be throttled, I'd suggest you let the matter lie."

"Let it lie!" Samantha cried out. "Are you protecting her perchance, my lord?"

"Don't be a goose," he said dampeningly. "There is nothing chivalrous about my suggestion. However much you relish a good mill, the *ton* doesn't. And I think you can rely on Mademoiselle Cartier, however unlikely a champion of your cause, to extract justice for you!"

"Why should she?" Samantha asked, completely confused.

"The woman scorned," Sheffield said blithely. "Mr. Shakespeare's phrase applies to ladies of all quality. I shouldn't be the least bit surprised if Mademoiselle Cartier deals Chauncy a facer every bit as good as the one you dealt me last night." Her sudden blush made him smile. "On second thought, she probably would deal him a better one. French ladies are notoriously prone to violence."

"Do you speak from personal experience, my lord?" Samantha asked in a voice of ominous sweetness.

The viscount winced. "No, by Jove, I don't. And that's quite enough about French ladies. Why in heaven didn't you tell me the truth about Compton last night? Wilhelm told me he had offered for Miranda, and why any female should be so skittish as to pretend she were doing something illicit in the room with him is beyond my comprehension!"

"I made no such pretense!" Samantha denied, infuriated at such an idea. "It was you, my lord, who made a cake of yourself, accusing me of acting in a very coming way with the earl—which is only too stupid, for you must have seen yourself how Compton was overset by Miranda's refusal. So that I felt it incumbent on me to soothe his ruffled feathers."

"Very incumbent," Sheffield agreed, unable to keep his eyes off her figure storming about the room. "You forget, however, that I was in the cardroom for most of the evening, having been dispatched there by the accusation of a certain female that I had betrayed her trust. And this did not set well in my dish." As she paused, somewhat mollified by his remark, he went on in a gentler tone. "You should have told me what had happened, instead of trying to shield the earl."

"I was not trying to shield him!" Samantha exclaimed. "And you, I might add, were in no mood to listen to any explanation, bursting in upon us like a gudgeon."

The viscount had been called many things in his life but never to his knowledge or face a gudgeon, and he was rendered a trifle unsteady by this epithet.

"A what?" he asked shakily.

"A *gudgeon*!" Samantha repeated with awful emphasis, the look in her eye practically daring him to take issue with her.

"I see, a gudgeon. How kind of you to point out this character defect in me, for I vow I would otherwise be totally ignorant of it. As it is, I shall take immediate steps to eradicate it."

"Oh, fustian!" Samantha laughed.

His laughter joined hers. "I know I lost my head," he said ruefully. "I hope you shall forgive me for bursting in and for what later transpired in the room."

By which, she supposed, he meant the kiss. "Of course I forgive you," she said, trying to sound lighthearted even though her heart quickened at the memory of the touch of his lips on hers. "After all, it was the merest trifle. Stealing a kiss. Something you have long experience with!"

"What a strange conversation this is. French ladies and now my long experience with kissing. Anyone overhearing would think you considered me a libertine."

"By no means!" Samantha answered. "You assured me yourself when I first arrived in London that you were no rake. And I took you at your word. But I have cut my wisdoms, and a gentleman like yourself over the years must have had numerous barques of frailty under your wing."

"Miss Curtis!" The viscount said in a voice of mock outrage. "I beg you to allow me some remnant of shattered dignity. I have never spoken of my barques of frailty to any gently nurtured female."

"If you call me that one more time today, I think I shall go into strong convulsions," Samantha promised.

"That would be enlivening," Sheffield answered. "But I for one have borne with enough theatrics for one day. Let's have no more of my barques of frailty. As though I were deep in the petticoat line, which I am not."

"Of course you aren't," she agreed. "Your travels take you away a good deal of the time, did they not?"

Shoulders shaking, Sheffield lifted a hand. But he could not dismiss the notion that perhaps to Samantha their exchange in the anteroom had amounted to little more than a trifle. He would have sworn that she had responded to him during the kiss. But had that been reality or mere wishful thinking?

For the first time since his comeout, the viscount who had regarded himself as a matrimonial prize of the first water was at point non plus and feared to put his fate so soon to the touch.

"There is something I should tell you," Samantha said, breaking the silence that had fallen. "I have consented to the match between Miranda and Roddy."

Sheffield stared at her. "Forgive me, Miss Curtis, but I thought you did not wish my cousin to marry Miss Miranda. How comes this sudden reversal? You do not strike me as a lady who changes her mind with every wind."

"You wouldn't speak that way if you had seen Miranda crying her eyes out last evening at Lady Alice's," Samantha informed him.

"I shall take your word for it," he said, looking unmoved by this account. "And while I know it must be tedious to attend to a watering pot, I don't see the need of your capitulation!"

"I had no choice but to capitulate," Samantha said. "I know it's idiotish and unreasonable, but they are young and have fallen in love with each other."

"Just because they make a Cheltenham tragedy of their love is no reason for you to give in," Sheffield pointed out.

"Take Miss Miranda back to York. No, I daresay she would merely hatch up a plan to make for Gretna. Well then, let me see. Banish her to a nunnery unless she agrees to behave. No," he shook his head at this plan, "she shan't like that, and probably neither would the good sisters. I see your point. It's much better to allow her to marry and starve to death with Roddy."

Samantha shook her head. "It won't come to starvation. I have a plan."

"Oh, a *plan!*" Sheffield exclaimed. Samantha dealt him a severe look and asked coldly if he wished to be enlightened.

"I am all ears! Do you mean to take them under your wing? An idea of note, but I beg you to reconsider, for even a saint would find it intolerable within a day. Such cooing and clucking that you would be surrounded with!"

"I realize that," Samantha said with a laugh. "My solution is simpler. I shall divide whatever remains of my Aunt Kendall's inheritance between myself and my two sisters."

"What!"

"It is a surprise for them," she went on, ignoring his attempt to interrupt, "so I bid you not to say a word. The money could just as easily have gone to them as to me, and it does seem injust that I should benefit, the most especially when they are in need. Pamela will then be able to assist Donald in buying those Arabians he is coveting at Tattersall's, and that might turn his estate around. As for Miranda, she will be able to live on her portion until Roddy receives his inheritance, if they exercise prudence."

"Your sisters may be prudent, but I know you are not. Did you call this concoction a plan?" he railed. "A better word for it would be folly. Do you never spare a single thought on yourself and your future, Miss Curtis? And don't nauseate me with tales of your advanced dotage. You should have better use of your funds than to bestow it on my dimwitted connection!"

"I am not bestowing it on Roddy," she contradicted. "I am giving it to Miranda, and there is nothing you can do to prevent me."

He looked grim for a moment. "Perhaps not. But has it

occurred to you that you do entirely too much thinking about those precious sisters of yours and might spare some thought on yourself?"

She laughed. "Heavens, what a drudge you think me. I am no such thing. And as for my sisters, I have always been accustomed to taking care of them and see no reason to stop now."

"We shall see about that," he announced. And on that cryptic note, he bowed himself out of the drawing room.

～ NINETEEN ～

With Mademoiselle Cartier-Battiscue successfully foiled, Samantha returned to her enjoyment of the London Season. For the first time since her mother's death, no vexing problems awaited her attention in the morning, and she found it a joy to sit back in bed drinking morning chocolate from a tray and contemplating the day's tasks in front of her. Usually these proved no more strenuous than accompanying Lady Alice on rounds of dressmakers in preparations for her wedding or indulging in brief outings with several of her own callers, including, strangely enough, Sheffield.

In this agreeable climate Samantha bloomed, growing even more radiant than ever. Sheffield drove her about the Park almost daily, and this had caused a considerable flurry in the breasts of several matrons, including Lady Alice, who said to her captain that perhaps Warren wasn't such a nodcock as they had supposed.

On a bright Monday afternoon Samantha sat in the high-perched phaeton enjoying her drive with the viscount and pausing now and then to chat with friends, a circumstance that occurred rather too frequently to suit Sheffield.

"Have you heard anything more on Lady Battiscue?" Sheffield asked, taking a narrow turn in the path, thus preventing Lord Coodle from riding next to Samantha's side of the carriage.

As Coodle dropped off, Samantha nodded. "Mr. Phelps has learned that the real Lady Battiscue has been enjoying the waters at Worthing with numerous assorted pugs."

"That removes the last vestige of doubt from the bogus affair, does it not?" Sheffield asked as he turned the carriage toward the path leading to the Serpentine. "Do you know, after hearing so much about her I am curious to meet her, dogs and all!"

"No doubt to compare her with your Aunt Gertrude?" Samantha asked solicitously.

He grinned. "Well, no. Actually it would be to compare her with my Aunt Mary. She was Aunt Gertrude's twin sister, and she dotes on dogs too."

"You are trying to hoax me, my lord!" Samantha said, laughing. "I doubt you even have an Aunt Gertrude!"

Sheffield looked aggrieved. "Now, I can't have that. Nor could Aunt Gertrude if she knew about it, for she likes to be noticed. The next time she is in London with Aunt Mary, they usually travel together," he confided, "I shall inflict them on you for afternoon tea!"

"Oh heavens, there is no need for that!" Samantha said with some alarm. The idea of two elderly griffins descending on her put her in a quake. "They shall think me one of those hurly-burly modern women!"

"It doesn't matter what they think," Sheffield said, darting a quick look at her. "I think you a delight."

The sincerity in his voice struck home at once, and Samantha colored up instantly. What did he mean by such flummery? And why was he being so gallant of late? He had not only accompanied her to the Park but had invited her to Drury Lane with him on the coming Saturday. She did not know what to make of it, unless he were trying to fix his attention on her.

"Just because you are skipbrained enough to imagine yourself in love with someone is no reason he must be," a voice chided her, and she was almost relieved to see Mrs.

Drummond Burrel approach in her barouche. The Patroness acknowledged Sheffield's "good afternoon" with a nod and a grim set to her mouth.

"That is one Patroness you are not at first oars with," Samantha murmured after she had passed.

Sheffield grimaced. "To be at first oars with Mrs. Burrel would boggle my mind. And if I were, my consequence would be so puffed up there would be no bearing me."

She laughed, then noticed that his smile had faded. Puzzled, her gaze followed his to an approaching tilbury. There could be no mistaking Sir Cyril's vehicle and the Beauty on the seat beside him. As it neared, Samantha noted with unholy glee that the baronet was sporting a large bruise over one eye, courtesy no doubt of Mademoiselle Cartier's gallic fury. Amused, and reasoning that this was no doubt what had kept the baronet from the Park during the fashionable hour for several previous days, she darted a quick look at Sheffield, expecting to see some amusement on his face. She was surprised to find his countenance dark and unreadable.

To Samantha, as he glowered at Chauncy he looked the very image of a man nursing a sorely bruised heart. Blinking hard, she gazed off to the side.

The viscount, of course, was nursing no such emotion. He did, however, find the sight of Frieda and Cyril reprehensible. After all, they had sought to perpetrate an odious hoax on the woman he loved, and he was not inclined to stop and speak with them with anything approaching civility. He contented himself now with a look that spoke volumes as he led his team briskly past them on the path.

Samantha had settled on a more agreeable target by now. Mr. Philip Hancock, handling a high-spirited pair of perfectly matched bays, was taking the turn toward them with a pretty young lady on the seat next to him. She no doubt was the latest candidate to undergo inspection by his mama.

Samantha had assumed that any awkwardness between herself and Mr. Hancock was behind them, but as the two carriages met, she discovered that this was not so. Mr. Hancock acknowledged her civil greeting with one of his own, but he could not keep himself from flushing deeply when his eyes locked momentarily with hers. As though, she reasoned later, he was still feeling the sting of her refusal. And she could not help feeling guilty for that.

No further intrusion on their drive around the Serpentine occurred, although Sheffield thought his companion rather more quiet than usual. He put her down safely at Cavendish Square and drove off. But he could not help dwelling on the meaningful exchange of looks between his passenger and young Hancock.

How must he look to someone of Samantha's discrimination, he wondered. He was also forced to concede the odious possibility that Samantha might actually prefer the suit of another—say, young Hancock—to *his*!

He had thought it best to woo her slowly, but now a change in that strategy seemed dictated. But even if he did pop the question tomorrow, there was no telling what her response would be. Sheffield frowned even more darkly. And just what the devil was Hancock to her?

He wrestled with this question during the rest of his journey home and even after he had reached his Berkeley Square establishment. He resolved to ask Wilhelm what, if anything, he knew of an attachment between Mr. Hancock and his cousin Samantha.

Unfortunately for Sheffield, Wilhelm did not return to Berkeley Square that afternoon or evening. He was instead enjoying the play at the green baize tables of Watiers. It was not until well into the morning of the next day that Sheffield had his first chance to speak with his guest. The viscount found him overseeing the removal of his clothing and other personal possessions.

"By heaven, Wilhelm," he ejaculated, "never tell me the play at Watiers has grown so dear that you are reduced to selling your possessions!"

Wilhelm's stomach heaved with genial laughter. "Good God, no, Sheffield. As a matter of fact," he confided naively, "I had a streak of good fortune last evening."

"Then what prompts your removal?" Sheffield asked with a frown. "I do hope you don't mean to make good your threat and evict your lovely cousins."

Wilhelm chuckled. "Bless me, no. As though anyone could throw them out. Or perhaps they might if Samantha weren't there. No, Warren, I'm bound for Hereford."

"Another fishing trip?" Sheffield guessed.

Wilhelm smiled. "Different type of fish. Phineas Walker."

Sheffield stepped back and, perceiving the flush in Wilhelm's cheeks, deduced within the instant that he was in the throes of the grippe.

"It comes on very sudden," he said soothingly. "Perhaps if you retire to bed I shall have Alphonse send up a nourishing broth."

"What do I want with broths, Sheffield?" Wilhelm demanded. "I ain't sick, nor bosky neither. I'm offering for Walker's daughter, Kitty. I meant to wait until he got to London, but now the aunt tells me—and a more shatterbrained creature I have yet to meet!—that he has gone to Hereford straight away. And I'm dashed if I'll wait here a minute longer. Going after him."

Sheffield chuckled as he became aware that it was Cupid and not the grippe that was afflicting Wilhelm.

"Bit of a change from your bachelor bliss," he said to his friend.

"Yes," Wilhelm admitted, "but she's such a taking little thing."

"So I have observed. And she shall make you an excellent wife. I wish you happy."

"Thank you, Warren," Wilhelm said, much overcome, and shook the viscount's hand with some emotion. "I'm obliged to you. That goes without saying. Don't know what I should have done, what with Samantha taking over my establishment."

"Do you mean to depart straight away?" Sheffield asked, going down the stairs now with him.

"I must. Not a moment to waste. I'll stop at Cavendish Square first and tell Samantha where I shall be."

The mention of Samantha brought to mind the question Sheffield had been planning to ask. "Wilhelm," he said now, with a slight frown contracting his heavy brows. "Pray don't think me a gossip monger, but is there anything between your cousin and Philip Hancock?"

An oath broke out unbidden from Wilhelm's lips.

"Oh, lud! Don't tell me you've discovered it!" he wailed. "Samantha shall be livid."

Sheffield tightened his hold on the banister and turned quickly toward the other man.

"So there is something."

Wilhelm nodded and sighed. "But she ordered me to keep it a secret! And I don't doubt she'd cut off my tongue if I so much as breathed a word about it to anyone."

"What do you mean, *it?*" Sheffield asked sharply.

Wilhelm looked up vaguely distracted. "Hancock's offer to her, of course."

For a maddening moment a pulse raced somewhere in Sheffield's brain. "He offered for her?"

Wilhelm nodded once again. "Oh yes, nice and proper I think it was. And I don't see the point myself on keeping mum on the matter, for I'd call it a feather in my cap to have attached young Hancock. But there is no reckoning with females, is there?"

"No, indeed," Sheffield said, as pale as a ghost.

Wilhelm turned a worried face toward the viscount. "The thing is, Warren, Samantha did say I wasn't to tell a soul, so I'd be obliged if you didn't speak of the matter to her or anyone else."

"You may rest assured that Miss Curtis's secret is safe with me," Sheffield replied coldly, his outward manner giving no hint to the torrent of emotions flooding through him. Hancock and Samantha in a secret engagement? No wonder she had fallen into such a devilishly quiet mood after seeing him in the Park. But why the secrecy? That wasn't the mode at all. And he, for one, would never countenance such a thing.

"But then, I don't have a mother like Philip," he reminded himself, his memory delving up without difficulty the faces of other females Philip had sought to attach only to have his mama disapprove.

Unaware of the quandary into which he had plunged his friend, Wilhelm hurried over to Cavendish Square to alert Samantha to his pending visit to Hereford.

"But are you sure Mr. Walker shall be there, cousin?" Samantha asked. "You may be off on a wild-goose chase."

"All I can do is hope, coz. Used to think there wasn't much to this whole marriage business, but it's devilishly complicated."

"Especially when family is involved," Samantha agreed sympathetically. "But I consider it an arduous journey to ask of you. All the way to Hereford."

"Oh, I don't mind," Wilhelm said promptly. "It shall do me a world of good, for I have been fagged to death here in London. And if the marriage does come off in spite of everything, that's all we can ask, eh?"

"She is a lucky chit," Samantha replied. "I only hope she realizes what an excellent husband she is getting."

Wilhelm beamed. "Perhaps between the two of us we shall convince her of that, coz. And now I must away. I shall write to you as soon as a decision is reached."

"I shall be anxiously awaiting the outcome," Samantha told him.

Wilhelm's arrival had caused Samantha to delay some morning errands of her own, and as soon as he had gone she prepared to set out on them. She went out into the hallway and was startled to find Pamela standing stock still near the stairs, a peculiar expression on her face.

"Pammy?" she asked quietly. "Are you feeling at all the thing?"

Pamela looked to have been summoned from the depths of a dream. She raised her blue eyes to her sister's face and informed her that she had a headache. Since this symptom had been offered whenever Pamela had quarreled with Donald, Samantha knew better than to press her. She contented herself now with a sympathetic pat on the shoulder and took herself out the door, headed for the City.

Pamela, however, remained rooted where she had been by the stairs, the victim of neither a quarrel with her beloved husband nor a migraine. She had come down the stairs during Wilhelm's *tête à tête* with Samantha and had overheard some but not all of their remarks concerning his visit to Herefordshire. At first she had dismissed the words as of no possible interest, but when the remarks appeared to center on marriage to one of their family and a necessity that meant dispatching Wilhelm to Hereford, Pamela's disinterest melted into consternation.

And the fatal words uttered by Wilhelm: "Between the two of us we shall convince her of that!" acted like a blinding light to Pamela. There was only one person the family knew in Hereford. And there was only one reason Pamela could deduce that Samantha would send Wilhelm there on a family mission, a mission that had to do with marriage in particular.

Samantha, she saw clearly, had no intention of allowing Miranda to marry her beloved Roddy, and was in fact still scheming to marry her off to the Earl of Compton, who, Pamela knew very well, boasted estates in Hereford!

Astounded at her sister's duplicity, she decided to take action herself and went off to find Miranda to alert her to the problem they were facing.

~ TWENTY ~

Unaware that she was the target of many baleful comments through the afternoon behind Miranda's closed doors, Samantha went in to dinner that evening in a mood of happy anticipation. This was checked almost at once when she saw that Pamela's blue mood seemed to have affected Miranda. The youngest Curtis sat looking increasingly wan and out of curl, picking at the food on her plate with an idle fork and inclined to burst into tears whenever Samantha addressed a civil word her way.

By Thursday she began to wonder if the whole *ton* had been afflicted by this same lachrymose ailment. Not even Sheffield seemed immune during his daily calls on her in the phaeton. Ordinarily a fine conversationalist, his lordship of late barely stirred himself to utter a half dozen commonplaces to her during a drive, no doubt a sign of his rapid boredom with her.

Sheffield was not so much bored as obsessed, so much so that he decided to quit London in the near future. He came to this decision one evening. London, thanks to Samantha, was quite spoiled for him now. He would go off on another trip! At once! The location was of no importance as long as it was far from London. And he decided on the West Indies, a part of the world he had neglected so far in his travels.

Alerting his staff to his impending trip, he penned a quick note of apology to Samantha Friday morning, telling her that he would not be able to keep their engagement at Drury Lane on Saturday since urgent business drew him out of town. Grimacing at this baldfaced lie, he signed the note, blotted it, and dispatched a footman to bear her the message, knowing quite well he had taken the coward's way out. But he did not trust himself to take any farewells from her in person. And what was the use in complicating matters for her. She was happy with Hancock. So be it.

Now that the decision had been made, he decided to keep his own farewells to as few as were practical. He drove his phaeton to Lady Alice's, finding her with Captain Maybury.

"A trip, Warren?" Lady Alice exclaimed as Sheffield explained the journey he was undertaking. "I would have thought by now you would have exhausted your tolerance for exotic lands. And the Indies, of all absurdities. It is so frightfully hot there. You shall wilt within a day of landing."

"What a poor creature you do think me, Alice," Sheffield said, a glint of amusement visible in his eyes. "I am not such a weak kitten! And I assure you, I shan't wilt."

Realizing the futility of further speech, Lady Alice said no more. But her captain, hoping still to deduce Sheffield's real motives behind the sudden trip, managed to wrangle a ride back to Green Street with him.

"Where is your carriage, Edward?" Sheffield asked when they were underway. "Not in disrepair?"

"For Roddy's sake, I hope not."

Sheffield turned a puzzled face toward his friend. "What has Roddy to do with your carriage?"

"Taking care when he rounds a curve, I should hope," the captain said. "He borrowed it for a day's outing with Miss Miranda. They are bound for Hampton Court."

"Odd. Why didn't he borrow one of mine?"

Maybury shrugged. "I don't know. And another thing I don't know is how you expect me to swallow this twaddle about your trip."

"It's not twaddle," Sheffield said, hunching a shoulder. "I'm bored. Good Jupiter, Edward, you know yourself how wearying the *ton* can get. And you know my great love of travel."

The captain grunted. "Thought you had given all that over. You talked about settling down. That's why you had your eye on Frieda Horick, wasn't it?"

"One can't always have what one wishes for most in life, Edward," Sheffield said quietly. And before the captain could delve further into the mystery, he was being put down in front of his Green Street residence.

With that task completed, Sheffield swung his carriage over to Albemarle Street, hoping to catch Roddy before his visit to Hampton Court. But his cousin had already departed.

"Do you have any notion when he shall be back?" Sheffield asked the butler.

"As to the exact hour, I couldn't say, my lord," the servant replied. "But it shouldn't surprise me if it were much later than this evening, perhaps even tomorrow."

These words brought a frown to the viscount's brow. "What makes you say that?"

"Well, my lord, Mr. Monroe did command his valet to pack a satchel of night things for him."

The frown froze on Sheffield's face. "Why the devil would he need a satchel of overnight things for an outing to Hampton Court?"

Rather flustered at being the target of the viscount's glowering look, the butler hastened to assure him he didn't know.

"Just where is your employer off to?" Sheffield asked.

"I'm sure I don't know, my lord," the butler repeated. "I only know that he instructed Withers to pack a bag, and he had the captain's carriage with him—which now that I think of the matter, did strike me as rather odd."

The rest of the butler's ruminations concerning Roddy failed to move his lordship, for the viscount had already returned to his phaeton. As a rule Sheffield's imagination did not run to the lurid, but he did not need to think twice what to make of Roddy, a satchel of overnight things, a carriage, and, quite probably, Miss Miranda Curtis.

Muttering an oath at the folly of any chuckleheaded Romeo, and hoping that he might be wrong, he headed in breakneck fashion for Cavendish Square, overriding Horace's wish to announce him by striding into the breakfast room with his driving cape flung over one shoulder and his high-crowned beaver askew.

"Where is Miss Miranda?" he demanded of Samantha, who had been seated alone in the room drinking coffee and rereading the curt missive he had dispatched to her earlier in the day. She was more than a little startled by his entrance, but not impervious to the heroic figure he cut in the room—if, of course, she overlooked the hat being askew.

"Your sister, where is she?" demanded the heroic figure.

"If you mean Miranda, I believe she is on an excursion with Pamela to Hookam's," Samantha said in measured tones. "Would you care to take some breakfast or coffee, my lord?" she inquired. "I know that I am often rendered testy myself in the morning before I have drunk a cup of coffee."

"You may be testy despite the coffee if that sister of yours is half as skittlebrained as I think she is."

Samantha glared at him. "I fail to see why my sister, either of them, should exert such fascination for you so early in the morning that you would burst into my breakfast room unannounced!"

"Don't be missish!" Sheffield ordered. "If Miss Miranda is at Hookam's, I'll beg your pardon, but if she isn't—as I suspect—you'll be begging mine."

"Sheffield, must you speak in such riddles? You are worse than a Sphinx. What is all this talk about Miranda?"

Sheffield chose his words with care. "Roddy is not in his quarters. He wrangled Captain Maybury's carriage on the pretext that he was taking Miranda to Hampton Court, which must be a lie since you say she has gone off with Pamela to Hookam's. Moreover," he continued, noticing how the color had drained further from her cheeks, "his butler tells me he left with a satchel of overnight things. Now then, Miss Curtis, which of us is the airdreamer?"

"You are thinking of an elopement," she said, grasping the situation at once. "But that is preposterous! Why should they elope now, for I have consented to their match —unless *you* chose to cut up stiff with Roddy, forbidding him to marry?"

"It is not in my power to forbid Roddy to marry," Sheffield said acidly. "He is of age, and I haven't seen him for days. So I am in as great a fog as you."

"They might not have eloped," Samantha said. "You could be in error, my lord. Perhaps Captain Maybury mistook Roddy's destination. Miranda could be at Hookam's with Pammy."

"I suppose so," Sheffield said grudgingly. "And pigs could fly, too, if they only put their minds to it!"

"There is no need to be so rude!" Samantha snapped. "I know it is a dim hope, but you needn't be so sarcastic. They must be stopped, for I shan't have Miranda marrying in such a havey-cavey fashion." She noticed that, far from attending to her words, the viscount had begun to edge toward the door, and she followed him out into the hall, demanding to know what he planned to do next.

"Go to Hookam's." He flung the answer over his shoulder as he moved past Horace.

"I'm going with you," she declared, following him out the door.

This stopped him at once. "I have no time to waste, Miss Curtis."

"Nor I," she said, pulling on her gloves. "So I suggest we do not stand here gibblegabbling, and that you hand me up into that phaeton and we make for Hookam's as fast as you can. Otherwise I will be obliged to chase you down the street screaming for a constable!"

Under the circumstances Sheffield's hand was forced, for she would probably make good such a threat. He helped her into the carriage none too gently, complaining all the while about females with addlebrained sisters.

Samantha scarcely heard him. Her own thoughts whirled madly about in her brain. Miranda. Roddy. Pamela? An elopement? Never. They could not be so stupid.

Before she had a real opportunity to ponder just how stupid the three of them could be, the phaeton had arrived at Hookam's. She jumped down and led the way into the shop. To her dismay, none of the three could be found among the customers in the book-lined establishment. Sheffield, who had deduced as much in his first glance, unearthed a gangly bookseller, who furnished the information that a carriage matching the description of Captain Maybury's vehicle had been seen in the area not an hour ago and that three people fitting the description Miss supplied had boarded it. And to clinch the matter fully, the gentleman was carrying a satchel.

"Which way did they head?" Sheffield demanded.

"Can't be sure," the bookseller apologized. "But I did hear talk of Reading."

"Oh, no," Samantha ejaculated, turning and marching off. Sheffield gave chase.

"Must you always dash off?" he complained when he had caught up to her. "And what, pray tell, is the significance of Reading to you?"

"My parents eloped to Reading to be married! No doubt if this is an elopement, Roddy and Miranda wish to follow in Mama and Papa's footsteps."

Sheffield rubbed his chin. "That is fortunate for us, although I must own it bespeaks a deplorable lack of creativity on the part of my connection. But at least now I shan't have to follow them to Gretna. My Welsh-breds shall last the run to Reading and back. You'll excuse me if I leave you to find your way home."

"You'll leave me nowhere," she contradicted. "I am coming with you. And don't let's quarrel over it any longer.

It's my sister as well as your connection who has this maggot on her brain."

"I'll make much faster time without you," he said, still making no effort to help her into the phaeton.

"I hardly see that one more in your carriage will impede your progress so dearly. And what will you do if you find Miranda or Pammy in hysteria? Neither you nor Mr. Monroe would have the slightest idea of how to handle a vaporish female."

"I daresay you may have your uses," Sheffield said, recoiling from the vivid scene she had just described. He helped her into the seat again, took his own beside her, and applied his whip lightly to the back of the team. In seconds they were off.

"Too fast for you, ma'am?" he asked as they raced around a curve in the road.

"Not at all, my lord," she answered with aplomb. "You have on several occasions boasted to me about your prowess with a whip, and I mean to hold you to that claim. I give you warning that should you overturn the phaeton, I shall not let the matter pass lightly!"

In spite of the urgency of their situation, a smile creased Sheffield's face.

"And what if you did suffer a broken neck?" he quizzed. "What would you feel then?"

"If I did suffer a broken neck," her eyes glinted back at him, "I should be past all feeling, as the Reverend Sutter back in York used to say. But should you survive me, I think I can rely on you to feel all the paroxysms of guilt!"

"And I suppose I would have to," he agreed with an appreciative grin on his lips.

Once or twice during the first hours of their journey the phaeton came within an ames-ace of another carriage tooling down the narrow road, but Sheffield always managed to whip by with an inch to spare on either side of the wheel. He truly was a master whip!

They reached Twyford at last, and he pressed on without pausing to stop for lunch or a change of horses. Although Samantha was not hungry, she was worried.

"The bookseller may have erred," she said, voicing her doubts for the first time to Sheffield. "They may not have gone to Reading."

"We are only a half hour away," he replied, looking grim. "We'll soon see our error, and if we aren't wrong . . ."

He did not need to finish his threat. Had the situation been any less grave, Samantha might have spared some pity on young Roddy.

Samantha brushed back some of the curls that had spilled over her forehead. "There is a little parish where Mama and Papa were wed." She hesitated a moment. "Do you think if Miranda came all this way to be married—"

"She would undoubtedly wish to exchange her vows at the same altar," Sheffield concluded. "I think you have it, Miss Curtis. And we should thank heaven for a certain traditionalist strain in your family. Permit me to say how relieved I am your mama did not see fit to elope to the Continent!"

Samantha laughed. "That would have made it difficult for us," she agreed. "Not to say hard for Pammy, who is prone to seasickness, you know."

"I didn't," he replied shortly. "And seasickness is the least of Mrs. Langford's worries. Try as I might, I cannot fathom her role in this dubious affair. I know Roddy and Miranda are in love, and lovers have more hair than wit, but Mrs. Langford always struck me as a female of sense."

"She is," Samantha agreed. "But I vow, I cannot make head or tail of her part, either. She has been acting peculiarly of late too, but I laid that to a quarrel she had with Donald earlier in the week. Perhaps it unhinged her mind."

Sheffield gave a bark of laughter. "I should have interrogated Langford on this whole affair."

"Oh, Donald wouldn't know a thing," Samantha averred. "He is a pet and the kindest of brothers-in-law, but he's not the type . . ."

"To take a hand in problems?" Sheffield asked acutely.

She nodded, conscious that the same could not be said of her companion of the moment, who seemed to thrive on ordering people about in times of crisis.

At last they reached Reading. The viscount, with the

assistance of a passerby, was able to locate the small parish that Mrs. Reginald Curtis had so often described to her three daughters.

Hurrying, Samantha tried to keep up with him, but his longer stride made it inevitable that he should be the first to confront the guilty trio at the altar, where Roddy was speaking to the minister.

"Good day, Roderick," Sheffield said cordially. His connection turned an ashen face his way. The minister gazed over his spectacles at the viscount, rather surprised to find another member of the Quality in his modest domain.

"Good day to you, good father," Sheffield continued. "And Mrs. Langford, Miss Miranda."

At the sound of her name, Miranda shrank back with a cry against Roddy's shoulders. But the third member of their party was made of sterner stuff and launched a vigorous if somewhat muddled attack of her own.

"Miranda is marrying Roddy," Pamela proclaimed with unnecessary vigor. "You can't stop us, Lord Sheffield, for I am her guardian, after all. And they are in love. Roddy is of age, and we have a special license." She thrust the document out at him. "See for yourself. Roddy found a bishop who would grant him one."

"Then he must be lacking even more wits than the three of you," Sheffield said, without glancing at the document. He was, however, struck by one point in Pamela's impassioned catalogue and, turning to Samantha, inquired in a voice of bland interest if Pamela really were Miranda's guardian.

"Yes, of course," Samantha replied. "She is the eldest of us."

"A poor excuse if ever I heard one," the viscount retorted. "And I lay the blame on this whole affair on your mother. If she had been a woman of sense she would have borne her children with you in the lead, and none of this folly would have arisen."

"Don't you dare speak a word against my mother!" Miranda bridled, emerging momentarily from the safety of Mr. Monroe's arms, intent on picking up the cudgels in her mother's defense.

"Oh, don't be such a ninnyhammer," Samantha implored, taking a reluctant hand in a scene that was even more farcical than the ones Mr. Sheridan penned for the stage. "Sheffield is not trying to slander Mama, so there is no reason to act like that." She rounded on Pamela. "And while I could perhaps excuse Miranda for being foolish, I can't excuse you, Pammy."

"You needn't bother to act so superior, Samantha," Pamela sniffed. "We know the truth."

"The truth about what?" Samantha asked, staring at her.

Pamela sniffed again. "There is no need for your odious dissembling. I heard all."

"Perhaps you did," Sheffield said, a gleam in his dark eyes, "but I did not. And I am all agog to know just what queer notion you are laboring under, Mrs. Langford."

"The notion, my lord, that my sister never intended Miranda to wed Roddy. That her consent to the match was naught but an odious sham. That all along she schemed to attach Miranda to another. It was a cruel hoax to play," she said, turning a withering eye on Samantha.

"Don't be a goosecap," Samantha snapped, put out of patience by this recital. "I have never heard such drivel in my life. Pray, just which other was I scheming to attaching Miranda to?"

"The Earl of Compton!" Pamela announced with a flourish.

But her moment of triumph fell sadly flat. "That's rubbish!" Samantha exclaimed.

Pamela tossed her head back. "I heard you myself."

Alerted by the signs in Samantha's eyes that the sisterly skirmish might erupt into a full-fledged war and that he was in the direct line of fire, Sheffield now took upon himself the unfamiliar role of peacemaker, informing Samantha that she was a fool not to have been born an only child.

"And I speak from experience, ma'am. Had I a sister anything like either of yours, I would have strangled her by now."

"What an uncivil thing to say!" Roddy said, roused to speech for the first time since the viscount's arrival. His cousin dealt him a quelling look. "You be quiet." His eyes shifted from one recalcitrant face to the next until it fell on one wholly baffled.

"Good father," he said charmingly, "we are in the midst of a heated family altercation. Rather noisy affairs they can be, as you may have guessed by now. Would you happen to have a room where we five might retire to speak in private?"

With evident relief the minister yielded at once to the authority in Sheffield's voice and led them around in back to a small room that boasted no chairs but just enough room to stand. He then departed, claiming pressing matters of church to attend to.

"But you haven't married us yet," Roddy protested. Sheffield dropped a restraining hand on his cousin's arm. "Now, see here, Warren," the younger man blustered.

"Be quiet," Sheffield commanded again. "I have endured enough *Sturm und Drang* for one day, not to mention putting my Welsh-breds through a devil of a run. You have behaved like a coxcomb, Roddy, and your father is no doubt turning over in his grave in Sussex. Have you not an ounce of wit? Jeopardizing Miss Miranda's reputation with a harebrained scheme like this!"

Mr. Monroe's jaw worked furiously. "I haven't jeopardized her. I'm trying to marry her. And," he went on, "you can't stop me. Even if you do manage somehow to thwart us today, I shall find Miranda wherever you or Miss Curtis might hide her, and I'll elope with her again. I'll do it two, three, or four times if I must."

"Now that would be the queerest thing of all," Sheffield replied. "As though any man would wish to elope continually with the same female. Different ones I *could* see," he acknowledged, giving the matter more thought, "but the same chit—"

Samantha begged him to stop speaking fustian. "What I wish to know is what Compton has to do with any of this."

"I heard you the other day speaking to Wilhelm," Pamela spoke up. "You were dispatching him to Hereford, weren't you? And joking about the marriage in the family, and how together you would endeavor to convince the bride about the excellent husband she was getting! *Barbarous!* Everyone knows that the Earl of Compton has estates in Herefordshire."

"Is that what you thought?" Samantha felt close to hysteria. "To be sure, Compton does have estates there, I believe. But so do other people."

"Such as Phineas Walker," Sheffield supplied helpfully.

"Who is Phineas Walker?" Pamela asked in a voice of stone.

"The father of Miss Kitty Walker, the female who of late has so smitten your Cousin Wilhelm that he dashed off there to beg leave of the father to marry her."

Pamela hooted. "Marriage? Wilhelm? Now I know the two of you are hoaxing me. Wilhelm is a confirmed bachelor!"

"Quite true," Sheffield acknowledged, "but even confirmed bachelors have been known to take the plunge."

"I don't believe it either," Miranda annnounced. "This is a hoax. But it shan't work. You and Sheffield have hatched up this plot to take me back to London," she said to Samantha. "But I won't go. I'll die before I ever wed that odious earl."

"Good heavens, he's not that odious," Samantha protested, unwilling to have Compton's reputation besmirched in any way.

"Miss Curtis is right. Compton is not the least bit odious —a trifle prosey perhaps," Sheffield conceded, "but not odious. However, Miss Miranda is correct when she says she'll die before she weds him, for I fully believe he hasn't the slightest wish to marry her." He turned to look at the astonished Miranda. "Saw him myself on New Bond Street just the other day consoling himself with a new Beauty on his arm.

"What an insufferable thing to say!" Miranda exclaimed.

"Warren!" Roddy broke in. "Is this all a hoax?"

The viscount had reached the end of his endurance, and he threw Samantha a supplicating look. "I have half a mind to take you back with me to London, Miss Curtis, and leave these three to their ruin."

"That is even more insufferable!" Miranda burst out.

The viscount looked at her politely. "More insufferable, my dear? Miss Miranda, I have said much ruder things about the three of you than *that* during the course of this day. And I was merely pointing out that since our presence was so unwelcome, Miss Curtis and I might withdraw and leave you and Roddy to make micefeet of your lives."

Pamela had by now lost all interest in Miranda and stepped closer to Samantha. "Is it true, Samantha? Is Wilhelm really planning to offer for Kitty Walker?"

Having for once exhausted her words on a topic, Samantha nodded.

Pamela paled. "But I thought . . . Why didn't you tell me!"

"You weren't in the mood to listen!" Samantha snapped. "I vow, between the way you glowered and Miranda wept, I was convinced a new strain of influenza had struck the *ton*."

Sheffield strolled over to the two of them. "It was not the influenza, of course, but lovesickness. Fed, I am certain, by the current diet of lending library romances. My first act, Miss Curtis, if I were you, would be to ban such books from your establishment." He eyed Miranda's and Pamela's fallen faces grimly for a moment. "For how else would your sisters believe you to be such a villainess. Anyone can see you are rather too lovely for that. They, I am told, usually have warts on their noses. And your goodness is also bespoken by your willingness to divide your fortune with your sisters just so that Miranda would not starve and Pamela might assist her horse-mad spouse to invest in worthwhile horseflesh."

At this new evidence of their sister's generosity, both Pamela and Miranda broke out into tears.

"Oh, Samantha, I am sorry!"

"From clothheads to watering pots," Sheffield ejaculated with some revulsion. "Now, now, the two of you. Do give that up," he ordered at once. "You shall be turning your sister into a sponge if you persist."

This acid remark had the effect of sobering both Pammy and Miranda.

"You have spoiled my surprise," Samantha scolded him.

"Have I?" he asked blandly. "No matter, since none of it shall come to pass."

"Why do you say that?" she asked in surprise.

"Because I have already spoken with my man of business," he replied as he helped himself to a pinch of snuff. "I directed him to grant an allowance to Roddy. The exact figure escapes me at the moment, but it is sufficient to ensure his and Miranda's comfort until he inherits. So there is no reason for you to part with your blunt on his expense."

"I say, Warren, that is good of you!" Roddy broke in, every symptom of anger gone from his face. "I shall pay you back every penny."

"You certainly shall," Sheffield agreed. His eyes, however, were not on his grateful relation but on Samantha. "And," he continued, "I've also spoken with Langford. For a man of his milky disposition he's not inclined to take help or money from anyone, especially his sister-in-law. I had a hard time getting him to take mine and was obliged to call it a loan. After he has invested in the cattle, he'll pay me back. So you see," he beamed at Samantha, "there is no need to speak any more of this dimwitted plan of yours. And now that the tears have finally dried, I suggest we return post haste to London." He nodded at Roddy and Miranda. "The two of you are practically betrothed, and Mrs. Langford is safely married, but Miss Curtis is not. And I should hate for any stain to her reputation to come from the day's events!"

~ *TWENTY-ONE* ~

Why should Sheffield be so preoccupied with her reputation, Samantha wondered as they drove away from Reading. Unless perhaps he was loth to have it appear in any way that he might have compromised her, for then, being a man of honor, he might feel obligated to offer her marriage. And that, she reasoned, would surely go against his grain if he were languishing after Miss Horick. Not, Samantha told herself, that she was inclined to accept anything from him, for a more vexatious, high-handed, and interfering gentleman she had yet to meet.

"Vexatious, high-handed, *and* interfering, Miss Curtis?" he queried as she scored him on all three points on their way back to London. "I confess that my reputation is hardly that of a saint, but you paint me a veritable Bluebeard. Wasn't your intention to prevent the wedding between Roddy and Miss Miranda today, or have you changed your mind and merely neglected to inform me? Quite understandable, since I have been at your side these several hours, and one is always prone to overlook what is right under one's nose."

"No one could overlook you, my lord," Samantha responded arctically. "And I have not changed my mind. I was not referring to Roddy and Miranda's elopement but to the way you usurped my plans for giving the money to Miranda and Pamela. And despite your ruining what should have been a splendid surprise, I intend to go on with my plans when we return to London. Mr. Phelps has already drawn up the plans."

"Then he can undraw them," Sheffield said languidly. "Your sisters aren't likely to take a penny from you. And if you do bestow the money on them, you'd only find it back in your recticule somehow. They are rather proud of their men, all in all, those two sisters of yours."

The truth of his statement infuriated Samantha. "This is all your fault! You've spoiled everything! What shall I do with the money?"

Sheffield was singularly unmoved by her reaction. "If all else fails, I would advise you to save it for your dowry."

"My dowry!" Her voice rose. "You speak as though I am on the scramble for a husband, which I am not!"

Sheffield remained silent as he wondered what she would do if he told her that, however much he hated the idea of her marrying Hancock, he could not allow her to undertake such a match without her full portion, and *that* had been his reason behind the loans to Roddy and Langford.

"I am well aware, Miss Curtis, that you consider yourself an old maid," he said with only the faintest hauteur.

"Then you see all your twaddle about a dowry is fustian, and that it sits badly with me that you are Miranda's and Pammy's benefactor!"

"Now that is doing it too brown," he retorted. "I am aiding Langford and Roddy, not your sisters. And you did not scruple to think how it would sit with me at your being the benevolent hand behind Roddy's change of fortune."

She colored slightly. "I know. But, still . . ."

"Do you know I can think of no stupider way to end an already long and bone-shattering day than to quarrel over which of us shall be allowed to part with our blunt to benefit that henwitted trio in front of us."

Samantha laughed in agreement. "You're right. Very well, my lord. But that is all the money you shall spend on us. I mean to pay for Miranda's wedding."

He shrugged. "I know very little about weddings and won't be here when it comes to pass."

Samantha looked up quickly. "Not be here? What do you mean?"

"If you must know, I'm bound for the West Indies."

The West Indies! Samantha did not need to hear another word. If she had desired further evidence of the wound inflicted by Miss Horick, here it was!

"The Indies?" she managed to say. "How exciting for you. No doubt you shall have many tales with which to regale your listeners when you return to London."

"Look here," he said, scowling fiercely. "I know it's none of my affair, but if Hancock should cut up stiff over your absence today—I know a little of how the prattle boxes work and someone might have seen us earlier at Hookam's or when we return to London—send him round to see me. I shan't be leaving for a day or two."

Samantha's brow knit in puzzlement. "Why should I send Mr. Hancock to see you?" she demanded.

Sheffield twisted his lips slightly. "Call it a mere precaution. In case any vexatious questions should arise."

"Vexatious questions about what, pray?" Samantha demanded. "And why should Mr. Hancock of all people question me about the day's affairs? I fear, my lord, you are not making a particle of sense!"

The viscount lifted a hand. "I know I shouldn't have spoken, and I realize it's still a secret, but it shan't be for long. That mother of his is a bit of a tartar, but she shall undoubtedly approve of you."

Samantha, who had been rendered mildly perplexed by Mr. Hancock's role in this conversation, was baffled by the intrusion of his mother, a female whom she had not yet met.

"Pray, what does Mr. Hancock's mama have to do with anything?"

Sheffield stared at the lovely face now screwed up in utter confusion. Abruptly, he reined in his team of Welshbreds.

"Let's cut line," he ordered. "There are only the two of us here, and you needn't scruple to keep up your ruse."

Her eyes widened. "What ruse? You are beginning to sound like Pammy earlier in the day!"

"I learned of the matter myself from Wilhelm," he said brusquely. "And don't eat him as he fears, for the suspicions were mine to start with. And I can't fathom why Hancock would wish to keep the news of his offer quiet. If I were he, I'd be in alt."

Samantha gave a shaky laugh. "You would be cast in alt

by a female refusing your offer of marriage?" she demanded. "I know you are not rumored to be so enamoured of the marital state, my lord, but it strikes me as wanting in conduct to offer for someone and then be cast into transports by her refusal!"

"Refusal!" Sheffield's jaw dropped, and he pounced on her words with such violence that Samantha wondered if the strain of the day's journey had caused an impairment of his wits. Although she had never seen a madman first-hand, and true, his lordship had been perfectly lucid not five minutes ago, she knew such fits were supposed to come on quick as lightning.

"Never tell me, you silly chit, that you refused young Hancock!" Sheffield said now.

"Well, I did," Samantha said, rather nervous of the wild expression on his face. "However, I fail to see why that should be of such concern to you! And since I know one does not bandy about such delicate matters, that is why I ordered Wilhelm to keep silent—" She broke off, perceiving now that her companion on the seat next to her was no longer attending to anything she said but had his shoulders hunched over in the midst of a laughing fit—also, she remembered, a common affliction of the mad.

"My lord," she said, striving to keep her voice calm and soothing, for such mellifluous tones were most comforting to lunatics, "if you would just hand me those reins, I shall endeavor to start the team up, and we shall catch up with Mr. Monroe. He shall bring you the services of a doctor."

"The services of a doctor?" Sheffield ejaculated. "What the devil do I need with a doctor?" he demanded as he wiped his brimming eyes. "Oh, I see. You think I have gone mad."

"No, of course not," she said hastily. "It's just the strain of the moment."

"Miss Curtis, I grant you I have been acting like an idiot, but that took place days ago. I am once again rendered lucid. I thought, you see, that you and Hancock . . ." His voice trailed off as Samantha's hands stole up to her cheeks.

"Mr. Hancock and I?" she repeated. "You didn't think that he and I—"

"Oh, I did think it," Sheffield said vehemently. "I committed the crime that I have scored you for on numerous occasions, leaping to conclusions. Not that it took much effort, for I did see the way you looked at each other that day in the Park. And when I quizzed Wilhelm, all he would say was that Hancock's offer was a secret. But what that silly gudgeon didn't tell me was that you had refused the offer, so all along I thought you were secretly plighted. Which, I know, makes me as melodramatic as those silly sisters of yours."

"But why should Mr. Hancock and I be secretly plighted?" Samantha demanded.

"His mother, of course. Philip has trotted females over to his mama for years, and none has been brought to the mark. My Aunts Gertrude and Mary couldn't hold a candle to that Hancock woman, and it wouldn't surprise me in the least if Philip eventually tires of bringing the chits home to meet her and just ups and elopes the way Roddy almost did." He stopped, realizing suddenly that however determined Mrs. Hancock was to play a part in her son's marriage proposals, she had no such claim on the viscount's.

"Why did you refuse Hancock?" he asked Samantha now.

"That is a highly impertinent question," Samantha said, stiffening. "And it's none of your affair."

"It wouldn't have anything to do with me, I suppose," he asked, picking up her hand and kissing it lightly. A light electric shock trailed up her arm, bringing an enjoyable glow to the rest of her body. She hurriedly snatched her hand away.

"No, indeed," she said with some emphasis.

A weaker man might have termed this a mortal blow, but Sheffield was not dismayed. "I suppose it's Coodle then," he said solicitously. "A bit prosey, I should have called him myself, but there is no accounting for tastes. And he is determined to please. Only think how he finally faced the monstrous Brutus!"

"I did not refuse Mr. Hancock's offer on Lord Coodle's behalf, my lord," Samantha said scorchingly.

"Oh, didn't you?" Sheffield said with an air of great interest. "I'm not surprised, for I did think you would lead him a cat and dog life."

Samantha fixed a baleful eye on him. "Your opinions on whom I should marry are of no possible interest to me."

"No, really? Then I'd better suggest you take me at once."

For a minute Samantha felt so lightheaded that she might have toppled from the carriage seat to the ground.

"What are you speaking of, my lord?"

"You. Me. Marriage," he said succinctly.

"Is that an offer, Sheffield?" she demanded.

"Of course it is," he said impatiently. "Not pretty enough for you, I suppose?"

Samantha wrenched her eyes away from his face. "You are speaking nonsense, my lord. Or else you are fearing that you must offer for me because we shared a carriage for most of the day and since it shall be coming onto night when we return to London . . . But truly there is not the slightest need. I don't feel compromised in the least."

Sheffield pushed back his high-crowned beaver, a thunderstruck expression on his handsome face. "Of course you don't feel compromised," he expostulated. "No gentleman of my acquaintance could compromise you. You've too great a head on your shoulders, although at the moment you are acting like a ninnyhammer."

Feeling somehow that she had been more insulted by his words than complimented, Samantha replied that she was of an age to make any chaperonage unnecessary.

"Yes, yes, I know. You're on the shelf!" he roared. "And I daresay I shall have to delay any trip I do take to the Indies to go off to Yorkshire and see what it is about the area that makes a charmingly young, lovely female persist in the misguided belief that she is in her dotage!"

A thrill ran unchecked down Samantha's back. "Oh, what did you call me?" she asked in spite of herself.

"A charmingly young, lovely female," he repeated with

great feeling, smiling at the sparkle in her eyes. "One who in fact attracted me at first glance!"

"My lord, I never so much as cast out a lure!"

"I know." His tone turned reproachful. "And that did puzzle me a good bit, for I was so accustomed to females setting their caps at me. I know it sounds odious, but it is the truth. And then I realized that a female like yourself would scarcely fling herself at my head while I was still practically betrothed to Frieda, and that did have me at sixes and sevens. How could I unengage myself from Frieda when I wasn't properly speaking even engaged to her to begin with? Fortunately," he said, a trifle distracted by the sunlight filtering through his companion's lovely hair, "Frieda took a liking to Cyril, so it was the easiest thing imaginable to let him cut me out."

"Then you weren't . . . you aren't . . . languishing after her?" Samantha asked with some trepidation.

Sheffield drew back in rigid shock. "Good God, no. You're as bad as Alice! Why should I languish after Frieda? You were quite right that first night we met: Frieda shall drive a man to an early grave. It was you I was languishing after, you silly chit, if you would only notice. And I was all primed to do the noble thing, thinking you secretly betrothed to Hancock, and retire from the ranks and go off to the Indies to nurse my broken heart. And if it hadn't been for those silly sisters of yours and young Roddy, I daresay I would have done just that, so I can't scold them too much for the day's idiocy. Furthermore, Miss Curtis," he said, looking down at her and taking her hand again, "I must tell you that secret betrothals are repugnant to me."

Samantha felt her heart pounding wildly in her chest and lifted her face to him. What she saw in his eyes made her twice as breathless.

"Why should you scruple to acquaint me with your feelings on betrothals, my lord?" she asked.

"Because I love you!" he said, almost shouting the words. "Why else would I fight that dashed silly duel with Bunting, or make for Reading in pursuit of your silly sisters." Feeling that he had exhausted all forms of proper address and deducing that the moment seemed to clamor for action rather than perpetual discourse, he pulled her into his arms, oblivious to her soft cry of protest that the horses might bolt, and crushed his lips to hers.

Samantha, who had once before experienced the intensity of his passion in Lady Alice's anteroom, now discovered that she was returning his kiss with a fervor that matched his own.

"My lord!" she said finally, struggling for breath as the kiss slackened. He had her locked in his arms now and ordered her forthwith to stop fidgeting—the same command, she remembered with a smile, that he had given when they had shared a saddle together back in London. But then he had belonged to Frieda Horick. Now, he was miraculously *hers*.

"I can't imagine how long it took me to detach myself from Frieda," he complained. "I fell in love with you the instant I clapped eyes on you, despite that dowdy rig you were wearing. And you?"

"In my case," she said demurely, "it took rather longer."

He drew back in mock dismay. "Was I so odious?"

"Oh, no. But you do forget that on first sight, I took you for Wilhelm!"

His arm tightened about her as he laughed. "Good heavens, yes, Wilhelm. Now there's a fellow who has caused no small distress in all our quarters." He dropped a kiss on her ear. "I should advise you that I'm in earnest when I say I loathe long engagements. I'd best marry you before another addled notion can strike your sisters, although I suppose we shall have to postpone the ceremony until my mama can rush in from Vienna. After three decades of waiting for me to step into Parson's Mousetrap, she'll be livid if she isn't here to see the trap sprung for herself."

"What if your mama doesn't like me," Samantha said, suddenly worried.

"She'll love you," Sheffield predicted. "In fact she told me herself that her fondest hope was that I would find a high-spirited lady who would lead me an awful dance to the altar."

"And am I this female?" Samantha asked, gazing at him with loving eyes.

"Undoubtedly, my dearest, you are!"

And then, deciding that that was more than enough talk of mothers for one proposal of marriage, he bent his head and kissed her soundly once again.